Run River Run

Also by Keith Remer

The Aristocracy of Caddo County

Blood City; Book Two of the Calamitous Breed Trilogy

Killing Bardoe; Book One of the Calamitous Breed Trilogy

The Hiding Place of Thunder

Run River Run

by

KEITH REMER

Honey Lee Press
Oklahoma City, OK

First Honey Lee Press trade paperback edition October 2019
Manufactured in the United States of America
1 0 9 8 7 6 5 4 3 2 1

Print ISBN 978-0-9998532-9-0
EBook ISBN 978-1-7341015-0-8
Library of Congress Control Number 2019915571

For my dear friend and brother-in-arms,

Colonel Pat Scully
US Army, Retired,

whose physical characteristics and mannerisms
I borrowed to bring River Yates to life.

1999

Wilburton, Oklahoma

Chapter One

River Yates stared at the dog and the dog glared back. The dog, Cheyenne, exhibited a nasty snarl reminding River of one of his ex-wives. He couldn't remember exactly which one, and didn't care to.

Although Cheyenne seemed to like most people, he'd never warmed to River. Until just recently, the dog's attitude had not been a problem. But for the third day running, Cheyenne blocked River's path to the door of the Silver Dollar Bar. Cheyenne belonged to Hank Sioux, who owned the Silver Dollar, and the mutt's new inhospitable ritual tended to piss River off. It seemed to him no bar owner should keep a dog around that wouldn't let a loyal patron on the premises.

But then, no other bar owner River Yates knew would name his establishment the Silver Dollar Bar when the establishment didn't display a single silver dollar. The joint Sioux named his bar after, the famed Silver Dollar Bar of downtown Oklahoma City, once had an ornate mahogany bar inlaid with hundreds of the large coins. Sioux often waxed sentimental about the original bar in Oklahoma City. It had been the place where his old man bought Sioux his first beer. Not long after that, Sioux's old daddy got stabbed in that bar. Fourteen times. In the chest. Hank Sioux established his rickety and dingy little place as a monument to his father. Hank could be a sweet guy. River Yates just wished his best friend had better taste in dogs.

From his experience yesterday and the day before, River knew if he stepped to the left, Cheyenne would move to the right. And if River shuffled to the right, Cheyenne would scoot a bit to the left. River already tried sweet words and those sissy little kissing sounds people used to call dogs When River would raise his voice or use foul words, Cheyenne would show more of his yellow teeth and growl an ugly little threat.

And just like the previous two days, River and the dog drew an audience. The Silver Dollar had a glass front, painted red about three quarters of the way up the glass. Inside of the bar and above the painted portion bobbed the heads of Hank Sioux, Moe Trendle, and Jim Duck. In the old days the sight of River Yates being held at bay by a dog barely two feet tall would prompt his three life-long friends to laugh their asses off. Now, they all simply stared. Pityingly.

* * * *

"Why don't he just kick the livin' shit outta that ignorant mutt?" Moe Trendle wondered out loud.

"Probably thinks it will bite him," Jim Duck responded with a sad shake of his head.

"Cheyenne don't bite," Hank Sioux joined in. "Besides, River ain't worried about a little ol' dog bite. Hell, remember when that cougar got aholt of him up in the mountains? Damned near tore his arm off, but River hiked nearly ten miles just to get back to his truck."

"That was the *old* River," Moe sighed.

"Yeah," Jim agreed, "the old River that wasn't afraid of horses and guns and danger."

Hank wasn't as readily willing to admit the changes in River were due to fear. He just couldn't bring himself to believe that. "You don't know that he's afraid of those things. Besides, he still rides that old Harley and ridin' a motorcycle is about as dangerous a thing as a man can do."

"Well, you got to admit, Hank,' Moe persisted, "it is strange for a rancher not to ride his horses, and for an ex-cop and war hero to develop a distaste for firearms."

After a few seconds of contemplation, Hank said the only response coming to mind. "People can and do change, Moe."

"Uh-huh," Moe nodded, "and it ain't always for the better."

* * * *

River Yates seriously considered climbing back on his scooter when Hank Sioux opened the door to his bar.

"Hell, River, you know that damned old dog don't bite."

"Damned sure acts like he'd bite," River said without averting his eyes from the disagreeable mongrel. "Besides, it ain't a matter of whether or not the dog bites. It's a matter of what a man has to go through just to get a cold beer. You know, I could do my drinking in friendlier places."

"No doubt you could," Hank admitted while shoving Cheyenne aside with the toe of his boot, "but you'd have to actually pay for your beer at other places."

While gingerly stepping around the dog and past Hank, River muttered a face-saving, "You know, I'd expect a rude comment like that from a Cherokee Indian named Sioux who calls his dog

Cheyenne and owns a Silver Dollar Bar with not a single damned silver dollar. Eccentric people are normally rude people."

* * * *

Billy Shiloh took great pains to treat his new bride carefully. He never, ever punched her in the face. Only in the stomach, ribs and breasts. Sometimes, when she really deserved it, he kicked her in those places, too. But never, ever the face. Such treatment would leave marks her ol' daddy could see. Billy Shiloh didn't fear Walter Bates. Hell, Billy held fear of no man. Old man Bates owned gobs of money and it just happened to be the old asshole's money providing Billy and his bride, Cindy, with food, clothes, a car, and even the house they lived in. Sure, Billy trained Bates' high-dollar horses and performed some odds and end work from time to time in any one of the old man's many businesses, but Billy Shiloh would give a dime's effort for a dollar's wage any day of the week. It just proved best that his daddy-in-law not know that Billy, on a regular basis, beat the living shit out of Cindy Shiloh.

Speaking of which, a day or two passed since Billy last took corrective measures, but he could feel the necessity drawing near. Cindy was getting a little too brave. A little too mouthy for Billy's likings.

"Now, I told you, Cindy, I'm going down to have a beer and I don't want no shit from you about it."

"I ain't givin' you shit, Billy," Cindy said in the tone Billy once considered endearing. "I just want you stay with me a while. You don't ever like spending time with me anymore. You used to always…"

Enough became enough and Billy Shiloh just heard one word over enough. This time he aimed for the left breast.

* * * *

River Yates shuffled up to the bar sans silver dollars and pushed aside the bittersweet memory of how he once strutted into such establishments. Evidently, Moe Trendle and Jim Duck remembered the same. Nowadays, they just didn't seem as excited to see River as they once were. Oh, well, he compromised, maybe a man of fifty-three was just too old to strut anyway.

"Howdy, River," Moe sighed.

"Hey, River," Jim followed suit with even less enthusiasm.

"Boys," River nodded while settling his lanky frame onto a cracked and peeling vinyl barstool. He took the draw Hank placed before him, blew off the foamy head and downed it.

"How's your bed and breakfast business going, River?" Moe asked with a grin.

Moe had always been an ornery shit. He knew the idea of the bed and breakfast had not been River's. River and his younger sister, Thelma, now shared the old Victorian ranch house their grandfather built. It had been her doings that converted the River ancestral home into a damned motel. Moe Trendle just aimed to harass River. River knew how to harass back.

"I guess it's goin' okay, Moe. Have you sold one of those novels yet?"

"You know I haven't," Moe responded, then concluded icily, "but at least I haven't given up trying."

River sensed a taunting insinuation, but chose not to dwell on it. The fat and balding Moe considered himself a writer. Back sometime before, he talked incessantly about writing River Yates' life story, or maybe creating a fictional character with River's characteristics. Moe many times pointed out what a fine name River had and how fitting it worked for a main character in an adventuresome action yarn. Moe hadn't mentioned that lately. This observation prompted River to run a hand through his prematurely silver hair. Moe always insisted that his main character would have the same color hair and wear it just like River did, shoulder length, parted down the middle and pushed behind his ears. Moe also liked describing River's eyes as "ice blue." His story's hero would also, Moe said, have the same color eyes. River suddenly felt bad about ribbing his friend about the books. River developed a conscience the past couple of years and didn't know if it came about as the result of all the bad he'd done, or because of all the bad done to him. But, regardless, River knew the sorrows of someone pissing all over your dreams.

"I'll bet," Jim Duck piped up, "that the extra income from the bed and breakfast comes in handy about now."

Jim seemed to be jabbing at him now, though it would've been unlikely for the very short man with the thick glasses to do so. Normally, Jim took serious care to give no man no reason to whip his tiny ass. Still, his words stung of a good jabbing. River knew his own financial woes were no secret. Because last year's cattle prices plummeted and the drought killed his hay crop, River was forced to mortgage his ranch. A $20,000 balloon payment fell due in months and River held no prospects for getting that kind of money. No way. No how.

If Jim took a poke at him, River decided to ignore it. Part of the price one paid for living in Wilberton, Oklahoma, was having everyone know everything about anything anyone ever said or did.

* * * *

Billy Shiloh preferred to do his beer drinking at the Boogie Mountain Lounge, as did most people his age around town. On a typical day he'd pass by the shit-hole Silver Dollar Bar and never give the dive a glance, but today was no typical day. His wife's nagging and his justifiable response left him in a particularly foul mood. Additionally, the Harley sitting out front picked at an internal sore, festering now for over a decade.

The bike belonged to River Yates, a man most people around town considered some kind of folk hero. Since the age of ten, Billy considered him an asshole, *and* a bully, *and* a man he'd for years fantasized about repaying a family debt.

Less than three blocks away, and all those years ago, Billy witnessed a grievous disgracing of his mama's only brother, and young Billy's hero. He did not understand at the time the full exchange of the by-chance meeting of Yates and his Uncle Trevor.

"Yates, you son of a bitch!"

The man Billy did not yet know stopped short of entering Blakely's Hardware, and turned slowly to face the calling out. This man's demeanor was calm, but a look in his eyes made Billy step back and behind his uncle.

"Ain't none of your business, Trevor. Stay clear of it."

"You're a married man, Yates, and she's my sister. That makes it my business."

"Not that you'd care to know the difference, but I'm separated from my wife, and your sister is a grown woman, capable of making her own decisions…"

Then Yates looked down and straight into Billy's eyes, and he lowered his voice a notch.

"…Besides, this ain't the time or place for this discussion."

Evidently, Trevor did not agree and moved in close to Yates in an attempt to grab the collar of his winter jacket.

Ever since, Billy had tried to sort out the blur of motions that left his uncle lying on the sidewalk, bleeding, and withering in pain. Billy understood only one point at the time, River Yates put a terrible hurt on the man he practically worshiped. In the days, months, and years that followed, Billy came to understand that Yates also took advantage of his mama, and Trevor came to her defense. Now as a grown man, Billy could give a shit about his mother. Too many times over the years she'd proven to be no more than a common slut. But when it came to Trevor, what kind of man would not seek opportunities to revenge the brutal ass kicking of a damned good uncle?

Shiloh whipped into the Silver Dollar and parked threateningly close to the Harley-Davidson.

* * * *

River sipped on his third beer when the sound of the tavern's door creaking open caused him to conduct a mental roll call. Hank was here. Moe was here. Duck was here. Yup, the Silver Dollar's regular afternoon crowd stood present and accounted for. Whoever stepped in the door would be a nonregular – something the Silver Dollar didn't get much of and a thing of real interest to the regulars. River turned on his barstool to face the door, and tensed at the sight of Billy Shiloh. This young man didn't like River, and River couldn't blame him for that. He'd watched Shiloh over the years grow into the kind of man that reeked of trouble. Because River knew so well the type from once living that kind of life, he knew instinctively that the boy could prove to be a dangerous kind of specimen. He wore his meanness on his handsome face like something to be proud of. Billy Shiloh, many decades shy of his fifties, still strutted. River swiveled back around to face the bar. Eyeballing men like Billy Shiloh worked like tossed gasoline on a fire.

Hank, Moe, and Duck muttered greetings. Shiloh mumbled a less than friendly response. In the traditional way of his type, he didn't ask for a beer. He ordered one. After tossing his money on the bar, Shiloh took his bottle and moved to the darkest, remotest corner of the Silver Dollar.

Moe and Jim seemingly carried on just like they had before Shiloh came in, but River could sense their trepidation. It took someone who knew Hank Sioux as well as River did to notice the change in the big Indian. It showed only in dark eyes darting continuously to the shadows that the intruder menacingly occupied. Somewhat like the smoke from Moe's cigarettes, something ugly now permeated the bar's stale air.

It only took two beers to unleash the predator in Shiloh. As predators do, he attacked first the obviously weakest member of the herd. "Hey, short shit," he hissed at Jim, "you must be blind as my dick! Damn, I ain't never seen glasses so thick. Bring them things over here and let me try 'em on."

River cut his eyes to look at Jim. The little man slowly turned on his barstool to face Shiloh. The thick lenses of Jim's glasses always made his eyes look at least three times the size of normal eyeballs. Now they looked four. The frail hands wrapped around the bottle of beer noticeably trembled. River took in a deep breath of air, held it a second or two, and then exhaled it in the form of a low moan. Jim Duck would need rescuing.

* * * *

Hank kept a baseball bat behind the bar. But it had been so long since trouble brewed in the Silver Dollar that he wasn't sure just exactly where he kept it. He set about inconspicuously searching when Shiloh repeated his demand.

"I said get your ass over here you fuckin' midget. I wanna try on them glasses."

The tone of the voice made Hank want the bat ten times more than he did before. The unadulterated maliciousness dripping from the words pretty much indicated Billy Shiloh held no qualms doing harm to a man half his size.

Hank couldn't tell whether Jim's brain didn't relay a persuasive enough message or if the little body just refused to obey. But either way, Shiloh obviously grew tired of waiting. The prey wouldn't come to him, so he moved upon his prey.

"Your fuckin' ears must not work any better than your fuckin' eyes," Shiloh growled before reaching to snatch the glasses from Jim's pallid face.

Jim offered no resistance, but out of the corner of his eye Hank saw River turning on his bar stool to face the exhibition. The bartender breathed a sigh of relief. Hank wished he had a dollar for every hard case he'd seen River dispense with over the years. River knew how to deal with the mean types like Shiloh.

"Hey, uh, Jim," River said in his gravelly voice to Duck, "ain't it about time for that meeting you had planned with ol' Walter Bates?"

Jim didn't catch on, but Hank did, and he couldn't help but grin. River was using his brain. Shiloh's father-in-law served as about the only man in Wilburton who Shiloh wouldn't cross.

Shiloh caught on as well. The muscular young man had already put on Duck's glasses. He turned an amplified stare of ugliness on River Yates. "Are you wanting in on this, old man?"

The way Hank figured, it seemed about time for River to come forward with a beer bottle, or his knife, or anything else he could turn into a weapon. River always worked damned good in turning just about anything into an ass-kicking tool. Too, being called an old man was not something Hank thought River would sit still for. But sit still he did.

"Well, now, Billy," River drew, "I just didn't figure you wanted to be messing with someone that's about to meet with your ol' daddy-in-law. That probably wouldn't be too good for your business."

Hank liked River's strategy, and the words he used weren't bad. But just the way River said them bothered Hank. The words just didn't have the, "I'll stomp your ass into next week" edge that River had always been so adept at applying to his sentences. Worse yet, Hank thought he detected a tremor in the gravelly voice. Shiloh must have as well. Just a few steps put him in River's face.

Shiloh jerked the ridiculous-looking glasses from his face and slung them into the far shadows of the tavern. "You know, old man, I always, still today, hear how bad-ass you are. How you are one mean son of a bitch, even at your advanced age. But let me tell you something here and now, you're looking at a man that grew up just wanting a piece of your ass. Are we going to make this the time and place…old man?"

That flung a challenge Sioux knew for sure would bring River off his barstool. But it didn't. River just sat there. If the look on his face wasn't nervousness, it appeared something real close to it. It pained Hank something seriously. He'd never seen that look on River Yates.

"I just thought Jim's meeting with Walter Bates was something you should know about, Billy. Just trying to help you out. That's all it was."

Shiloh spun on Jim. "Do you have a meeting with Bates?" he spat.

"Uh, yeah," Jim choked. "He wants to buy some land from me."

Hank knew it to be a lie, but hoped Shiloh didn't. Sure enough, he didn't.

"Well you better get to it you little sonofabitch. He don't like to be kept waiting."

As Jim scurried, in a pathetic groping sort of way, to find his glasses, Shiloh turned back to Yates.

"I don't like fuckin' has-beens and I think you're the king of fuckin' has-beens. You best stay the hell out of my way."

When Yates nodded and simply said, "Okay," Hank felt something similar to what he felt many years ago when he heard his old man had been stabbed in an Oklahoma City bar. Fourteen times. In the chest.

* * * *

After Billy Shiloh stomped out of the bar, nearly taking the rickety door off its hinges, River turned back to his beer. Jim found his glasses and walked up to stand beside him.

"Why'd you take that shit from him, River?" Jim's voice still held a quiver.

"Damn, Jim," Hank spoke up, "River saved you from that bully."

The words sounded supportive, but when River looked up and into the face of his old friend, he saw bewilderment in his brown eyes. River then turned to look at Moe. The man did not look back but seemed gripped by deep thought.

River knew they all thought him to have turned coward. Maybe he had. But they didn't know all of it, and River wasn't about to try explaining. They wouldn't understand about the voices that came from the old red barn. Hank, Moe, and Jim didn't know how much a man could change when dead men just wouldn't leave him alone. River downed the beer in front of him and shoved off toward the door. As the bright afternoon sunshine assaulted him like a slap in the face, River heard Moe addressing no one in particular.

"Billy Shiloh...Now, there's a damned fine name for a character in a book."

* * * *

With the scraps from dinner drying hard in porcelain plates, the sun seemed to rush toward the western horizon. River stepped out onto the wrap-around front porch of what people now called the Robbers' Roost Bed and Breakfast. River had shared his sister Thelma's famous chicken-fried steak with a newlywed couple from Kansas. The fine dinner earned Thelma another fifty bucks from the lovesick kids and cost River just another little chunk of his soul. His granddaddy no doubt threw a shit-kicking fit in hell over strangers paying for food in the house he'd built with his own hands. While massaging an uncomfortably full stomach, River belched long and hard, just hoping the Kansas people would hear it. Before stepping off the porch, River took a moment to study the shades of orange and purple the sun splashed on the rugged horizon of the Sansbois Mountains. He'd been a lot of places, but none knew how to throw a sunset like Oklahoma.

Only one place remained on the old Working Y Ranch that River felt belonged solely to him. Every evening he made the trek to that place, being careful to cut a wide swath around the monstrous red barn nearing its hundredth birthday. A tornado barely missed the barn last spring. River wished it hadn't.

River's destination, the newest structure on the ranch, sat back behind the barn. The fact that it couldn't be viewed from the house made the place dear to River. More importantly, though, it housed a project long past needing completion. Every evening he would go into his shop building, and saw and hammer and sand, and wish he'd done so twenty-five years earlier. When he grew too tired to work any longer, every night he would go up to his room and pray the same prayer to a God he felt certain didn't care to hear from him.

Chapter Two

For a period of time Carrie Deshazo took any role offered. Those times were long gone. Patiently, she flashed a trademark smile at the man who helped make her famous. "I do not want to go to Oklahoma. And I do not want to do this movie."

"It's going to be a hit, Carrie. A tremendous one," agent Todd Wald insisted.

"It's a western, Todd. Westerns went out before I was born."

"The occasional western is still a big draw. Do you have any idea how much the new *True Grit* grossed?"

"No," Carrie yawned while examining the results of her morning manicure. "Now, Todd, ask me if I care."

Wald drummed his fingers on his desktop for a few seconds before responding. "Just the other day you were saying how tired you are. How much you need to get away. Get some rest. Wilburton, Oklahoma, is small, remote, peaceful. Go there. Take the script, give it another long, hard look. Get a feel for the people, the country, and the history. Take the time to relax and recoup."

Wherein the thought of portraying some "Outlaw Queen" held no allure over Carrie, the thought of getting away to remote regions did. "I could use the rest," Carrie thought out loud. "Maybe Andre would go with me."

Todd Wald leaned back in his chair and laughed his triumphant laugh. "Good. Good." Then as a side note, he added, "Andre Norman in rural, redneck Oklahoma. Imagine that!"

"I can imagine that much easier than I can imagine myself playing Belle Starr," Carrie said before coming to her feet. "It's late, Todd, and I'm tired. I'll sleep on your proposal."

* * * *

Carrie had always been blessed with the gift of sound sleep. Until just recently. The norm for the past couple of weeks had been restless nights spent tossing and turning and wondering just why the hell she wasn't sleeping. Although she did not come up with specifics, she determined that it wasn't something that "was," which kept her awake but something that "wasn't." Something seemed missing.

But what in the world could that be? What could a woman possess that Carrie didn't already have in abundance? She had her fame, and it wasn't fortune that was missing. If Carrie never made another movie, she had enough money to live like a queen through at least two average life spans. And love?

The notion caused Carrie to roll over and consider the form that lay snoring beside her. Love? According to the tabloids, and of course the snoring form himself, women all over the world fantasized about sharing a bed with Clive Benz. Moonlight filtered through the balcony's French doors to illuminate the naked male body lying on top of Carrie's satin sheets. His splendidly defined muscles were always portrayed in the movies as resulting from a tough man's hard way of living. The women all over the world didn't know about the teams of personal trainers, the silicone implants and the sinful amount of money spent on liposuction. All those swooning women whose hearts and loins yearned for America's manliest of men had no way of knowing that on his best nights, Clive Benz performed near adequately for only a few minutes and only once in any eight-hour period.

Love? For Carrie it seemed a moot point if not a terribly overrated concept. After all, she made her life in a world where nothing was real and love was expected to be narcissistic. So, whatever she didn't have that kept her up into the wee hours of the morning couldn't be love because Carrie loved herself just fine.

* * * *

Carrie lounged beside her pool while sipping on the second cup of morning coffee when her cell phone started ringing. Carrie's phone displayed the name of her agent and she answered with little enthusiasm.

"Good morning, Todd."

"Have you given the trip to Oklahoma any more thought?" Todd made his living by getting right to the point.

She *had* given it more thought. A person can give a lot of things a lot of thought between three and five in the morning. The few hours of sleep after that had not extinguished the need for a getaway. Maybe time away in the wilderness of Oklahoma might relax her and provide insight into whatever it "wasn't" that robbed her of sleep.

"I'm thinking of making the trip, Todd, but not about doing the movie."

"Well just going there is a good start, and do I have a deal for you!"

Not all of Todd Wald's deals were good deals. Carrie took a deep breath of the morning air and stretched in the luxurious California sunshine before mumbling, "And what would that be?"

"I located what sounds to be a charming bed and breakfast on a real working ranch. It's secluded and private and in the foothills of the mountains Belle Starr hid out in."

"I hope it's not rustic, Todd. I don't do rustic."

"I checked. It's not rustic. It has all the conveniences of home. You know, Carrie, they do have running water, indoor plumbing, and electricity in Oklahoma nowadays."

As with most agents, Todd excelled in the use of smart-assed comments. "Okay. Book two rooms, Todd. I'm sure Andre will go with me."

Todd always laughed at the mentioning of Andre's name and that always tended to piss Carrie off. "Don't be snide, Todd. And don't get your hopes up. I'm not playing Belle Starr."

Carrie hung up only seconds before Clive Benz joined her at the pool. Carrie often thought Clive too pretty to play the parts he did. The steaming cup of cappuccino in his manicured hands worked yet another contradiction. His characters were eternally the type that drank coffee. Black.

"Morning, gorgeous," he greeted before kissing her gently on the cheek. The movie version of Clive would have taken her in his arms and ravaged her right there at poolside, which would have been a welcomed change of pace.

"Morning, dear," Carrie yawned.

"You look tired. Another restless night?"

"I am tired, Clive. I'm going to take a trip. A getaway."

Clive Benz showed his concern like only a big screen action hero could. "I have a facial scheduled at ten."

* * * *

Carrie Deshazo and Andre Norman chose to enjoy a late dinner on the patio of the Pane e Vino in the heart of West Hollywood. While sipping a Cabernet Sauvignon, Carrie proposed the trip to Oklahoma.

"A bed and breakfast? On a ranch? My, my, honey, I need some cowboy clothes!" Andre exclaimed gleefully with wide sweeping motions of his delicate hands.

Carrie giggled. The man never failed to make her feel happy. "It's an actual working ranch, Andre. Not a dude ranch."

As he often did, Andre ignored her. "I'll buy some of those satin shirts with the adorable little pearly snap buttons. And pink cowboy boots. I have to have pink cowboy boots!" Andre made a toasting motion with his glass of Merlot.

Andre Norman played well his role as the stereotypical flaming homosexual. None could be prouder of the designation. Still, he exhibited more heart and guts than any man Carrie ever knew. For that, and a hundred other little reasons, she loved him dearly.

"Please, Andre, no pink cowboy boots. Just me being there will draw enough attention."

"Oh, all right," he grinned. "I'll just buy regular cowboy boots. But I will need some rhinestone spurs and a pair of patent leather chaps!"

"You're just wanting some real cowboy to kick your ass, aren't you?" She grinned back.

"Ooohhhh, honey, don't mention real cowboys and my ass in the same sentence. It gives me goose bumps!"

Andre was nearing seventy, but didn't look or act his age. His copper-colored hair still grew naturally, and his brown eyes danced with the life of a man half his years. Andre made his millions as one of the most sought-after screenwriters in Hollywood. He wrote the screenplay for Carrie's first really big movie almost ten years earlier, and they had been close friends ever since. Carrie often thought it ironic that Andre possessed most of the characteristics she wanted in a man. Besides his fortitude, Andre was honest, hard-working, and sincerely caring.

"Please, Andre," Carrie chuckled, "no rhinestones, or chaps. And don't even suggest one of those huge, obnoxious cowboy hats."

"Oh, all right," he sighed with an exaggerated pout. "But when we do get there, I hope you won't deny me a young cowboy or two."

"You are charming, Andre, and most definitely irresistible. But true cowboys? Do you think it's actually possible?"

Andre offered only a knowing wink in response, and Carrie pursued the matter no further. After all, everyone knew it a fact that the screenwriter seduced more than his fair share of Hollywood's leading men. So, one or two cowboys out of all the cowboys in Oklahoma? Carrie wasn't about to bet against it.

"So, sweetheart," Andre purred after sampling his wine, "what is this movie you are adamant about not doing?"

"It's about some old gangster named Belle Starr. Have you ever heard of her?"

"Of course. But she was no gangster, dear. She was an outlaw. The queen of the outlaws, as a matter of fact," Andre said smugly. No one could be as smug as Andre.

"So I've heard," Carrie retorted distastefully. "What do you know about her?"

"Oh, not a whole lot. I know she was murdered. Shot in the back with a shotgun if I remember correctly."

Carrie's wineglass was poised at her lips for a drink and it froze there momentarily before she lowered it without partaking of the contents. The shock must have registered clearly in her expression.

"Oh, Carrie, how insensitive of me. Please forgive me. I just wasn't thinking," Andre gasped as he reached and took one of her hands in both of his.

Carrie's mother had died of a shotgun blast. But she wasn't shot in the back.

Carrie fought back a sigh with a glimpse of her watch. "My, look at the hour."

"The night's still young," Andre responded.

"But it's midnight in Oklahoma," Carrie said and immediately wondered why that seemed to matter.

* * * *

"Hey, Jesse, you out there, man?" Billy Shiloh's words erupted into the engulfing darkness and then returned to him in the form of an echo. Words echoed well in the Sansbois Mountains. Especially in the still of night. Billy had been calling for Jesse ever since the former had been just a runt kid. And so far, Jesse never answered back. Though maybe someday he would. The thought of being answered by a ghost gave Billy a thrill and he laughed out loud. The echo made it seem like the mountains laughed with him.

Billy liked the mountains for many reasons. At the top of his list sat the fact that old Jesse James hid out in the Sansbois. And so had Frank James and the Younger boys and Belle Starr. Some of the old folks would tell that, years later, even Pretty Boy Floyd hid out in these very mountains from the G-men. Billy liked being way up in the Sansbois at night all by himself. At night there were no damned tourists. At night the mountains belonged to Billy Shiloh.

Billy didn't know why, but he always felt a tie to the outlaws who sought refuge in the Sansbois. It felt kind of like a kinship of sorts. Also, Billy always thought he'd been born a hundred or so years too late. The outlaw life called to him. Beckoned him.

So much so, that he often daydreamed of being a modern-day outlaw. Hell, no one would be able to catch Billy in these mountains. He'd been hiking and exploring the Sansbois since before starting the first grade. He'd practiced moving through the thick forest and across the rocky bluffs quickly and quietly, both at day and at night. He grew so good at hiding that there had been times deer and other animals stumbled right upon him before catching his scent.

Billy harbored a secret, too. One of the places the old outlaws hung out now served as a state park named Robbers' Cave. Even though this place still remained secluded up in the rocky bluffs and crevices of one of the mountains, it wasn't really a cave at all. It was really no more than just an indention of twenty or so feet in the side of the mountain. But Billy held as a secret the location of a real-by-God cave. One that a man could get lost in if he wasn't real damned careful. And one, if need be, that a modern-day outlaw could hide in forever.

If he ever did have to run, and someone did by luck find his cave, Billy felt prepared for that, too. Hours upon hours of shooting made him a deadly shot. Billy couldn't remember the last time he'd missed something he shot at. And he was quick, as well. He religiously practiced his quick-draw techniques with his two revolvers for three or four years now and Billy needed no other religion. If it ever came down to a gunfight, Billy didn't have to pray to win.

* * * *

River tried to keep his eyes closed. There seemed no sense in looking. He knew where he'd find himself standing and what he would see if he looked. He also knew what would happen next. The

22

only thing he did not know, that he never knew, was which voice would summons him tonight.

"That's you out there, ain't it, Yates?"

It sounded of the deep, mean voice of Moose Boggs. Breathing suddenly became difficult for River. He could feel the beat of his heart quicken. And though he didn't want to, never wanted to, he opened his eyes. The night stood darker than even the darkest nights should be. But the old barn looked illuminated. Glowing. As if alive. River stood only feet from the closed double doors. Close enough to touch them, but too terrified to do so. Even though he never did it, he knew he could move forward. Because he had tried so many times, he knew he could not back away.

"I know that's you, River Yates. I don't have to see you. I can feel you. It's one of the few good things, Yates, about being dead. When you're dead, you just know things. Why don't you just come on in here, you sorry son of a bitch? Why don't you just come on in here and get what you got comin' to you?"

Then, like he did every night, because he could do nothing else, except move forward, River began to scream. But it did not drown out the voice.

"We're all in here, Yates…waiting. And we can wait forever, man, because forever is all we got left. But you, Yates, you ain't got forever. Sooner or later, you gotta pay for what you done to us."

And, sooner or later, River knew he would.

Chapter Three

Although there were no guests at the Robbers' Roost, Thelma got up at six and started breakfast. Guests or not, she and her older brother had to eat. Since it was just the two of them there would be nothing elaborate this morning. Just eggs and bacon. And none of her homemade biscuits, either. When there were no paying customers, toast worked good enough.

Thelma prepared a pot of coffee when she heard River starting to move around upstairs. Their two bedrooms were located directly above the kitchen and far down a long hallway from the guestrooms. A fact for which Thelma increasingly gave thanks. There were few nights now that River didn't wake her up with his dreadful screams. When they first started, a month or so after the terrible accident in the old red barn, Thelma asked River about the apparent nightmares. River insisted she must be the one dreaming. She knew better. That was just her now lone sibling's way of emphasizing that he wasn't much for sharing feelings of pain and fear. Now, he'd been waking her up in the middle of the night for well past a year, and indications were River still intended to keep to himself whatever tormented him so terribly.

It broke Thelma's heart. River was four years her senior. He had always been a good older brother, and she had been the doting baby sister. As a small girl, she worshipped the ever-protective River. In so many ways, he never stopped being her hero. Even though he changed so much over the past year or so.

Where River had once been swashbuckling, he now acted hesitant. Now instead of boisterous, he seemed more reflective. Subdued rather than confidant. Worse yet, what Thelma always thought gleamed as her brother's crowning glory, even over his dashing looks and swagger, was his booming devil-may-care laugh. Thelma couldn't remember the last time she'd heard him even snicker, much less laugh.

But, still, he had that certain something. When he walked into the kitchen, Thelma – like she did every time River entered a room – felt it. Her brother still had that special presence about him that made people take note of him anytime he made an entrance. It seemed this certain something that always had and still did make River so popular with the women. Even now, he could take his pick of any of the town's available women, and most of those who weren't available. But River just didn't seem that interested in the ladies nowadays. Thelma just figured four wives and four divorces pretty much dampened his enthusiasm for the opposite sex.

This morning River had pulled his thick silver hair into a ponytail. This style accented his strong jaw and rugged good looks. It always seemed to make his electric blue eyes just that more piercing.

"Sure is good to wake up to an empty house," he mumbled while pouring himself a cup of coffee.

"An empty house doesn't make us any money," she responded pleasantly while placing a plate of eggs and bacon on the table in front of him.

For a brief moment Thelma thought he might argue the point, but he just shrugged his square shoulders. To her disappointment, River had lost his passion for debate.

* * * *

As he did every morning after one of the nightmares, River forced himself to step out on the back porch and face the source of the dreams – the old barn. He thought it ironic that, as a child, the barn had been his very favorite place on the ranch. It had been his castle. His hideout. A fortress from which he'd fought off hordes of imaginary Indians, Nazis and slant-eyed little men from Far Eastern places. And with that, more irony. One of the voices that haunted him from within the dream barn belonged to a Vietnamese.

Even as an adult he'd taken refuge in the barn, enjoying the hours he spent there grooming his horses, nursing sick livestock back to health, or any one of the other dozen tasks that ranchers performed in their barns. All that changed the day his only brother, Sky, bled to death on the barn's hay-strewn earthen floor. River had not been in the barn since that day.

The thoughts of Sky and the Vietnamese brought River back around to Moose Boggs. After all, his voice had last called from the lurking structure. Thinking of the man quite naturally led River to think about the day he killed him.

Boggs didn't die quick or easy. He damned sure didn't die like people shot with large-caliber handguns on TV or the movies. There was none of that dramatic flying backwards and landing in a manly spread-eagle-face-up position. River knew for sure though that the many who told and retold of the now famous gun battle had Moose going out in that manner. Hell, there were probably as many fictionalized accounts of the shooting as there were on the gunfight at the O.K. Corral. It had been nearly thirty years since River had gunned down Boggs, but he remembered it like it happened only the night before. And River remembered how it really went down, and it didn't come close to any of the glorified versions.

At the time, River worked as the youngest of the seven police officers on the Wilburton police department. He'd only been on the small-town force for six months. Only back from Vietnam a little over a year. Legend had it that the two men met by chance in the graveled street in front of a now long-gone little tavern, and that a drunk and always mean Boggs called out the young cop – just like the gunslingers did in the movies. Only River knew the truth.

They had not met by chance. Earlier that day, Boggs made some suggestive remarks to Sally Harris while Sally toiled for her minimum wage at the Dairy Queen. Everyone in town knew Sally was River's woman, and soon, everyone in town would know Boggs was trying to take her away from him. Or, at the very least, receive some favors from Sally that River wasn't willing to share. That night, while on duty, River searched the town for Boggs and finally found him heading into the little tavern.

Even though it had been close to thirty years, River could still remember the chill of the night air, the sound of the Credence tune reverberating from the tavern, and the exact exchange of words.

"You owe me and Sally an apology, Boggs."

"I don't owe either of you shit."

"You ain't gonna talk to my woman that way."

"Your woman? Hell, she's fuckin' practically the entire town!"

"You're a lying son of a bitch!"

Boggs evidently had a thing about being called a liar. He went for the .38 revolver in his inside coat pocket. The response definitely surprised River. Sure, the words were heated, but men usually just went fist to fist over angry words and name-calling. River simply underestimated Boggs' propensity for nastiness.

A cop with more time on the streets would have assumed that a man pulling a gun intended to use that gun. River didn't make that assumption. Instead, he assumed Boggs would wave the gun around a little – make some threats – call some names. So, Boggs got off the first shot.

By this time there were bystanders. The most popular and predominant version of what happened told how the two men stood their ground, took aim and blazed away. In fact, they did blaze away.

But neither stood their ground. As a matter of fact, River jerked his .357 from his holster while on the move. By the time he got off his first round, Boggs too was moving. And they weren't moving toward each other. Each moved backwards, and not in any smooth, coordinated fashion either. Both dodged and ducked and stumbled and fumbled. Their movements were too damned spastic to allow for aiming. Basically...it was ugly.

River had no idea how many rounds he fired before Boggs screamed and collapsed to the ground. When River made it to Boggs, the big man had curled up on his side, bled from the mouth and cried like a baby. What bothered River very much then and still did today, was the fact that Moose Boggs died calling for his mama.

Now, mentally back to where he stood physically on the back porch, staring at the red barn, River let out a tortured sigh. He hunted Boggs down because he'd asked Sally Harris for a piece of ass. The man ended up dying over mere words. And of all the different parts of this River most wanted to forget, was the part about Boggs knowing what he said as the truth. It took River a month or two after the shooting to find out, but it proved a fact that ol' Sally dallied with practically the entire town.

River bought a bulletproof vest after his shoot-out with Boggs. The gunfight had been wrong. All wrong. And wrongs always had ways of trying to right themselves. River wore the vest for what little time he remained a cop. Now, it laid put away with all his guns. Far away. River thought it a true pity that all things couldn't so easily be put out of sight and out of mind.

Such as the hulking red barn. River took a deep and strengthening breath of the fresh morning air before descending the steps and covering half the distance between himself and the barn. From what he considered a still safe span from the structure, River raised an index finger and wagged it at what had transpired to be a foe.

"Damn you. Why do you house them? You and me were once great friends. Hell, we shared secrets. Now, you mock me. You let them in, and you keep me out. Damn you."

River turned from the barn and started back for the house not feeling any better about speaking his mind. What awful things did it say about a man, he wondered, who'd been reduced to talking to a barn?

* * * *

Cindy Shiloh carefully crawled out of bed. Billy didn't like being awakened. She didn't know exactly when her husband came home and to bed the night before, but she did know it had been very late. Billy especially didn't like being awakened after being out until the wee hours of the morning. Billy liked his breakfast the minute he got out of bed. Having to wait for his breakfast put Billy in one of his hitting kinds of moods. He hadn't hit or kicked Cindy lately, and she wanted to keep it that way.

She lovingly fixed his favorite breakfast and was careful not to overcook his eggs or undercook his sausage. Sure, Billy had a mean streak, but Cindy knew she was lucky to have him. Billy looked to be by far the most handsome man in Wilburton. His coal black hair, emerald eyes and sculptured body never failed to catch the eye of the town's female population. Cindy loved Billy with all her heart and knew that in his own special way, he loved her, too.

Cindy didn't expect her man to sleep as late as he did. Try as she might, she couldn't keep his breakfast warm. She hurried through the process of frying up more eggs and sausage when he stalked naked into the kitchen. The second breakfast remained several minutes from perfection.

"You've had all this fuckin' time and you ain't got my breakfast ready yet?" he stormed.

"I fixed it once, Billy," Cindy sobbed, "but it got cold."

In the next instance Billy grabbed her by the hair.

"You ain't never goin' to learn, are you?" he screamed in her face while shaking her violently with the grip he held on her hair.

"I think it's time you had a special lesson on how to treat a man," he bellowed.

Jerking Cindy off her feet and dragging her across the floor by the hair of her head, Billy moved to a kitchen chair. He plopped onto the chair, spread his legs and forced Cindy's head to his lap.

"You don't have to make me do this, Billy," Cindy cried. "I'll do it on my own. I love you, Billy!"

When his free hand punched her hard on the left breast, Cindy provided what Billy wanted. It only took awful seconds to complete the task.

"Now, I want my fuckin' breakfast," Billy moaned while jerking her to her feet. With a brutal shove, he sent her stumbling backward toward the range.

The middle of Cindy's back collided violently with the edge of the stove. What seemed like lightening shot through her body and she crumpled to the linoleum floor. The terrible pain lasted only a second, and as Cindy gagged on the salty taste in her mouth, her world faded to black.

* * * *

River had an arm buried nearly up to his elbow in the cow's vagina when Thelma walked into the corral.

"I have news you are just not going to believe!" Thelma nearly squealed. Then, in a more moderate tone, "Jeez, that is so disgusting."

Artificial insemination was expensive, but much cheaper than owning a prize-winning bull. "Oh, I don't know," River droned, "this ol' gal don't seem to mind it."

"Then why do you have to lock her head in that chute?"

"Foreplay," River said under his breath. "So, what's the big news?"

"Oh, yeah," Thelma squealed again. "You will not believe in a million years who I just booked to stay with us for nearly two weeks!"

"Two weeks?" River moaned. "Whoever it is must not have much of a life. Who in the heck stays in a bed and breakfast for two weeks?"

"Rich and famous people. That's who!"

Thelma's enthusiasm did not prove contagious. "Getting ready to pull my arm out. Might want to turn your head."

Thelma did, and even shut her eyes. "Don't you want to know who it is?"

"Not really," River sighed as he pulled off the elbow-length plastic glove.

"Okay, I'll tell you," Thelma giggled, "but you have to promise not to tell anyone. Our guests want their privacy. They don't want to be bothered by a town-load of autograph seekers."

River released the chute, and the cow didn't hang around. River wished he didn't have to. "Famous people? Why would famous people want to come here?"

"For privacy and seclusion. That's why you can't tell a single soul. You know how things get around in town."

River did. "Well? Who in blazes is it?"

"Carrie Deshazo!" Thelma all but screamed.

"Who?"

"Who? I said, Carrie Deshazo!"

"Never heard of her."

"You've never heard of Carrie Deshazo?" Thelma gasped.

"Now, Thelma, why the hell would I say I never heard of her if, in fact, I had heard of her?"

"Oh, my God, River! Carrie Deshazo is one of the biggest movie stars of this decade!"

"I don't frequent the movies, Thelma. I don't even have time for television. Never heard of her."

"She starred in *Heritage Park Rumors* and *A Dozen Miami's* and, oh, what was that movie about the little boy that was adopted by the Jewish couple in..."

"Thelma, I don't want to live two weeks with some snooty Hollywood star!"

"Well, then, you better just find you someplace else to live for two weeks," Thelma growled before stomping away. Then, over her shoulder, "And don't tell anyone that they are coming."

"They?" River shouted after her. "Who else is coming?"

"She's bringing a famous screenwriter with her," Thelma shouted back.

"I don't like screenwriters, either!"

Thelma didn't seem to care.

* * * *

"You're two hours late this time, Billy."

There existed no malice in the words. They simply stated a fact. It was Walter Bates' way. Billy never knew a nicer man. Billy stood as living proof that Bates could be generous to a fault. Bates' goodness almost never failed to make Billy want to smash the old man's head in.

"Sorry, Walter. Cindy had some things she wanted me to do around the house."

"A woman will do that," Bates chuckled. "How is that daughter of mine doing?"

"Doing fine," Billy lied. She hadn't come to by the time he'd left the house. But he believed she would be up and around by the time he made it home. Also, she'd no doubt be wiser in the ways of how a wife should act.

Bates toiled at the process of changing the oil in his John Deere tractor. Had Billy been to work on time, he'd be the one performing this grimy, demeaning task. The old man already drained the dirty oil and strained at loosening the oil filter. The thought of volunteering to jump in and help occurred to Billy, but he ignored it. The too-nice old bastard seemed to be doing just fine all by himself.

"Heard you had a little run-in the other day with River Yates," Bates grunted while wrestling with the filter.

"I didn't start it," Billy lied again.

Bates looked up from the filter and arched his eyebrows knowingly. He was just too damned nice to call Billy a liar.

"I didn't," Billy insisted. "He's the one that started shit with me."

"Well, I guess that's possible," Bates said as he turned his attention back to the stubborn filter, "especially if ol' River was drinking. I just feel obliged to tell you, Billy, that he isn't a man you want to mess with. He can be meaner than a rattlesnake."

"Didn't seem so mean to me," Billy sulked. "Word has it that he's gone coward."

Bates managed to break the filter loose and now wiped his oily hands on an old towel. "You know, River was highly decorated in Vietnam for bravery. One time, years ago, I saw him take on two ol' boys at the county fair. They were both a lot bigger than River. Of course, he's always been stronger than a darned ox, but anyway, he whipped both of those men. And whipped them unmercifully. One was in the hospital for a month.

"Yeah, I've heard all that noise about him losing his guts," Bates said as he tossed the towel aside and started screwing on the new filter. "But let me tell you something, Billy, a rattlesnake can lose its rattlers, but it still has its fangs. I'm sure ol' River has calmed down a little. Age does that to a person, but a man like that, he doesn't ever really change. You take my word on this, Billy, don't mess with that man. Way down deep beneath whatever River Yates is today, is still a dangerous man. You catch him just right, and he'll kill you, or make you wish you were dead."

Billy did listen to the advice and drew one conclusion – he had some things to prove. River Yates would be the way he did it.

* * * *

Hank Sioux had not seen River since the day Billy Shiloh started the trouble in his bar. Since his old friend weighed heavy upon his mind, and since it turned out such a glorious spring day, Hank decided to drive out to the Working Y Ranch. Hank didn't expect River to tell him what bothered him. It just wasn't his way. But, maybe just having someone to shoot the shit with might make whatever tormented River just a little bit better. A real friend was something hard to find, and nobody made a better friend than River.

Hank made it halfway to the ranch and crested Copperhead Hill when he spotted River and his motorcycle. The bike sat parked beside the asphalt road, and River stood alongside looking at it.

Hank brought his rickety old pickup to a stop and said out his window, "You having problems?"

"Nope," River grunted.

"Then what the hell are you doing?"

"Looking at my bike."

"Why?"

River turned his gaze from the bike to the countryside and seemed to consider his surroundings. "I bought this bike when I was still married to Alice," he said, apparently more to himself than to Hank. "First new Harley I ever owned. I've ridden them since long before it was a craze."

River always liked to point that out nowadays, and Hank always thought it seemed a waste of effort. Hell, considering the looks of both the man and bike, no one would confuse River for a yuppie weekend rider. "Yeah, I know. Hey, where were you headed?"

"I was considering leaving town."

"But you ain't got nothing packed," Hank pointed out.

"Thought I'd just hit the road. Go someplace I never been. I could find work along the way to buy whatever I needed."

It wasn't the first time River talked of up and leaving. But he never exactly said what he was running from or to. Hank would never be surprised if one day River simply disappeared.

River looked back at his bike and seemed to consider it profoundly. "Alice was a damned good woman. I should have treated her better."

"You know, River, what we ought to do is just head into town and open the bar a little early today. Hell, you can pick some other day to leave town."

For the first time during the conversation, River looked at Hank. "Is that damned mean dog of yours going to be there?"

"No. Left him at home today."

River nodded his head a couple of times and then crawled on the bike he'd bought when married to his last wife.

* * * *

Billy stepped through the front door of his little house and called his wife's name. No answer came in return.

"Cindy? Hey, Cindy!" he shouted louder this time. Just as he started to think maybe she'd gone out to pick up some groceries, he heard the sobbing. Billy tracked the pitiful sounds to the kitchen.

Cindy lay on the floor in the same spot Billy left her nearly seven hours earlier.

"What the hell..." Billy started.

"I can't move my legs, Billy!" she cried out. "I think you broke my back!"

Billy froze in place. 'Bullshit," he muttered.

"I can't feel them either, Billy. I can't feel my legs," Cindy said before starting to cry louder.

Shiloh shook his head to clear it. She had to be mistaken. Did Cindy realize if she broke her back what kind of trouble he would be in? The house, the car, all that money for so little effort - he would lose it all.

"I need help, Billy," she screamed. "Call an ambulance!"

"No. Oh, no. We can't do that, Cindy," he said as he fell to his knees beside her. "Your back ain't broke. You just need some rest. You need something to eat. I'll get you to bed."

Billy reached to put his arms beneath her. Something might be wrong with her legs, but not her arms. She slapped his hands away.

"Don't move me! I laid here all day afraid to move! Don't do me more damage!"

While Billy tried to lift her, Cindy attacked with her arms and hands, slapping, pushing, and scratching. Until Billy grabbed her around the throat.

"Listen to me, God damn you. I ain't losing all we have, and I damned sure ain't going to jail for a worthless bitch like you! Now, I'm going to put you to bed and nurse you back to health, and if you keep fighting me...I'm going to break the part of your back that controls your arms."

Cindy gave Billy a look he'd never seen her give. It wasn't just fear. He'd seen that on her before. No, this looked like real, deep, scared-shitless kind of terror. And it shut her up. When he hoisted her off the floor, Cindy passed out.

* * * *

River got his fill of Thelma's excitement long before he did her fried pork chops. She just went on and on and on about what it meant to have such special guests staying in their home. River pointed out that it wasn't a home, but a make-shift Holiday Inn. She just ignored him.

Had he told anyone in town they were coming? Hell no. He didn't see it as that big of a deal. Besides, he couldn't remember the big-shit actress's name. To get away from all the ranting, River stomped out to his workshop to busy himself on his project.

Even though this particular job evolved from a long-ago broken promise, it soothed River to work on it. After all, it was penitence. Just one way of making up for a life of broken promises. One day he would be finished with it. When that time did come, he knew neither what he would do with the finished product...or himself. Sometimes he truly believed this undertaking solely kept him from completely going insane.

Chapter Four

Billy moved through the dense woods under the cover of darkness. No breeze existed to ease the night's humidity, and sweat coated his body. Still, he progressed quickly and effortlessly with the confidence of a man who knew exactly his destination. Like he had done so many nights before. Billy found the entrance of his secret cave without difficulty. He quickly moved aside the logs and branches concealing the small opening just barely big enough for Billy to slither into like a snake.

The entrance gave way to a small area that allowed Billy to almost stand upright. In seconds he found the flashlight he kept hidden in the cave's "foyer." He used the light to illuminate the chamber that spiraled lazily into the depth of the cave's belly. Billy came to check his stored provisions.

For years he smuggled cans of food and small bottles of water into his hideout. He also squirreled away a sleeping bag, a kerosene lamp, several gallons of kerosene and a twelve-gauge shotgun he'd stolen from a friend's house when only fourteen-years-old. Since then he'd pilfered enough shells to hold off any posse that might come looking for him. He checked it all and nothing seemed disturbed.

After lighting the lamp, Billy sat down on the cool floor to finalize the plans he hoped would get him out of his current predicament. The light of the lamp danced on the moist rock walls and helped soothe Billy's jittery nerves. He knew what he had to do. He just didn't know exactly how to do it. If the plan didn't work – if he couldn't pull it off – the cave would become his home. Or, more appropriately, the base-camp for the outlaw Billy Shiloh.

* * * *

River bolted upright in bed and grabbed his head with both hands. Trembling fingers worked to massage the pain from his temples. Tonight, he'd heard the voice of the Vietnamese. Although he had long forgotten what little words and phrases he knew of the singsong dialect, he somehow understood the high-pitched foreign words that beckoned him to open the door and enter the old red barn.

It had been so many, many years ago, but the voice always took him back. Once again, he was a mere teen and frightened beyond imagination and far too young to be a squad leader – much too inexperienced to be held responsible for the lives of ten other frightened youths.

Every time he went back, it all remained the same. Nothing ever changed. Still the floor of the jungle stood tangled and moist and alive with insects that stung and bit and demoralized. Still as dark as if someone painted the canopy above their heads in black and extinguished every star in the heavens. Still eternally hot, the air heavy and hard to breathe, saturated with the odors of rotting foliage, sweat from filthy bodies, and the unmistakable scent of fear. And always,

always, no matter how hard River Yates fought to keep from going back, he went back all the same...

* * * *

...River swatted at the mosquito buzzing around his ear and wondered why he bothered. If he got lucky enough to kill it, a dozen more would just take its place. In defense, he tried to push his steel pot far enough down his head to cover as much of his ears as possible. His stomach ached from a tinge of dysentery and his left foot itched miserably from the fungus raging between his toes. Just another shit detail in a shit land and all River really wanted to do was get the fuck out of there.

Stone and Bensen argued again in hushed tones – their way of dealing with the shit detail in the shit land. River didn't know what they disagreed about this time. Their tones were hushed, but still dangerously audible.

"Stone, Bensen, shut the fuck up," River hissed in a whisper.

Profanities were returned, and then near-silence reigned once again.

River's squad had been tasked to set an ambush. Two of the other squads in his platoon were in place further down the narrow jungle path. Intelligence suspected the path to be a supply route used by only small teams of NVA to provision nearby villages. It had been River's experience that intelligence seldom got things right. This mission counted the third time in a week and a half that his squad deployed on an ambush. So far, their efforts netted absolutely nothing. That didn't bother River even a little bit, because it all made so little sense. The war had all but ended. The bulk of U.S. forces were pulling out of Nam. Being here, now, made no damn sense at all. Why run up a body count for a war all but lost?

An hour passed, and then two. Try as he might, River could not keep his mind on the business at hand. It kept slipping away from him – escaping from the misery of his hiding place in the jungle to the place he longed to be. Home. His mom was not in good health. He doubted that his girlfriend remained loyal. He wondered if his brother had taken good care of his motorcycle and horse. He thought of hot showers and a real bed and...

Suddenly he heard a noise – the snapping of a twig. Slowly, carefully, quietly, River raised his M-16 and peered through the attached starlight scope. The air in his lungs turned to ice.

A lone figure moved methodically along the path with a Chinese assault rifle held at the ready. River could make out the shape of a pith helmet. The head gear distinguished an NVA regular – the point man. Further behind the enemy soldier shimmered the blur of other figures. River couldn't get a count, but knew for sure that this was no small team.

Although he could feel the pound of his heart clear to the tips of his fingers and his guts clenching like an angry fist, River reverted to his training – don't execute on the point man. Let him pass – wait for the main body. River's only signal to his squad would be him opening fire.

When the mass of bodies filled his starlight, River pulled the trigger. Instantaneously, the dark exploded into light and the silence erupted into a deafening roar as his men let go with all they had. River had his selector switch on semi-automatic. Several of his men had theirs set for fully automatic. The ground actually seemed to move. The squad's night vision disintegrated to blindness and the starlight scopes were rendered useless. The massed weapons spit fire and lead for what seemed like an eternity, and as far as River could tell, they caught the enemy so unaware that they could not return a high-rate of fire. River didn't even try to give the order of cease-fire. He just let his men go until they were spent. Just as suddenly as it started, the shooting stopped. No one moved a muscle as the darkness returned with a vengeance. The radioman made the only sound as he reported in a gasping whisper to platoon headquarters.

After long seconds of catching his breath, River tried his voice. "Is anyone hit?" No response meant a good response.

Even longer seconds ticked by before he spoke again. "Payton, Michaels, follow me. Everyone else stay put."

River pushed to his feet and he saw two other forms doing the same. His legs felt like jelly. They did not want to respond to the task at hand. The damage, though, had to be surveyed. Any remaining source of danger demanded elimination. River already loaded a fresh twenty-round magazine into his M-16 and moved the selector switch to automatic.

The narrow path was strewn with bodies and heavily-laden bicycles which were pushed down the supply line. The guerrillas used them like wheelbarrows to transport their supplies.

Carefully, and poised to fire, River and his two men worked in and around the devastation. Just when he began to think the destruction complete, what should have been a dead body raised up just feet in front of River. The singsong high-pitched voice cried out, and River responded by emptying the twenty rounds at practically point-blank range.

He had been deep in this shit land for nearly nine months, and, for the first time he knew, without a doubt, that he hit an intended target. The flash from his muzzle once again blinded him, and River could not clearly see the results of his response. Nor did he want to.

He only wanted to quickly move away, but he couldn't. It felt as if the bloody muck of the trail held him in place. Finally, after what seemed an eternity, he felt hands pulling him away.

Corporal Tim Payton's voice seemed to call from the far end of a very long tunnel. "Come on, River, the company's coming up. We've been relieved. It's over, River. Let's go. It's finished man..."

* * * *

...But three decades had come and gone, and River now knew that it would never be over. He would never be finished with what happened that night in the jungle.

With his head buried in his hands and his sheets soaked from sweat and tears, he didn't have to remind himself that it wasn't what happened that night that kept the memory alive, but instead what he learned about the ambush days later that would not let it die. The news of what intelligence revealed came directly to River from his company commander. The CO didn't want him hearing about it from any other source. He wanted to make sure his young sergeant understood that in war, well, shit happens. Sometimes, it's really ugly shit that could stay with a man for a long, long time. The captain, probably no older than twenty-five himself, had taken a fatherly approach to telling River that, yeah, it was a fuck-up, but not one he should take blame for.

Eleven human beings were shot to shit on that trail — the one who had suddenly sat up, who should have already been dead, nearly got cut in half by River s gunfire. Three of those found dead were NVA. The rest had been taken by force from a small village by the NVA and forced to push the bicycles down the trail. None of them were armed. Four of them were women. One of the men was in his seventies. The one who sat up, the one who should have already been dead, turned out to be a mere boy of thirteen.

The high-pitched singsong voice that wailed from the barn had never grown to sound older over the years. No matter how many times River begged him in his dreams, the boy refused to forgive.

* * * *

Billy returned home at a little past midnight. He expected Cindy to be awake, but she wasn't. She still lay on the bed just like he had left her with her hands bound together with duct tape and a sock stuffed in her mouth held in place with yet more of the tape. Now, he started being quieter. He didn't want her awakened. It would be easier this way.

Billy stripped off all his clothes and then grabbed the pair of cotton gloves off the nightstand. He'd worn them earlier in the day when he'd tied and gagged Cindy with the tape. Billy once again put on the gloves and then carried his clothes into the kitchen. While there, he removed a butcher knife from the drawer next to the sink. Without further hesitation he padded back to the bedroom. He didn't want time to talk himself out of doing what had to be done. He went directly to Cindy's side of the bed and reached across her to get his pillow. In one quick movement he shoved the pillow down over her face with his left hand and used his right one to plunge the knife into her chest.

Billy expected a reaction. Some movement, moaning, something – but there was none. His first attempt must have gone smooth in the heart. See, he reaffirmed to himself, he'd simply performed a by-God mercy killing. Still, he had to make it look like something else. So, he jerked the knife out and plunged it in again and again until his arm grew tired of doing so. The sound it made going in and out kind of gave Billy the creeps. He anticipated lots of blood, but little appeared. He'd expected gushing but it only seeped. Taking his clothes off had been a waste of time.

With the dirty part of the work completed, Billy yanked Cindy's T-shirt up around her neck and used the knife to slice her bra apart in the middle of the cups Cindy's left breast had a nasty bruise on it. A wonderful effect, Billy thought. Next, he unbuttoned her jeans and worked them and her panties halfway down her thighs. While he still had on the gloves, he pulled one drawer out of their bureau and dumped the contents on the floor. Only then did Billy remove the gloves and cram them into a small plastic trash bag.

Considering all finished and smartly done, Billy took the knife and climbed in the shower. He didn't have much blood on him, but better safe than sorry. He scrubbed his entire body and the knife with a little brush Cindy kept in the shower. Then he carefully washed the brush. After drying, he went back to the kitchen, got dressed, and tossed the knife back in the drawer. After grabbing up the bag that held the gloves, Billy went out the front door, remembering to lock it behind him. He disposed of the gloves in the sewer grate on the curb in front of the little house, and then went back to the front door and gave it a sturdy kick. It only took one. The cheap lock and flimsy door easily gave way, and thankfully, the noise didn't sound loud enough to wake any of the neighbors.

Now came the time for the truly hard part. Billy had to somehow act distraught. He went back in the house and dialed 911.

* * * *

As the chief of police of the Wilburton Police Department, Mike Simms didn't normally work the graveyard shift. But one of his nine officers stayed home sick while another enjoyed vacation. Filling in where needed just came with the turf of running a small department. Simms didn't mind. He had the education, smarts, and experience to work in a larger department, but he preferred the less hectic life of policing a rural community. It functioned as a trade-off, and Simms believed that trade-offs were just a part of living.

Simms cruised the outskirts of town when Tammy Welcher's shrill voice came across the police radio in a near scream.

"Chief Simms are you out there?"

The night dispatcher was the excitable type and normally forgot radio procedure when anything out of the norm occurred.

"Adam One, to headquarters," Simms responded irritably. "Of course, I'm out here, Tammy. What do you have?"

"A murder, Chief! We have a report of a murder!"

Now, Mike Simms' heartbeat quickened. Wilburton, Oklahoma, didn't get a whole lot of murders. "What's the location, Tammy?"

"It's at 265 East Tulsa. A Billy Shiloh is screaming that someone has broken into his house and murdered his wife," Tammy huffed as if out of breath.

Simms sat clear across town from Tulsa Street. It would take him a good three minutes to get there. The chief knew Billy Shiloh and thought of him as trouble just looking for a place to happen. He considered telling Tammy to start a county deputy or highway patrolman that way to help, but decided he'd hold off. If Shiloh killed his wife, he probably wouldn't be calling the police. Plus, Simms didn't want too much hoopla just yet. Shiloh's wife was Cindy Shiloh and Cindy's daddy did, after all, own most of the town. Sims didn't believe in causing a stink when stink could be avoided.

Shiloh awaited Simms out in front of his residence. The young man looked noticeably upset – pacing, ringing his hands, and crying out loud. He sprinted out to the curb to meet Simms.

"She's dead!" He screamed. "I just came home to find that someone had raped and cut up my wife! They kicked the fuckin' front door in and raped and killed my Cindy!"

Shiloh's face practically dripped from apparent tears. Damn, Simms thought, it looked as if the boy splashed water on his face. The cop took a few minutes to try to calm Shiloh, and finally persuaded him to wait in the patrol car while Simms investigated.

The door had surely been kicked in. Simms entered the Shiloh place with gun in hand. One never knew. He encountered no one in the living room or kitchen. One lone light glared in the back of the house, and Simms slowly made his way back to it.

And there she laid – a young girl gagged and tied and half-naked and most assuredly dead. Chief Simms turned away in disgust, repulsed by the sight and one single memory. Just last summer he saw Cindy downtown in a tight, short summer dress. Like a man will, he quite naturally wondered what the fine woman looked like beneath that dress. Now he knew. He wished he didn't. Chief Simms' stomach lurched and he fought to hold in the burger he'd eaten earlier in the night.

* * * *

Billy sat in the car and went over the story in his mind over and over again. Try as he might, he couldn't work up one single, real damned tear. Finally, the unusually tall, skinny cop practically bounded out of the house. He didn't look so good. Billy fought back a snicker.

When Simms opened the driver door to get in, Billy sounded as concerned as he could. "See, she's dead, ain't she? I told you, raped and murdered."

"Yeah, Billy, you were right," Simms said as he seemed to melt into the driver's seat. His voice actually trembled. "Tell me what you know, Billy. How long ago did you find her?"

"Hell, just minutes ago. I came home, found the door kicked in and I just about went crazy. I started screaming Cindy's name, but there wasn't no damned answer. I went running into the bedroom..." Billy paused and tried to cry. When he couldn't, he went on, "...I couldn't believe my eyes. Somebody had killed my new wife. I ran back in the kitchen and called for help."

"Where had you been this time of night, Billy? What had you been doing?"

The question didn't bother Billy. It didn't sound like the man held him in blame. Billy was ready for the question anyway.

"I work for Cindy's dad, Walter Bates. I was stocking the shelves of his little grocery store over on Tenth Street. I got keys to the place."

"You have any idea who would do a thing like this?"

Billy sure wanted to grin. He was ready for this one, too. Billy often felt amazed at his own brilliance.

"I sure do. It was that sorry bastard Yates."

Simms turned and looked hard at Billy. "River Yates?"

"It had to be, Mister Simms. I had trouble with him the day before yesterday in the Silver Dollar Bar. And then, just yesterday, he came right here to my house and threatened to do me harm right in front of Cindy. And Cindy, she butted in and told him he better get off our property. That's when he looked her over real good. I could just see the lust and hate in his eyes. Hell, I should have killed him right there and then. Oh, God, I'm to blame that she's in there now all raped and dead!"

Billy covered his face in his hands and made some damned good sobbing noises. The cop patted him on the shoulder and said some soothing words. Billy wished to hell he could work up some tears.

* * * *

Mike Simms idled up the long gravel road to the Robbers' Roost bed and breakfast with his lights out. Oklahoma Highway Patrolman Steve Payne pulled in behind him. Steve had his lights out, as well. The big house sat dark and peaceful looking. Of course, it was nearly four in the morning.

Simms knew River Yates well and didn't think it possible for him to commit such an ugly act, but the accusation demanded an investigation. The chief fancied himself somewhat of a historian on the period of Oklahoma's territory days. A time when Wilburton and the surrounding area became settled by a rough breed of man that often came to the mountainous country seeking refuge from the law in Fort Smith, Arkansas. A common and unusual characteristic of the type that occupied the countryside was that they were somedays lawmen, and other days outlaws. Many of the modern-day citizens of Wilburton were descendants of such men and still bore the same rowdy characteristics. River most definitely fit the mold. Simms wanted Trooper Payne with him on the slight chance River murdered Cindy Shiloh. If he did, River would not be a man Simms would care to try to take in by himself. And if he didn't do it, Simms wanted Payne by his side because you never knew what kind of mood you'd find River in. The man would most likely not take kindly to being questioned about a rape and murder.

* * * *

River awakened to Thelma tugging on his shoulder and calling his name.

"What? What the hell is it?" When he could sleep, River slept soundly.

"River, are you awake?"

He awoke enough to detect the fright in his sister's voice.

"Yeah, I'm awake. What time is it? What's wrong?"

"Mike Simms and Steve Payne are downstairs, River. They want to talk to you. They wouldn't tell me what it's about."

Then a voice sounded from behind Thelma. It made her jump.

"Hey, River, it's me, Mike Simms. Why don't you get your hands out of those covers so I can see them?"

"What?" River sat up in bed and tried to shake the sleep from his head. Inadvertently, he did bring empty hands into clear view.

"Thanks," Simms said as he stepped up beside Thelma. Steve Payne moved around to the other side of the bed.

"Looks like you got me surrounded, boys. Now, you want to tell me what the hell is going on?"

"Why don't you crawl out of bed, River," Payne spoke up.

"Because I'm naked, Steve,"

"Okay," Payne replied, face reddening.

"River, we sure hate to disturb you," it was Simms again. "But we have to ask you some questions."

"Well, okay. I don't know what the hell you have to question me about, but could you boys step out a minute and let me throw on some pants?"

"No, you're just fine right where you are, River," Simms grinned. "I kind of like you there empty handed and nude. It makes you seem just a little more agreeable."

"Yeah, I guess it does. No matter what you think I've done, I ain't about to fight you buck-assed naked in front of my little sister."

"Good," Simms nodded. "Now, where were you tonight between the hours of about nine and midnight?"

"He was right here," Thelma butted in. "He was home for dinner by five thirty and he's been here ever since."

"Yeah. I went out to my shop at about seven, but I was back in the house at nine. Now, what the hell do you think I've done?"

Ignoring the question, Simms turned to Thelma. "You saw him come in the house at nine?"

"Of course, I was watching television in the den."

"What time did you go to bed, Thelma?"

"About ten-thirty."

"Then, you really don't know if he was here from ten-thirty to midnight, do you?" Simms' tone sounded gentle.

"I damned sure know he was here at eleven-thirty." Thelma's did not.

"And how do you know that?"

"Hey!" River inserted, "I want to know right now what this is all about, or neither one of us has another word to say."

"You can talk here in the comfort of your bed, River, or you can talk to us down at the police station." Simms' words had taken on a little edge.

River allowed himself the same privilege. "A man ought to do whatever his balls are big enough to allow him to do, Mike. So, go ahead. Take me to jail on a false arrest. I just wouldn't mind a damned bit owning a chunk of our fine little town."

Mike Simms seemed to seriously consider his options for a good long minute. "Do you know Cindy Shiloh? Walter Bates' daughter?"

"Sure," River nodded, "known her since she was a baby."

Mike Simms stared intently at River. River recognized the look of being studied and evaluated.

"Well, she was murdered tonight," Simms said with a grimace.

Thelma let out a moan before plopping down on the edge of the bed.

"Murdered?" River didn't want to believe it. Cindy had always been a sweet child, and Walter Bates a fine man.

"Maybe raped, too. An agent from the Oklahoma State Bureau of Investigation and a medical examiner are at the scene now. We'll know more here in a little bit. Just might get some hard evidence on the perpetrator," Simms said testily.

The shock of the news caused River to dwell solely on poor Cindy and her father. The mentioning of the word "perpetrator," however, brought his well-being quickly to mind.

"Whoa! You wait just one damned minute here," River allowed his voice to boom as he sat up as straight in his bed as he could without exposing himself. "Are you accusing me of murder and rape?"

"No, I'm not," Mike said with a vehement shake of his head, "but Billy Shiloh is. Why don't you tell me about the fight you had with him?"

"Fight?" River all but shouted, unable to fathom why Shiloh would make such a damaging accusation. "Hell, that wasn't no fight. Maybe an argument, but it was damn sure no fight. Why in the world would that man think I killed his wife?"

"Tell me about going over to his house yesterday," Simms said with eyebrows arched.

"I didn't go to his house yesterday or any other day. I don't even know where the sonofabitch lives!"

Mike Simms seemed to suddenly grow tired of the questions and answers. He rubbed at his temples for a few seconds before proceeding. "Okay. Thelma here can vouch for your whereabouts from late afternoon until ten-thirty last night. And, Thelma, you say you know he was here at eleven thirty. So, if this is true, River, you couldn't have made it into town, done that dirty deed and gotten back out here in an hour's time.

"Now, Thelma," Simms said as he started to pace, "you never told me how you know River was here at eleven-thirty. Did you see him at that time?"

River's mood sunk even lower. Thelma hadn't seen him after he went to bed. She must have heard him – the nightmare – the screams. Before saying a word, his sister looked him in the eyes, and must have read what weighed on his mind.

"My bedroom is next door," she began cautiously. "You know, Mike, River suffers from...a lot of old wounds. From the war, and from his rodeo days. He does quite a bit of moaning some nights. You know, like when he rolls over, or gets up. Right at eleven-thirty, I heard him moaning."

River breathed a sigh of relief. Screaming was not something he wanted people knowing that he did.

"You're sure?" Mike said, sounding hopeful.

"Of course I'm sure, Mike Simms. Sure as I am that you're standing in my house this very moment accusing a good man of a terrible deed."

Simms chuckled, and looked relieved. "Good, Thelma. I hope you both understand this is something I had to do. And, I hope you both know that I might be back, you know, considering what evidence might turn up."

"I ain't worried about it turning up a damned thing, Mike," River said pointedly.

"Well, you just stick around these parts for a few days. Don't be leaving town," Simms said with little conviction. "And, you might keep an eye out for Billy Shiloh. He doesn't seem to care much for you."

That did worry River.

* * * *

The sun was nearly up before the lawmen left the Working Y, and Thelma prepared a light breakfast. River barely did more than pick at it. Accusations of hideous crimes tended to play hell with a man's appetite. Once the sun popped over the horizon, River took his place before the red barn.

"Guess you and all those inside of you find my current predicament particularly amusing. You want that boy, Shiloh, to come for me, don't you? Yeah, you want another occupant...him... or me."

River paused to take in a deep breath only to release it slowly from pursed lips. He looked at the ground and shook his head. *Talking to a damned barn...and dead men.* The realization, although disturbing, didn't stop him from doing more of the same.

"Well, let me tell you all one thing for sure. I'm not contributing to your body count. No way in hell. And one more thing, I'm real close to losing this entire ranch. The very last thing I will do before they come to drag me off my land...is burn you to the ground. That's a promise."

River signaled his resolve by spitting in the direction of the barn. With that, he turned and started back to the house, throwing over his right shoulder the middle finger of his right hand.

Chapter Five

"See? We should have hired a limousine and a driver."

Carrie Deshazo laid her head down on the steering wheel and took several deep breaths. This was the second time Andre had said this since leaving the airport in Oklahoma City. The first time, she took a wrong exit off the interstate that ended up taking them thirty miles out of their way. Now, parked on the shoulder of the highway, just five or so miles outside Wilburton, she wished she'd taken his suggestion when they planned their travel arrangements. Her decision to get a rental began to really look like a poor one.

"Well, surely you know how to change a flat," she rebutted.

"Well, surely I don't," Andre said in his smug way. "Never have done it. Never intend to."

"You expect me to change it?"

"No. I expect you to call Avis. Have them send assistance."

Carrie felt stupid for not thinking of that on her own. She grabbed her purse from the back seat and pulled out her cell.

"Oh, shit," she blurted, "there's no service."

"My, my, now, we do seem to have a situation," Andre said with nervous nods of his head.

After taking a few seconds to collect her thoughts, Carrie reached across Andre to the glove compartment. "The owner's manual should have instructions. Changing a tire isn't brain surgery, Andre."

"Let's hope not. I've never done that either."

The manual did have instructions, and the process didn't seem all that complicated. After unloading their luggage from the trunk, they found the jack, lug wrench, and an exceptionally small spare tire tucked tidily away in their own little compartments.

"The book says the first thing we do is loosen the lug nuts," Carrie instructed.

"All right then," Andre said enthusiastically, "where are they?"

"They're on the wheel, Andre," she said patiently.

"I don't see them."

"They're beneath the wheel cover, Andre."

"As well they should be," he chuckled.

The wheel cover came off easily. The nuts wouldn't budge.

"Are you turning them the right way?" Andre asked.

"The book says counterclockwise, Andre. I'm trying to turn them counterclockwise. You're the man. You ought to be doing this part."

"You are probably stronger than I am," Andre said without shame.

He was probably right. After a few more minutes of experimentation, Carrie figured out that it best to position the wrench so she could push down on it with the entire weight of her body. Soon, all lug nuts were loosened. She could feel the sweat soaking through her cotton blouse.

"Damn, it's hot here," she huffed.

"Tell me about it," Andre said as he fanned his face with delicate movements of both hands.

"Okay. There should be a slot in the frame right in front of the tire, Andre. Find it and screw the top of the jack up and into the slot."

"You're already down there, and already quite a mess. Why don't you do it?"

"For God's sake, Andre, you're wearing cowboy clothes and cowboy clothes are made to do work in," Carrie said while wiping the sweat from her forehead with the back of her hands. Her fingertips were coated in grease.

"Do I look authentic? You've never said," Andre scowled.

Carrie had been pleased that Andre dressed conservatively western. He wore starched Wranglers, a denim shirt that didn't have the pearly snap buttons and a pair of exotic skinned black boots. The oval-shaped belt buckle with the bucking horse at first seemed awfully large. But, in both the Dallas-Fort Worth and Oklahoma City airports, she'd seen much larger ones. She also felt pleased he'd not found a cowboy hat suiting his taste.

"You look very authentic," she replied while standing to stretch.

Carrie allowed herself a break while she considered the wonder of their surroundings. The countryside changed drastically during their three-hour trip. The land just outside the sprawling capitol city had consisted of the rolling plains she'd expected to find in Oklahoma. Even there, however, there had been many more trees than she expected to find. Along the way they marveled over fields of brilliant green, and cattle seemed to be practically everywhere. In just the past thirty miles the terrain turned more mountainous, nothing like one would find in the Rockies, but rugged and beautiful all the same. Here, where they sat stranded, wild flowers bloomed in vivid purples and reds and yellows all along the roadway. The air, although humid, smelled clean beyond belief and carried the wonderful scent of all the flowers. It truly was a beautiful place.

"My goodness," Andre exclaimed, breaking Carrie's revelry, "you won't see a sight like that in Los Angeles."

Carrie followed Andre's pointing finger down the stretch of road behind them. Coming toward them was a large green tractor. A dark young man, bare from the waist up, pulled the imposing machine off the highway and pulled to a stop behind the rental car.

"The Gods have sent us an angel," Andre clucked appreciatively.

The nicely-muscled man with the thick black hair, Carrie had to admit, was handsome to a fault.

"You folks need a hand?" he asked cheerfully as he crawled down from the tractor.

"Oh, yes, yes, we most certainly do!" Andre giggled with quick little claps of his hand.

The man stopped in his tracks and stared quizzically at Andre. "Ya'll ain't from around here, are you?"

"No, we are not," Carrie said, stepping in front of Andre, "but we certainly could use your help. We have a flat and neither of us has changed a tire before."

The man craned his neck to look around Carrie and frowned as he considered Andre. His expression offered no comfort. Then he turned cold green eyes on Carrie. Now, he smiled again, but the eyes didn't portray the same sentiment. For seconds, he unabashedly scanned those eyes over Carrie's entire body. She quickly decided she didn't like the man. Quite literally, he gave her the creeps.

"Hey, don't I know you from someplace?" he asked while moving up uncomfortably close.

"I told you we're not from around here," Carrie said as she took a step backwards.

"Yeah, I heard you, but...well. I'll be damned!" He suddenly laughed out loud as he started circling Carrie, taking her in from different angles. "I know who you are!"

"Would you please help us with the tire?" Carrie didn't really want him to. She really wanted him to leave, but felt certain that wasn't going to happen.

"You're that actress that played in that movie about that female cop, ain't you!" the man said gleefully.

"Well, I'll be double damned. Now, what's your name?" he persisted.

Carrie considered lying, but knew it would only prolong the inevitable.

"Carrie Deshazo," she said coolly.

"Why hell yes! You damned sure are Carrie Deshazo. Well don't that beat all! My name's Billy Shiloh," the man beamed while extending his right hand.

"I have grease on my hands," Carrie responded.

"Hell, I don't care. You're Carrie Deshazo. Put it there Carrie Deshazo," Shiloh said as he extended his hand to within inches of her right breast.

Reluctantly, Carrie took the hand and gave it a quick shake. The man didn't let it go easily. She had to jerk her hand from his. Andre did not fail to notice and stepped up alongside Carrie.

"Will you help us change the tire, Mr. Shiloh?" he inserted. His words rang as effeminate as usual, but they were calmly firm.

Shiloh's smile faded away. "You're a little light in the britches aren't you, dude?"

"I beg your pardon?" Andre said forcibly.

The mean look the man gave her friend made Carrie's stomach lurch, but in the next instance Shiloh threw back his head and laughed joyously.

"Hell, you don't have to beg for nothing, man. I'll change that tire."

Billy Shiloh immediately began the task of finishing the job Carrie started.

"What brings ya'll to our neck of the woods?" he asked while positioning the jack.

"We're just passing through," Carrie lied, "on our way to Little Rock, Arkansas."

"Well, you best be careful passing through this here area," he moaned while cranking the handle to the jack. "Had us a terrible murder here just two nights ago."

Shiloh paused and looked hard into Carrie's eyes. "It was my wife that got murdered. Stabbed and raped. I know who did it, but the damned chief of police hasn't done a goddamned thing about it. Guess I'll have to take the law into my own hands."

The words bore no emotion whatsoever, but still gave Carrie a chill. Andre offered a response.

"Sorry for your loss," he said icily.

Shiloh turned to stare momentarily at Andre, and then slowly, deliberately gave him a wink. Shiloh finished changing the tire without another word.

After placing the flat tire in the trunk, and without bothering to help them with the luggage, Shiloh climbed back up on the tractor.

"Hey, Carrie Deshazo, what was the name of that movie that you played the female cop in?" He asked with a smirk.

"*The Lighter Side of Darkness*," she mumbled.

A snide smile worked its way across the face she no longer found attractive. "You showed a lot of tit in that movie. Your ass, too. I liked that."

Andre again moved to her side, and she felt him stiffen. She placed a hand soothingly on his arm. Shiloh started the tractor and took off with a taunting, cruel laugh.

* * * *

Carrie and Andre made the last miles of their trip mostly in stunned silence. They found the Robbers' Roost bed and breakfast with relative ease. The sight of the well-kept Victorian had an immediate calming effect on Carrie. It looked friendly, inviting.

Before they could get out of the car, the front door of the house flew open. A stout, middle-aged-looking woman came bounding down from the grand porch that all but circled the large house. She met them at the car with arms literally wide open.

"Miss Deshazo, Mr. Norman," the woman said sweetly with a warm smile, "I'm Thelma Mayhue. Welcome to the Robbers' Roost." Warm hugs for both of them followed the greeting.

Carrie immediately liked Thelma and sensed Andre did, as well. She seemed so...sincere.

"You have such a beautiful place, Mrs. Mayhue," Carrie smiled.

"Indeed," Andre confirmed.

"Oh, please, call me Thelma," the innkeeper giggled. Her excitement dripped.

"And I'm just Carrie."

"I'm simply Andre," he said with a curtsy.

Thelma Mayhue seemed to pay no mind at all to Andre's flamboyance. She simply curtsied in return.

"Please, come inside. Let me show you to your rooms. I'm sure after that terrible drive you will want to freshen up. I have fresh-squeezed lemonade and warm oatmeal cookies when you're ready for them. Dinner is still hours away."

Carrie popped the trunk. She and Andre made a move for their luggage.

"Oh, no you don't," Thelma scolded. "I didn't get this build by letting my guests lug their suitcases around! I'll bring them to your rooms while you settle in."

Carrie instinctively knew it would do absolutely no good to argue with her doting host.

* * * *

After a hot shower, Carrie put on a seersucker sheath dress and didn't bother to dry her hair or reapply her make-up. Andre opted for a nap, so Carrie went downstairs by herself. Thelma insisted on giving her the grand tour of the fine old home. It wasn't the Beverly Hilton, but it looked clean and comfortable and furnished with delightful antiques. The wonderful aroma coming from the large country kitchen permeated the entire house and made promises of something tantalizingly fattening. Carrie inquired as to the source of the aroma, but Thelma told her it was a surprise.

In the five or so minutes it took Thelma to show her around, Carrie learned not only of the home's history, but of Thelma's, as well. Her husband, Bill, died ten years earlier of cancer. She had taught school, the sixth grade, for nearly twenty years. She loved to garden and bake and read romance novels, and she lived in the house with her older brother, River – a good man who, "has no idea just how really good he is...down deep inside." The words came out tender and made Carrie wonder about their meaning.

Thelma concluded the tour by taking Carrie's hand and telling her she looked even more beautiful in real life than she did in the movies. Wet hair and all. Carrie's years in Tinseltown taught her to distance herself from her fans, hold them at arms length. Too many experiences taught her that most just wanted to take from her one thing or another. Thelma seemed more intent to give. Carrie warmed to her like she had no others in far too many years.

Carrie sat in a fan-backed wicker chair on the tremendous front porch while Thelma went about her work, but not before placing a plate of cookies and a pitcher of lemonade on the wicker table in front of Carrie. She settled back and sipped the lemonade and found it heavenly. For the moment, she found pleasure in just smelling the fat, warm oatmeal cookies.

A gentle breeze, warm and humid, felt good on Carrie's bare arms. There existed plenty to look at from her position on the porch. Flower beds and large, ancient looking trees adorned the front yard. Across the drive rested a pasture of lush green and, beyond that, the mountains and a forest of pines. To her left protruded a grouping of outbuildings and a corral. To her far right a magnificent red barn invited exploring. As she contemplated the possibilities of doing so, a torrent of profanities burst from the direction of the smaller structures on her left. She turned her head just in time to observe a man running for dear life across the corralled lot. Right on his heels charged a very large and apparently agitated black cow. To her amazement, the lowered head of the charging beast connected with the man's backside and literally sent him flying and screaming through the air. The man landed flat on his face, but leapt up and took off with a flash, and again, his adversary followed in hot pursuit. In the next instance both man and animal disappeared behind one of the buildings that blocked Carrie's view. Before she could catch her breath, the cow darted back into view, running at breakneck speed back across the lot. The man, this time wielding a large club, now became the aggressor. Carrie, wide-eyed with mouth agape, watched until yet another structure obstructed her view.

Carrie leaped from her chair and nearly cleared the porch when she heard the creak of the front screen door opening. Out popped Thelma and Andre.

"I saw a man being mauled by a cow!" she exclaimed, "and the man now has a club and I'm afraid he's going to kill the poor thing!"

It surprised Carrie and left her appalled when Thelma simply burst into laughter.

"That's just River and Bobo, and Bobo isn't a cow. He's a steer," Thelma said around her laughter.

"But it was just terrible," Carrie objected.

"Well, dear," Thelma said with an amused shake of her head, "it's River's fault. Every time we raise a steer for slaughter, he makes a pet out of it. He wrestles with them and chases them and gets them to chase him, and that's okay while it's a fifty-pound calf. But when it gets to be a full-grown, eight-hundred-pound steer, it still wants to play, and, well...sometimes it gets a little ugly."

Carrie turned to Andre for his input, which she knew inevitable.

"You won't catch me playing with something that large that has been deprived of its testicles," he said dryly.

Thelma laughed heartily at the revelation. "Tell you what, Carrie, why don't you mosey on down there and meet River while I fix Andre up with some lemonade and cookies?"

"Well, I, uh..." Carrie started to object.

"Do go," Andre agreed. "The man and his pet are apparently in need of a mediator, and I am in need of Thelma's hospitality."

With further insistence from both Thelma and Andre, Carrie reluctantly set off to find the man and the cow that wasn't really a cow at all.

Carrie worked her way in and around two of the sheet metal outbuildings and prepared to round the corner of a third one when she heard the murmuring of words she could not make out. The gentleness of the voice caused her to pause and consider that she might be intruding. The guilt of eavesdropping, however, pushed her onward and she stepped around the corner of the building.

The sight before her again brought her to a halt. Several yards in front of her, Bobo, the steer, stood alongside a split-railed fence. His large head draped over the fence – his eyes closed.

The man, River, had his back to Carrie. He had his left boot propped on the lower rail of the fence, his left elbow rested on the upper one. His right hand lazily scratched the wide area between the steer's closed eyes. Carrie still couldn't make out the words he used, but they were most assuredly kind and loving. The club she'd seen the man with earlier lay tossed aside.

Carrie marveled at the long, gray hair that fell across the broad shoulders topping a lanky frame and slender hips – surprised she had failed to note the hair in the earlier melee. Carrie always preferred long hair on men.

After standing there a few seconds, Carrie determined she did not wish to interrupt the "moment" being shared between the man and his pet. Intending to disappear back around the corner of the nearby building, Carrie took a step backwards and her shoe fell on something that made a snapping sound.

It startled both man and animal. Bobo reared his head and snorted and River quickly spun around into a crouched fighter's stance. A savage look in the stunning, practically silver eyes caused her to gasp and take yet another step backwards. Carrie could not imagine what lifestyle or past experiences made the man react so explosively to surprise.

Instantaneously, and to Carrie's relief, his aggressive posture dissolved into fidgeting shyness while the hard look in the rugged face faded to embarrassment. The amazing eyes dropped from her face to the ground at his feet.

"You scared the hell out of me," he mumbled in explanation.

"You're kind of jumpy, aren't you?" Carrie responded without thought. The man's reaction both frightened and embarrassed her as well as it did him.

"Just not used to people sneaking up on me, that's all," he said defensively.

"I wasn't sneaking up on you. I just saw you and your cow... playing, and your sister insisted that I come down here and meet you." Carrie turned defensive in turn, and really didn't know why.

"He ain't a cow."

"I know that...I'm no idiot," she shot back, wondering why in the world she argued with a total stranger over such a trivial matter.

"Besides, he was the one playing. It wasn't a whole lot of fun for me. My butt still hurts."

Carrie tried to stop it, but a smile worked its way across her face all the same. She liked the contrast between the man's dark, rugged face and his pale eyes. His face, although younger looking than the hair would suggest, was chalked with deep lines and enhanced with a strong jawline. The face brimmed with character.

"We're not getting off to a great start here," she said, lowering her defenses.

The man brought a work-worn hand up to swipe across his mouth, leaving in its wake a sly, fetching semblance of a grin. But he offered no verbal response.

Carrie pressed her initiative to lighten the mood. "I'm Carrie Deshazo," she said while extending her right hand.

"Figured as much," he responded not unkindly. "I'm River Yates," he added while stepping up and shaking her hand with a firm, callused grip.

Carrie liked a man to shake her hand with disregard for her gender. She'd always considered it an act of respect. "I'm sorry I startled you. I didn't mean to intrude."

The unique ice-blue eyes softened, but were still alert and hinted of intelligence. "Oh, it wasn't really an intrusion," he said, hitching his thumbs in the front pockets of his jeans and simultaneously scuffing the ground with a boot heel, "but I would appreciate you not spreading it around that I converse with my livestock."

Carrie responded with laughter. "Your secret is safe with me."

A shy smile worked its way across a face Carrie began to find uncommonly attractive. Not at all like the pretty face of Clive Benz and the other Hollywood types she'd grown accustomed to.

"Have you ever petted a steer?" he asked evenly.

"No. As far as I know, that's the first one I've ever even seen," she said nodding at the animal that looked on curiously.

"Want to?"

"Does it bite?"

"Cattle will kick you and, uh, as you've seen, charge you, but I've never known one to bite."

"I don't care to be kicked or charged," she chuckled, warming to River's now easy-going manner.

"Come here," he said as he moved to the fence. "Don't worry, Bobo likes being rubbed on."

Hesitantly, Carrie took his word on it and walked up beside River. The man smelled of the outdoors and Carrie found it pleasant.

"Here, pet him under the neck," River said as he reached beneath the great head. "It's the softest part."

Slowly, Carrie reached out and touched the steer's luxurious coat to be surprised by both how soft it felt and how much Bobo did in fact seem to enjoy the attention. For the first time since she couldn't remember when, a living creature seemed appreciative of her touch.

* * * *

After the woman walked back up to the house, River tried to busy himself with his chores. But she occupied his mind. She had not at all been what he'd expected. She'd seemed so...regular. She had what Thelma referred to in a woman as "spunk." Whatever one chose to call it, River always harbored a weakness for women with that particular quality.

She did look a little familiar to him. Maybe he'd seen her in a commercial or something. He liked the fact she seemed comfortable without make-up, and didn't mind being seen with her hair less than perfect. That made her just more...regular. River knew he'd seen women more beautiful than this one. He just couldn't remember when.

A few silly flirtatious thoughts crossed his mind about her, and each time they did, he busied himself just a little more. After all, he kept reminding himself, this woman enjoyed fame, success, and probably banks full of money. And him? Well, he was a middle-aged man who could offer absolutely nothing to a much younger woman with fame, success, and bunches of money. Just thinking such thoughts made him feel stupid. He decided he would make a conscious effort to stay clear of the movie star. There'd prove no sense in saying or doing something that could only embarrass him.

Besides, the woman came here with a man. He wondered why they'd bothered to get separate rooms but surmised that the man more than likely had a wife out there in California. Hell, for all he knew, this Carrie Deshazo could be married, as well. Relationships like that, he imagined, were commonplace in Hollywood, but then, where were relationships like that not commonplace?

River worked at working, out of view of the house, until minutes before Thelma's scheduled time for dinner. Set times for eating, and what he'd always called supper now being referred to as dinner, all came about with Thelma's prostituting their birth place out to total strangers. River deeply contemplated the shame of it all when he stumbled upon the snoozing figure stretched out in one of the wicker chairs on his front porch – and he did a double take.

The shirt and jeans on the man were acceptable enough. River owned a closet full of the same style. It was what the man had on his feet that held River spellbound. They were bright purple and fuzzy house slippers – the kind women wore. River finally managed to look up to find the man awake and staring back at him.

"What'cha wearing those for?" River heard himself gasp.

"Aren't they simply to die for," the man giggled.

Giggled. River cocked his head and squinted an eye at the fellow. Surely, his leg was being pulled. The man's voice, how he said his words, sounded as girlie as the shoes on his feet.

"I purchased a pair of adorable cowboys boots for the occasion," the man cooed with fluttering waves of his hands, "but they were just killing my tender little feet." For emphasis, the man kicked off one of the slippers and brought up the foot to wiggle toes practically in River's face.

When River all but tumbled backwards off the porch, the man broke into shrill laughter.

"Hey, that shit ain't funny," River huffed once he'd regained his balance and moved out of toe range. He wanted to be angry, but felt just too damned shocked to be anything but shocked.

"Oh, but it is!" the man squealed with delight. "Your sister anticipated that you might be just a little homophobic, but you're a hoot!"

"So, you ain't joshing? You're really a, uh, well...homosexual?"

"Well, yes, that's the clinical word for it, and I do appreciate your being so sweet about it, but frankly, dear, I'm a died-in-the-wool queer!"

"And my sister knows it?"

"She seemed to pick right up on it. Imagine that," he giggled again.

"I'm trying to," River said with a sigh. For a mind-clearing break, he turned his head to survey the grounds surrounding his ancestral home. Times were damned sure changing around the old Working Y.

* * * *

River picked at his pot roast and, for once, thanked God for Thelma's gift for gab. The more she talked, the less he had to. The dinner conversation bounced mostly between Thelma and the fellow named Andre, another person who didn't lack for words. The Carrie woman hadn't said much either; she'd just laughed a lot. Only when she spoke, or laughed, would River look up from his plate. He'd tried not to, even then, but the woman just seemed to draw his attention like manure did flies. She seemed kind of shy when talking about herself, but did graciously answer all the questions Thelma threw at her. She appeared humble, and River liked that about her. But, she wasn't shy about eating. She displayed a hearty appetite, and River liked that even better. Try as he might, he couldn't find one damned thing about the woman he didn't like. Still, nothing being said truly interested River until Thelma asked them about their trip from Oklahoma City.

"Well, other than getting terribly lost and having a flat," Andre said in his way of talking that really made River uncomfortable, "it was pretty much uneventful until we met one horrid creature by the name of Billy Shiloh."

For the first time, River looked up from his plate to stare at Andre. Thelma all but choked on a mouth full of food at the mentioning of the name.

"So, you know him?" Andre questioned.

"Oh, yes, we certainly do," Thelma said, cutting her eyes at River.

"Was his wife really murdered?" Carrie asked abruptly.

Thelma gasped, "Oh, no! I hope he didn't tell you River did it!"

Four wide eyes and two gaping mouths turned on River.

"Oh, Thelma," he moaned.

"Well, River, they are going to hear the whole ugly mess sooner or later. It's best they hear it from us." Thelma then smiled sweetly at her astonished guests. "You can't keep anything a secret around these parts."

Carrie and Andre continued to stare wide-eyed at River.

"Why, hell, I didn't do it!" he exclaimed.

Andre moved to the edge of his seat. "I, for one, can't wait to hear the whole ugly mess. Do proceed, Thelma!" he said gleefully.

Of course, Thelma did just that while River picked up the pace at picking at his food. Never once did he look up from his plate.

"...And since I provided River with an alibi," Thelma finally concluded, "they, of course, didn't arrest him, but they did tell him not to leave town."

"Absolutely fascinating!" Andre squealed.

"I think it's absolutely terrible," Carrie said softly.

"My God, girl, where is your sense of adventure?" Andre exclaimed with hands in the air. "Can't you see we've been dropped right in the middle of a murder mystery? And you *do* know that murder mysteries are my forte. And don't you dare forget how many awards I've accumulated for the mysteries I've composed."

"I wouldn't dare," Carrie chuckled.

River almost looked up from his plate. Damn, but he loved the woman's laugh.

"You're patronizing me," Andre huffed. "Don't you think for one minute, girlfriend, that I don't possess the skills to solve this mystery and bring to justice..."

"Oh, could you?" Thelma jumped in. "Could you solve this mystery and clear my brother's name, Andre?"

"Thelma!" River protested.

"Well, I do have a good while to spend here," Andre inserted.

"Andre!" Carrie echoed River's tone.

"By God I will, Thelma!" Andre thundered, in a girlie sort of way. "River, you can count on me to champion your cause!"

"Hey, I ain't got a cause," River tried to protest.

"Andre," Carrie said sternly, "I don't want any undo attention drawn to us."

"I'll need an introduction to some of the town folk," Andre said to Thelma.

"You can go into town with River tomorrow," Thelma nodded.

"Thelma!"

"Andre!"

"Oh, come on, River," Thelma pleaded, "you can take Andre to the Silver Dollar Bar tomorrow. He goes there every day for a beer or two," she added as a side note to Andre and Carrie.

"I can't take him in the Silver Dollar!"

"And why not?" Andre huffed. "I'll have you know, mister, that I've done some acting in my time, as well as writing. I can hide my persuasion when the need arises!"

"Andre, this is not a good idea," Carrie moaned.

"Please listen to her, Andre," River moaned in.

"Oh, it will be a blast, Carrie. We'll dress like the locals. We'll fit right in!"

With that Andre sprang from the table and did what River hated to admit was a damned good imitation of John Wayne.

"I'll walk like this!" Andre said with an exhibit of the famous stutter step. "And talk like this...pilgrim!" he said in a deep, metered voice.

Both Thelma and Carrie broke into laughter.

River failed to see the humor. Andre acting like the Duke seemed downright blasphemous.

* * * *

River stayed in his workshop much later than usual. He'd actually tried to go back in the house a couple of times earlier, but each time lights still burned in the windows, so he'd retreated back to his project. A few minutes after midnight he climbed the steps to the dark front porch of what used to be such a wonderful place to live. River reached for the handle of the screen door when the voice erupted from the shadows at the far end of the porch.

"Keeping late hours, aren't we?"

Startled nearly to the point of pissing himself, River performed a few quick steps of a little involuntary jig. Shrill giggles from the dark served as applause.

"Damnit, man!" River gasped, "that's a good way to get your ass shot!"

"You have a gun?" the dainty voice quickly grew serious.

"No, but if I did, I would have damned sure lit you up."

"'Lit me up'? I like that. It's cute. I might use that in a script, 'Joe Bob said to Henry Don, I'll light you up, son!'"

"What the hell are you doing out here, Andre?" River still nearly gasped to catch his breath.

"I'm lonely. I need a hug."

River's last gulp for air caught in his throat.

"Just joking," Andre giggled again.

"Well, you got a sick sense of humor then," River all but coughed.

"And you need to develop a sense of humor, my boy. And relax. Believe me, I won't be trying to get in your pants!"

"That's a damned good thing 'cause I'd light your ass up for that, too!"

"Glad we got that out of the way," Andre snickered. "Now, for a serious answer to your question, River, I'm out here having a nightcap of the finest Irish whiskey money can buy. I never travel without it. Would you be so good as to join me? Knowing now, as you should, that my intentions toward you are strictly honorable?"

River could never easily say no to good whiskey, and the man did seem sincere. "Okay. But you got to promise me that you won't be scaring the shit out of me no more. That's just not a smart thing to be doing to a war vet."

"And what war did you fight, my boy?" Andre asked with seemingly sincere interest.

"Viet Nam," River answered hesitantly, not caring to discuss such things with this – "man."

"You're terribly young to have fought in Nam."

Feeling Andre might be challenging the fact, as others had done because of his age, River begrudgingly explained, "I joined the army at sixteen and a half. I stole my older brother's identity to do so. He was born with a heart defect and couldn't serve on his own behalf."

"That's quite a feat to pull off, I'd imagine," Andre responded.

"It took some doing, but I got it done."

"Yes, I don't doubt you did. It's also an honorable feat. So, I do promise not to startle you ever again," Andre said ceremoniously, "from one Nam vet to another!"

River started over to Andre but stopped in mid-stride. "Huh? Is this another one of your sick jokes?"

"Absolutely not. I served in the earliest years of the conflict. Marine Corps. Semper Fi, sweetheart."

The tone sounded somber. Inherently, River knew it was true. Suddenly more at ease, he took the chair next to Andre.

Still, River had a question he could not hold back. "But, uh, how did you, well, uh..."

"How did I fool them? How did I keep from constantly having my ass whipped by my fellow marines?"

"Yeah, I guess that's what I'm askin'."

"Unlike you, I did not have to act like someone I was not. That was long before I'd accepted who I am. I didn't, as they say, come out of the closet until much later. I was one hell of a marine, and was damned proud to serve my country. I still am."

Moments of silence passed while River struggled with a feeling he couldn't immediately identify.

Andre filled the void. "I only have one glass. Do you mind drinking from the bottle? I promise it has never been to my lips. Besides, I'm tested religiously for AIDS."

Suddenly, River found a name for his feelings. It was shame with a thick coating of guilt.

"Hand me that bottle...Marine."

They shared no other words. They simply passed the bottle back and forth while staring into the darkness. In his mind River retuned to Vietnam and he guessed Andre went back with him. River figured they both returned to the battles of their past and both fought gallantly to the point of passing out in Thelma's wicker chairs.

* * * *

For no apparent reason, Carrie suddenly awoke from deep and peaceful sleep. The clock beside the bed displayed "3:10." She felt instinctively that rolling back over and drifting off would not be possible. Besides, moonlight through open shades seemed to beckon her to a window across the room.

Carrie tiptoed so as not to detract from the permeating silence of the old house. She could not remember ever being in a place so void of anything audible. She made the trek across the room with no sense of anything other than peace and tranquility. The moment she peered out the window, that feeling diminished just so slightly. Framed almost perfectly in the distance was the grand old barn.

Although it seemed fitting of a calendar photograph, beautiful in its own right, Carrie sensed something a tad unsettling about the wooden structure. She studied it in silence for several minutes before realizing what she sensed. Then she felt ridiculous. How could it be possible that a mere object could truly be *alive*? Surely it could only be the time of night, or the unfamiliar surroundings, or even the situation that brought her here in the first place. Still, Carrie felt an inclination to address the barn. Eventually, the appropriate words came to mind.

"You hold secrets," she whispered.

Release accompanied the declaration, and Carrie padded back to bed, drifting immediately into peaceful slumber.

Chapter Six

A little before noon Chief Mike Simms rang the doorbell to Walter Bates' home. Simms normally starved for his lunch by this time of the day. At the moment, however, eating proved the furthest thing from the cop's mind. It took two more rings of the bell before Bates opened his door. The old man didn't look good. Simms didn't expect he would. In just a couple of hours Bates would be burying his only child.

"Hey, Walter," Simms nodded, "sure hate to bother you, but can I come in a few minutes?"

Walter Bates blinked bloodshot, swollen eyes at the bright morning sunlight, but nodded back a greeting. "Sure, Mike, come on in. You'll have to ignore the mess. I haven't felt much like picking up after myself the past couple of days."

Simms said he understood and noted that the house didn't look bad at all for a man not that used to being a bachelor. Bates' wife of nearly forty years, Donna, died of a brain aneurysm a year-and-a-half earlier. Simms wondered why so much bad had to happen to such a good man. The chief of police took a seat on the couch when invited to do so. After several deep breaths, Simms started what he'd come to say.

"Walter, I have more bad news. I got the Oklahoma State Bureau of Investigation's and the county coroner's report a little while ago. Cindy didn't die of stab wounds. She suffocated from that gag in her mouth." He paused when the old man choked back a sob, but quickly picked back up so as not to lose his nerve. "She was stabbed after she'd been dead for quite some time, and her back was broken, too, Walter. We think that happened someplace else in the house, and that she was then moved to the bed afterwards."

"I, uh, don't understand, Mike...who...why?"

Mike Simms reached out and placed a hand on Bates' trembling shoulders. "We think it was Billy, Walter. We think he killed Cindy."

For a second, maybe two, Bates made an effort to fight back the tears, but they came all the same. The good man who had been done so wrong dropped his head into his hands and cried without restraint.

"I treated that boy like a son," was muttered in heartbroken sobs.

* * * *

Billy crouched in the woods behind his house and cursed his luck. They knew. The cops were watching his house. From his hiding place, he could see Wilburton's one and only unmarked police car parked at the end of the street. Two cops sat in it. Did they really think he'd be stupid enough to come be-bopping up to the front door?

Billy spent the night in his cave. He'd come home to get the few remaining things he needed from the place. The cops could no doubt see the front and back door from their location, but they couldn't see the windows on the side of the house facing Billy. He wouldn't be able to get all he wanted from the house. He might have to run, and he couldn't afford to load himself down. But, the two things he wanted most would fit snugly in the waistband of his jeans.

* * * *

Carrie spent the first half of her day doing nothing more than relaxing. She slept wonderfully the night before after engaging the barn, and believed she'd not moved a muscle until crawling out of bed at nine-thirty in the morning. Afterwards she ate too much of Thelma's magnificent breakfast and did a repeat performance for lunch. Between meals she'd lounged on the front porch, strolled around the beautiful flowerbeds that dotted the front and back yards and visited at length with Thelma.

She'd only caught glimpses of River throughout the morning as he went about doing, what she guessed, were the things a rancher did. Each time she did see him, however, the man caught and held her attention. It had something to do with just the easy-going way he moved and the way he seemed to concentrate fully on the tasks at hand. Too, she hadn't failed to notice the few interactions between River and Andre. It wasn't that they had been chummy by any means, but when their paths did cross, River seemed more at ease. Although she had not caught their words, the men's actions appeared relaxed, natural. The transition puzzled her, but, for some reason, she found it pleasing. For reasons that made no sense at all, she, too, felt more of a *connection* to River than she had the day before. Carrie chalked it up to a good night's sleep.

The day had grown increasingly warmer, and now, at three-thirty in the afternoon, it grew uncomfortably so for Carrie. She was not accustomed to the humidity. She and Andre were sitting on the front porch when River pulled an ancient truck to a stop in front of them.

"If we're going to do this," River scowled from the driver's window, "I guess we might as well do it now."

"That's a 1953 Chevy," Andre responded as he bounded from his chair. "Don't see many of those around anymore."

"Yeah, it was my daddy's truck," River nodded. "Awfully special to me," he said under his breath.

Although concerned about the vehicle's ability to get them to and from town, Carrie found the connection between man and machine charming.

Andre opened the passenger door and said mischievously, "I'll sit in the middle."

"Don't think so," River shot back dryly.

"You're no fun," Andre giggled as Carrie stepped around him and scooted in next to River.

"And start practicing your manly talk," River said with another scowl.

"Okay, partner, I'm getting ready to light yo' ass up," Andre said in an impressive baritone.

Carrie laughed out loud at the absurdity of the ploy upon which they were embarking and about her disguise in particular. The baggy jeans and a huge untucked denim shirt belonging to Thelma certainly concealed her figure, but she wasn't sure tucking her hair beneath a ball cap would keep anyone from recognizing her face.

"Do you think I'll really fool anyone?" she asked River.

"You look like a down-home girl to me," River confirmed with what she took to be an appreciative glance.

Carrie found River's response to her presence refreshing. Normally, men outside the movie business reacted to her in one of two ways. They acted either intimidated shitless by her fame and beauty, or swooned unabashedly as a result of the same. River, on the other hand, interacted with her as if she were simply a woman.

Other than Andre's typical observances on everything and anything, they made the trip into town mostly in silence. The warm wind that whipped through the open windows made Carrie drowsy. But when River stopped the truck in front of what looked no more than a shanty, she came immediately to full attention.

"This is it?" she asked.

"Yup," River sighed. "Welcome to the Silver Dollar Bar."

Then, with what seemed to be an afterthought, he added, "But don't look for no silver dollars in the bar 'cause there ain't none."

* * ⨯ *

Billy made it in and out of his house without the police catching him. For the past fifteen minutes, he'd been sneaking his way through backyards and alleys toward the outskirts of town. As luck would have it, just as he prepared to cross the street separating town and countryside, a single approaching car made him dive for cover. Concealed in some bushes at the side of the road, he'd watched the old piece of shit truck go bouncing by. He didn't recognize the two passengers, but he damned sure knew the driver.

Billy tried to talk himself into doing the sensible thing. He was less than three minutes from being in the woods and safely on his way to the cave. But from his place in the bushes, he'd watched the old truck pull into the otherwise deserted parking lot of the Silver Dollar Bar just a couple of blocks down the road. It'd be smart to just keep on going, but sometimes, for the sake of building on a reputation, an outlaw had to take a few chances.

To build his confidence, Shiloh patted the two pistols he'd taken from his house, now concealed beneath his shirt. After a deep breath, he darted off in the direction of the Silver Dollar.

* * * *

River silently thanked God Hank Sioux's dumb-assed old dog wasn't posted at the door of the bar. Knowing the mutt could simply be around the corner licking himself, River hurried to the front door and prepared to lead his entourage through the entrance, but suddenly remembering his manners, stepped aside and allowed Carrie to go before him.

He was glad going from bright sunshine to smoky darkness temporarily blinded him. He didn't care to see the look of disgust that had to be on Carrie's face. The Silver Dollar resembled no place for a lady. Of course, he'd tried to tell her that.

Throughout the day, and especially during the trip to town, River tried to come up with how he would introduce his guests, or more precisely, what explanation he'd give for bringing the strangers to the dump in the first place. As best he could remember, River never brought anyone into the Silver Dollar before. Neither had the other regulars. Somewhere in the process of coming up with what to say, River decided to say nothing at all. He just hoped to direct Carrie and Andre to the nearest table and sit them down as inconspicuously as possible.

Hank lurked behind the bar as usual, and Moe Trendle and Jim Duck perched at their usual places at the bar. When his eyes did adjust to the dark, River regretfully determined that the inquisitive staring of the owner and the other two regulars demanded some explanation. River tried never to be intentionally rude.

"These are my friends," was the only thing he could come up with on the spur of the moment.

"Well, do your friends have names?" Moe shot back.

"Why, hell yes, they have names, Moe. Everybody has names," River responded gruffly. Trendle's ever-curious nature of a writer sometimes just really pissed River off. It didn't help that he now found himself in a quandary. River had not discussed with Carrie and Andre the names they would use. After all, they were supposed to be incognito.

River did not have to puzzle over his predicament long. It took mere seconds before Andre stepped in.

"I'm Andre and this is Carrie."

The fake voice sounded masculine enough, but River decided to take no chances. "Andre here served our country in time of war. He's a former Marine."

Hank piped up over the subsequent introductions and greetings, "My ol' daddy was a Marine, and fought in Korea. But he's dead now. Had a little trouble in a bar. I named this place in memory of him."

"There is no memorial more honoring to a father than the display of a son's love," Andre said with several nods of his head to the bar owner.

River thought the words just a tad bit flowery, but they brought a proud smile to Hank's face. Still, River did not want much more conversation between Andre and his friends. He wasn't just real confident in Andre's ability to keep up this charade. River wasted no more time in pointing Carrie and Andre in the direction of the bar's most remote table. But before they could reach it, Moe spoke up.

"Hey, River, have you heard the big news?"

"No, Moe, guess I haven't." River had gotten the man and woman into the Silver Dollar with little fanfare. He now wanted only to get them out with more of the same, and as quickly as possible. He didn't care about any kind of news, big or small. Or, at least, he thought he didn't.

"The cops found out who killed Cindy Shiloh. It was Billy. They're looking for him now."

River pulled a chair out from the table and prepared to sit, but the words kept him upright. He spoke his thoughts out loud. "Well, I'll be damned. I know he ain't no good, but I never figured him for the type to rape his own wife and then stab her to death."

"I did," Carrie spoke for the first time since entering the bar. "I could see it in his eyes. He's evil."

"I certainly won't disagree with you about him being evil, ma'am," Moe said, "but Cindy wasn't really raped. Billy staged it to look like she was. And he didn't stab her to death. She suffocated from a gag he'd put in her mouth. He didn't stab her all those times until she'd been dead for a little while. He was trying to cover up whatever it was that really happened."

River went ahead and took his seat, but repeated his words, "Well, I'll be damned."

Andre, already seated, leaned close and whispered dejectedly in his true voice, "He was most assuredly my prime suspect. I would have solved this mystery posthaste. It sorrows me that my services here are no longer needed."

"Then you're ready to get out of here?" River blurted enthusiastically.

"Not until I've drowned a good portion of my sorrows. Tell me, River, is your fine-looking friend, Hank, a single man?"

Carrie chuckled. River didn't.

* * * *

Carrie found it perplexing that she liked being in the Silver Dollar with River. It most definitely was not her kind of place, and until now, she would not have thought River her kind of man. The owner brought cold beers to the table, and Carrie contemplated the attraction when the door of the bar startlingly banged open with an apparent vengeance. The bright sunlight beyond the door tended only to silhouette the human form standing in the doorway, lending the shape a menacing quality.

"I'm the outlaw Billy Shiloh and I'm here to kill River Yates!"

The booming words from the ominous silhouette would have been humorous if scripted in some melodramatic B movie. But this was no movie, and there was no laughter. Shiloh took a step into the bar, and the door slammed shut behind him. The sudden absence of the glaring light left Carrie blind, but she heard River's chair scoot backwards, and could see just well enough to watch him slowly come to his feet.

"I ain't got a beef with you, kid," River said in a calm voice that helped to still Carrie's pounding heart.

"No need for you to have one, old man. I got one with you that's big enough for the both of us."

The intense hatred in the words negated the effect of River's last ones and Carrie's heart raced now at full speed.

"Hey, Shiloh," Hank barked from behind his bar, "I don't want no trouble in my place. You just go on and get the hell out of here."

"Don't you be trying to tell me what to do, blanket ass. I came in here to kill one old man. The way I look at it, killing two at a time ain't nothin' but a bargain."

"Hank," River said evenly as he slowly made his way up to Shiloh, "let me handle this. Let me do the talking."

Billy made a half-turn to face the bartender, but spun to confront River. In the same instance his hands shot beneath his shirttails and flew back out with a pistol in each.

"These are the only things going to do the talking in this dump!" he bellowed.

Carrie jumped to her feet and unleashed her frantic breathing in a shrill scream. "NOOOOOOOOOOO!"

Shiloh leveled one of the pistols in her direction. "Hey, who the hell are you two? Get your asses over here so I can see you."

"You leave them out of this, boy!" River thundered while taking a step that put him face to face with Shiloh.

Billy Shiloh thrust the other pistol beneath River's chin, and pushed hard enough to tilt his head backwards. River stood his ground.

"We're coming!" Carrie screamed. "Come on, Andre. River, don't move. Don't do anything stupid, River!"

It relieved Carrie that Andre had to this point been quiet. It didn't surprise her when he moved to her side and up to Shiloh with a confident air of indignity.

"Well, cut my legs off and call me shorty!" Shiloh hooted when Carrie and Andre stepped into what light the bar provided. "Now, I wouldn't have known who you were, sweet thing, all dressed up like some kind of Okie woman. But, I damned sure recognize your fuckin' faggot friend! What the hell are you two doing here?"

"Oh, we didn't tell you?" Andre spat in his arrogantly effeminate manner.

The sound of the voice, Carrie noticed, caused River to exhale heavily. The man behind the bar and the two at the bar cut their eyes curiously at Andre, then back at River.

"Tell me what, queer?" Shiloh asked with a confused look.

"You asked what the hell we were doing here. Didn't we already tell you?"

"Hell, no, you didn't tell me shit."

"Oh, well, then I guess it isn't any of your fucking business then, is it?" Andre hissed.

Billy Shiloh's face twisted into an ugly grimace. It became painfully apparent to Carrie that Shiloh intended to do something terrible with the gun in his free hand, but then River intervened.

"That's a damned good one, Andre," River laughed out loud.

"You shut the fuck up!" Billy bellowed in River's face, thrusting even harder on the pistol beneath River's chin.

"I want to know what the hell Carrie Deshazo and this goddamned dick-licker are doing here with you, Yates," Shiloh all but screamed.

"Carrie Deshazo?" Moe called out from the bar. "*The* Carrie Deshazo?"

"Shut up, motherfucker!" Shiloh did scream at Moe.

"Yeah, Moe," River inserted, "this is *the* Carrie Deshazo and Andre Norman, a very famous screen writer. They're staying with us at the house. They sure are awful famous and powerful people to be put through this kind of shit."

"Is that supposed to scare me, old man?" Shiloh growled.

"No, kid, I'm just letting you know. You do something stupid in front of, or to these people, they can sure bring some mighty big troubles down on your sorry little ass."

"Well, that don't scare me. Nothing fuckin' scares me. Now, I'm going to get back to the business at hand. You see, Yates, killing you is going to make me even more famous than I am now. And killing you in front of these important people will make me just that much more famous. Hell, now it will probably even make the movies."

With that, Billy started barking out orders. He made Hank come out from behind the bar. Then he moved everyone but River to the nearest table and had them sit down with their hands in clear view up on the table top. He moved River in front of the table and told them all how lucky they were to have a front row seat to an event that was sure to someday make the history books.

"You put your hands up on top of your head, now," he told River, "and don't move an inch until I say you can."

After River complied, Shiloh took the gun in his left hand and stuck it into the waistband of River's jeans. Then Shiloh took several steps backwards before stuffing the other gun into his own waistband.

"This here will go down as one of the greatest shoot-outs of this century. We gonna do it like they did in the days of Jesse James!"

Carrie already felt terrified to the point of nausea. The demented grin on Shiloh's face brought the taste of metallic bile to the back of her throat. She could not control the tears welling in her eyes. When Carrie started to shake, Andre reached and wrapped her trembling hands into his soothingly strong grip.

Billy Shiloh brought his arms up to shoulder height, parallel with the floor, palms open and facing downward. "Now, when you're ready, old man, you go for your gun."

"I'm not going to go for the gun, Shiloh," River said after a deep breath.

"Why the hell not?" Shiloh huffed like a spoiled child. "Are you afraid, goddamn you?"

River Yates turned his eyes to look directly into Carrie's. For the first time since the terrible ordeal began, the astonishing eyes registered emotion. River held a deep, foreboding look of dread. In the next instance, River dropped his eyes to the floor at Shiloh's feet and emitted a great sigh.

"Yeah, Billy, I'm afraid."

One of the men at the table, the balding and rather fat one, sighed his own sigh. The little man with the thick glasses emitted a soft, sad moan.

"Well, kiss my ass!" Shiloh said as he threw back his head in laughter. "You are a cowardly old bastard after all! Well, guess I'll just put you out of your misery."

When Shiloh took hold of the gun protruding from his jeans, Hank stood up.

"You better sit your ass back down," Shiloh warned without taking his gaze from River.

"To kill River now makes no sense," Hank said in the choppy way of talking that Carrie always thought was just the Hollywood version of how Indians talked. "You came to fight him, to give yourself a big name. And had River decided to fight, and had you killed him, you would have had that big name. You would have deserved it.

"But now, if you kill River, you are simply shooting down a man that no longer has the...will...to fight. Instead of everyone here talking about the great gun battle, we will talk about how you shot him down in cold-blood.

"And, besides, your name has already grown here today. You are the first man we have ever seen to..." Hank Sioux stopped and took a deep breath. When he started again, his tone was softer, sadder, "...back River Yates down from a fight. Don't destroy this magnificent feat with the actions of a deranged maniac."

An arrogant grin slowly worked its way across Billy's face. "You know," he nodded at Sioux, "you're pretty goddamned smart for a dumb-assed Indian!"

"And for a smart outlaw," Hank said with a nod back, "you're staying here far too long. The cops were here just a little while ago. They know of the trouble you have with River. They know River is always here at this time of the day. I expect them back at any moment now."

Billy seemed to study the comment for several long seconds, then he began to nod his head agreeably. "You're probably right there, Tonto. I best be going. Well, folks, someday you'll wish I'd stayed long enough to sign a few autographs, but I do gotta go."

With that, the Outlaw Billy Shiloh retrieved his gun from River, and backed out of the Silver Dollar with a revolver in each hand.

* * * *

Hank knew for a fact he'd just saved River's life, but he felt like shit all the same. In the three or four minutes since Shiloh cleared out, River had been the only one to move. He'd turned his back on the table and now faced away while leaning against the bar on outstretched arms.

"River," Hank said after loudly clearing his voice, "I, uh, didn't mean to offend you, I was..."

"Hank," River interrupted, "you don't owe me an explanation anymore than I owe you one."

Without turning around and with everyone else still seated solemnly at the table, River called Andre's name.

"Yes, River?"

"When you two are ready, take the pickup and go on back."

Without another word, River turned and walked out of the bar.

* * * *

No one spoke for the longest time. Andre was the first to do so.

"I had determined our friend River to be a man of action. I was surprised if not disappointed by his pacifism."

The observation annoyed Carrie.

"We weren't surprised," Moe responded.

"Not anymore," Jim Duck added.

"He has changed," Hank confirmed with a sad nod of his head.

The comments unleashed something ugly from deep within Carrie. "What is wrong with you people? What did you expect him to do?"

"We didn't expect him to be afraid," Moe mumbled.

"He wasn't afraid," Carrie shot back vehemently.

"He said he was," Jim said while averting his owlish eyes from Carrie's glare.

"I know what he said, but I don't think...well, I don't know what to think," Carrie blurted. "But what if he was afraid? Does it really matter?"

The answer came to her before any verbal response and it shamed her to feel that it did matter. She'd lived a life among men that were paid to act like real men were expected to act. Now Carrie feared that what she found attractive about River seemed an archaic perception of him being what a real man was supposed to be. Chivalrous. Confident. Brave. Suddenly, Carrie grew as disgusted with herself as she was with the others.

"Ms. Deshazo," Hank spoke softly, "we don't mean to be disrespectful of River, or sit in judgment of his actions. He is, after all, my oldest and dearest friend. And in the situation, he was in earlier, any one of us would have been scared to death.

"But to know what we are feeling and why, you would have had to known River the way he once was. There was a time, Ms. Deshazo, that River would have drawn that gun, or taken Shiloh's gun away from him, or died trying to do one or the other. It's just that our friend has changed so much and we miss the old River."

"Why has he changed?" Carrie wondered out loud.

"I can only speculate. I think only River can give you the true reasons."

River had left, and now Carrie had no other reason to remain a moment longer in the Silver Dollar Bar.

"Andre, will you take me back to the ranch?"

As they were going out the door, Carrie heard the voice of Moe Trendle addressing no one in particular.

"By God, there's a hell of a novel coming together here. I'm going to start writing it tonight."

Chapter Seven

Billy crawled out of his cave at straight-up midnight. This time he took particular care in covering and concealing the entrance. If what he intended to do didn't work, then there would most likely be cops crawling all over the mountains in the next day or two. If they found his cave in his absence, all Billy's plans would be ruined for sure.

Billy carried his two pistols with him and all the cash he had to his name, which only totaled two hundred bucks. The only other thing he'd taken from the cave was the big ring of keys that Walter Bates entrusted him with shortly after Billy went to work for him. Billy clutched the keys in his hands as he set off into the pitch dark, dense woods. He didn't want them jangling. Billy needed to practice moving through the woods as quietly and quickly as a panther. The way he moved through the night, and the pine forests, would become part of the legend people would spread about him. Very soon, no one would dare come into the forest looking for Billy Shiloh, especially at night.

Gripping the keys belonging to Bates made Billy first think of the old man and then the old man's daughter. He hadn't spent too much time thinking about Cindy, or what happened. It wouldn't do any good anyway. What was done was done. But all in all, Billy did think it a little bit sad that she'd forced him to shove her backwards into that stove. Suddenly he started missing her, especially in a sexual sort of way.

Stop it, Billy thought as he practically glided through the dense forest of pines. He couldn't afford dwelling on the special love he'd held for a woman never cut out to be a wife in the first place. He didn't need to be wasting time on what had been. Instead, he needed to concentrate on the task at hand. Billy would soon show them all that he wasn't just a brave and daring outlaw, but a cunning one as well.

* * * *

Carrie bolted upright in bed. She knew in an instance what ripped her from the grip of sound sleep. She knew for sure what a scream in the middle of the night sounded like. It had been the last sound she heard her mother make. Although Carrie was only twelve at the time, she could still remember vividly the terribleness of that scream and the thundering boom of the shotgun blast that followed.

But tonight, she would not let herself dwell on the memory. She would not let it consume her as it had so many times in the past. Although she tended to be obsessed by it, Carrie never talked about it. Sure, she told a few people, like Andre, that her mother had been murdered, and how, and by whom, all the facts, except one. That very fact she most needed free of, she'd never shared with another. In her world of pampered people with make believe lives who experienced only self-imposed problems, she'd never met anyone she felt could relate to the depth of her anguish. Until just moments earlier, she'd not harbored hopes of ever meeting anyone that could.

The scream came from a man, and did not sound as near as next door, so it didn't come from Andre. That left only River, and on the heels of this realization came another. Carrie suddenly understood completely why she'd found him so attractive, and only a very small portion of the allure stemmed from the "real-man" bullshit she'd first contributed it to. She simply could not understand how she failed to recognize the look in his eyes and the tone in his voice. After all, how many long years had she stared at that same look in the mirror and heard her own words echoing the same sentiment? The link between them became so very clear for Carrie. River, just like Carrie, understood anguish.

* * * *

Billy made good time on foot. It took him just over an hour to reach his destination. A couple of old sheds and one large and much newer barn were the only structures on the ranch Walter Bates owned outside of town. One of the keys on the key ring would open the big padlock on the barn's double doors. As Billy hoped and expected, the place looked deserted. There just weren't enough cops in the county to watch every place he could show up.

Billy fumbled in the dark with the key ring until he finally found the key that fit the padlock. Once he got the doors open, Billy wanted to turn on the large floodlights that lit the interior of the barn, but he didn't think that would be too smart. Instead, he paused just inside the barn to let his eyes adjust to the deeper darkness of the cavernous structure. What he'd come for sat at the far end of the barn. Billy could see it looming back there, just waiting for him to liberate it. He worked at the keys in his hands as he made his way across the concrete floor, feeling for the one that would open the way for the next leg of his journey.

Bates kept the ten-year-old Chevy pickup in the barn for hauling hay out to his cattle. Like everything else the old man owned, it had been maintained in good condition. It was always gassed up and always ready to go. The big engine kicked immediately to life, and Billy Shiloh let out a laugh as he worked the gearshift into first and eased out on the clutch. It made him remember the first time he'd done so.

Billy hadn't owned a car back then, and Walter Bates hadn't been willing to let his precious daughter go on her first date with young Shiloh on foot. Billy learned fast not to look a foolish old gift horse in the mouth. Hell, Bates even gave them money for the movie theater. Billy, no less sly then as now, used the money to buy beer. But he didn't fail to pay the old man back. No, sir. To show his appreciation that long-ago night, Billy gave the father's daughter her first fuckin' right there on the bench seat of the pickup truck. Cindy hadn't really wanted to give it up that night, it being her first time and all. Billy remembered having to get a little tough with her, but give it up she did, and she cried afterwards. Billy found her tears amusing. Shit, he'd just fucked her, what did she have to cry about? The only part he remembered not liking was the blood she'd gotten on his private parts. He'd almost smacked her right there and then, but Billy had his principles. Punching a girl on a first date just wasn't gentlemanly.

The sentimental little trip back in time caused Billy to again laugh out loud as he pulled the old Chevrolet onto the county road and pointed it south. He knew exactly where he intended to end up. He just didn't know exactly how he'd get there.

* * * *

Long before anyone else in the house woke up, River stood outside in the early morning darkness taking the crisp air into his lungs in quick, shallow breaths. The two heavy wooden doors loomed only feet in front of him. He had not come this close to the old barn since...since *that day*.

"Sky, you're wrong. I won't do it again."

He hoped saying the words out loud would strengthen him, take the shakes out of arms and legs. It didn't. The dream still loomed too vivid.

"Never. I'll never do it again."

In the dream, neither Boggs nor the Vietnamese summonsed him to the barn. Sky Yates took his turn this time. But it had been different than all the other dreams about his brother. Unlike Boggs and the Vietnamese, Sky never spoke to him from within the barn. River just always knew he lurked just beyond the big doors...waiting. In those dreams, only River did the talking. Time and time again, nightmare after nightmare, he pleaded for Sky to forgive him. But Sky never responded. Unit last night. For the first time, Sky spoke to him from behind the closed doors. In a whisper.

"No more, Sky," River now insisted, "No more guns. No more horses. No more promises. See? That means I can't do it. Ever...ever...again."

The words weakened him even more, and River lost his resolve. He'd come out to the old barn to burn it to the ground. For a myriad of reasons, he simply couldn't do it. Maybe someday, but not this morning.

As he turned to hurry away, Sky's whispered words sounded once again in his mind and reverberated throughout his body with the force of thunder.

"I know things you don't, River. I know you can keep on running from who and what you really are, but it ain't going to change a thing. There will be more voices. Soon. Real soon. So, go ahead, run River...run."

* * * *

Billy drove all night, stopping only once to get gasoline, drink a Coke, and take a leak. He'd intentionally filled the tank only halfway. Two hours passed since the stop and he now sat parked alongside State Highway 95 just south of Temple, Texas. The old Chevy ran out of fuel just about where he'd hoped it would. Before crawling out of the cab, he wrote out a note and left it in plain view on the seat.

"I'm headed to Mexico," he scribbled. "Any lawman that tries to stop me better be prepared to meet Jesus." He signed it, "The Outlaw Billy Shiloh".

With one pistol tucked in the small of his back and the other stuck in the right pocket of his jeans, and both concealed by a light jacket, Billy continued south in a trot. He wanted to put as much distance as possible between him and the pickup before trying to thumb a ride.

* * * *

Thelma prepared the biscuits for the oven but looked up when Carrie walked into the kitchen. "My, dear, you're up awfully early. Did you not sleep well?"

The lovely famed eyes darted from the kitchen to the adjoining breakfast nook as the beautiful face flushed red. "I was hoping to catch River," Carrie responded hesitantly.

"He's already up and gone," Thelma said apologetically.

"Oh." The single word and face expressed disappointment and a hint of worry.

River did not show up for dinner the night before, and Thelma's roasted duck had been picked at solemnly by Carrie and Andre. Thelma tried her hardest to simply concentrate on serving her guests and fought off all urges to pry. But that was last night. Now, Carrie's mood and her expressed urgency to see River encouraged prying.

"What happened yesterday...at the bar?" she asked gently.

Carrie's eyes fell to a spot on the tiled floor. "It was awful. Just awful. I was so frightened, and I felt so terribly sorry for River."

The first few sentences seemed forced, but when Carrie looked up and into Thelma's eyes, the words began to flow as she recounted what happened in the Silver Dollar Bar. Thelma's heartbeat kept pace with Carrie's crescendoing account of the horrifying encounter. Well before Carrie finished, Thelma had moved to and fallen into the closest kitchen chair. When Carrie finished, she took the chair next to Thelma and both sat recouping their wits for several long seconds of silence.

Eventually, Thelma summarized her feelings. "Poor River."

Seemingly, as a result of the comment, Carrie stared intently into Thelma's eyes. "I heard him scream out during the night."

Thelma took several deep breaths. "Yes. He does that often these days...or nights, I should say."

"Why?"

More deep breaths. And one very long sigh. River would absolutely die if he even thought this conversation took place. But, Thelma justified, there would be no divulging of great, dark secrets. Because if such secrets even existed, Thelma didn't know them.

"I don't really know exactly why. All I know is that he started doing it just shortly after our brother died."

"Oh, I'm sorry...I didn't know..." Carrie winced.

"Well, of course you didn't," Thelma tried to chuckle. "His name was Sky. River and Sky. Like all true born and bred Okies, we have some Indian blood. A little Cherokee and even a little less Choctaw. But, our father took our heritage seriously and wanted to name his children in the Indian tradition of taking names from nature and surroundings. He wanted to name me Doe. Thank God, mom interfered on that one!" This time, Thelma truly laughed.

"Sky and River were always close," she continued. "We all were. Sky was the oldest. He, uh, well, he was killed a little over a year ago. Out there in that old red barn. He was stomped to death by a horse."

Thelma took a second to wipe at moistening eyes. Carrie reached out and took her hand. "River bought the horse. Paid a lot less for it than what it was worth, or so it seemed at the time. He'd bought it from a rancher in Tulsa who had been up front and honest in saying the horse, a mare, simply couldn't be broken. Told River she was simply unmanageable...dangerous.

"I remember River saying to Sky, 'Hell, there ain't no such thing as a horse I can't break.' And, at first, Sky also thought River had made one heck of a deal. But, it didn't take Sky too much time working with the horse before he was agreeing with the guy up in Tulsa. He soon wanted the horse gone. He kept after River to get rid of it, saying, 'you brought her here, you get her out of here.' Well, River finally agreed to do so, but he just never seemed to get around to it. I guess Sky got tired of waiting on him and went out there one afternoon and tried to load her into a stock trailer.

"River came home that evening for dinner and when Sky didn't show up, I sent River out to get him. River found him in the barn. He lay in there and bled to death. Maybe, if someone had been with him at the time, or had gotten to him shortly thereafter...he might have lived."

Thelma took a deep breath through her nose and blew it out loudly through her mouth. "I think that's probably why River screams. Bad dreams of blaming himself for his brother's death. Oh, he's changed so much since then," Thelma concluded with a wistful smile.

"How has he changed?" Carrie asked with a look of intent interest.

It did not fail to register with Thelma that one of the most famous women in the world held an interest for her older brother, nor did it surprise her. "Girl, you should have met him back when!" Thelma laughed heartily. "There was no man like River...still isn't, but what you see now is such a toned-down version of what he once was. He was so...electrifying. So very full of life. Did you know he was a rodeo star?"

"No, I didn't," Carrie smiled broadly.

"Oh, yes! Competed in the National Finals three years running. Won lots of money. I've never seen anyone that could ride like River."

A sigh involuntarily followed Thelma's last observation as her smile faded away. "Could. Note the past tense. River doesn't ride anymore. River doesn't do a lot of things he used to do. And those things he does do, he just doesn't do them in the same electrifying manner. River has simply lost his spark."

With that, Thelma looked Carrie blatantly square in the eyes. "River needs something...or someone...to help him get that spark back."

Carrie Deshazo did not turn away from the stare, but simply nodded her head slowly, thoughtfully.

* * * *

"Where you headed?"

"As far south as you're willing to take me."

"Well, I'm on my way to Austin. That ain't far."

"Austin will do damned fine for a start. My name's Billy Shiloh." Billy looked hard into the driver's scraggly face to see if the man recognized the name. It didn't look as if he did. Billy's shoulders drooped just a tad.

"Okay, Billy Shiloh, if you want to go to Austin, you better get your ass in this old car. I ain't got all day. And you can call me Stitch."

"Stitch?" Billy questioned as he pushed fast-food wrappers, beer cans and a pair of dingy, stiff socks out of the passenger's seat.

"Yup, Stitch."

"What kind of name is Stitch?" Billy said as he pulled the door closed and settled in. The pair of socks smelled as bad as they looked.

"It's a fucked-up name. That's what kind of name it is. Hell, everyone thinks it's a nickname, but it ain't. It's the name my sorry-assed momma and daddy gave me. I'm glad they're both dead. Shit, I never really cared for neither one of them."

Stitch had wide-set bulging eyes. He reminded Billy of a frog. Nothing in those bulbous eyes indicated that the man wasn't telling the truth about how he felt. Stitch wore a soiled and tattered white T-shirt. Tattoos, the blue and black homemade kind, covered every inch of exposed skin on his bony arms. Stitch gunned the engine of the 70's-something Dodge before pulling back onto the roadway. The old motor knocked louder than a door to door salesman. Billy cracked his window to get some air. The socks smelled more like ass than feet.

Billy pointed at the tattoos. "You been in prison, ain't you, Stitch? Ain't those shit-house tattoos?"

"Yeah, I did some fuckin' time, but it was a bum rap," Stitch said with a sad shake of a shaggy head.

"What did they get you on?"

"Armed robbery...of a grade school bus! Now, tell me that ain't a bum rap? Who in their right fuckin' mind tries to hold up a school bus load of kids? Hell, I was just aiming to get a ride home. I was drunker than shit and probably pulled a gun all right, but I got more class than to go robbing a school bus! Fuck, what kind of haul did they think I had in mind? Maybe twenty bucks of lunch money? Fuck 'em. I wish that judge and jury was as dead as my mom and pop!"

Billy couldn't help but laugh, and Stitch didn't seem to mind. "I hope you didn't tell the other convicts what you was in for!"

"Hell, no. I told 'em I was in for bank robbery!"

"Yeah, now that's a respectable crime. I just be might be pulling a few bank jobs in the near future my own self."

Stitch shot Billy a bulging look of suspicion. "You a criminal?"

"I'm an outlaw!"

"What are you wanted by the law for?"

"Murder."

"Damn," Stitch said with an appreciative expression of raised eyebrows and pursed lips. "Who'd you murder?"

"My old lady."

"Caught her with another man? Shot her ass?"

"Naw, she'd never fuck around on me. And I didn't use no gun. Broke her back."

All of a sudden Stitch no longer looked so impressed, or maybe that was just Billy's imagination. So, he went on. "Yeah, after she was dead, I grabbed what money I had, stole a truck and hit the road and here I am. On the run."

"A man runnin' from the law needs to keep a good deal of money on him for the just-in-case kind of stuff. How much you got on you?" Stitch said as he bent forward and started digging for something beneath his seat.

"Enough," Billy grinned. "About two-hundred."

Stitch's hand came out from under the seat with a gun in it. Billy burst into laughter. He'd already pulled the one from his front pocket and had the drop on Stitch.

"Now that wasn't too damned obvious, was it, Stitch?" Billy snickered. "I mention money, you ask how much and immediately reach for something under your seat. Damn, you know, I'll bet you are stupid enough to rob a grade school bus!" Billy laughed long and hard.

Stitch went ahead and brought the gun up and now had it leveled on Billy's mid-section. Stitch wasn't laughing. "Well, at least I don't call myself an 'outlaw' when I ain't really nothing but a goddamned woman killer!"

The words caused Billy to lose his sense of humor. He brought his gun up to within inches of Stitch's face. "Don't call me that!" he bellowed. "I'll blow you're fucking head off right here and right now!"

"Yeah? And then what you dumb fuck?" Stitch screamed back at him. "That will make me pull my trigger and gut shoot you, and then the car will crash and we'll just both be dead."

"Well, then, pull this piece of shit over. We'll settle this on the side of the road," Billy growled.

"You want it, you got it, asshole," Stitch snarled as he slammed on the brakes and jerked the steering wheel toward the right shoulder.

When the car came to a stop, both men still had their guns pointed at the other. "Let's very slowly stick our guns down the front of our pants," Billy suggested.

"Who died and made you the fuckin' boss?" Stitch spat. "This is my goddamned car and I'm at least five years older than you and I've been to prison. You ain't tellin' me what to do."

"So, you got a better idea, fuckhead?"

"Well, uh, no," Stitch mumbled.

Billy sensed Stitch losing his nerve. The bulging eyes started to twitch. Billy didn't want him backing down. "You are about a dumb fuck, aren't you? By God, I do believe you are stupid enough to hold up a school bus!"

It worked. The ugly face flushed again with anger. "All right, asshole. We'll do it your way. But you better move that gun real fuckin' slow."

Both men inched their guns into their waistbands.

"Okay," Billy grinned, "now we step out of the car and move off to the side of the road. Don't try nothing stupid. We'll face off just like they did in the old days."

"I'm going to shoot you down like the woman-killing dog you are!" Stitch said through clenched, decaying teeth.

Billy held his anger until they were in place, face to face, man to man, only a few yards apart. "You know, Stitch, I want this to be fair for you. Tell you what I'm willing to do. You go ahead and put your hand on your gun. I'll hold my hands over my head." Billy brought his hands up and rested them on his head.

Stitch didn't object to the advantage. The hand on the butt of his pistol began to tremble as if diseased.

"You're scared aren't you, chickenshit?" Billy taunted.

"I ain't scared of no woman beater," Stitch stammered.

"Then go for it," Billy smiled.

Other than trembling, Stitch didn't move a muscle.

"Know why your parents named you Stitch?" Billy hissed. "It's because that's what they had to do to your bitch of a mother when you shot out of her asshole. Yeah, you are no doubt a butthole baby, Stitch. A frog-looking butthole baby that ain't worth…"

Stitch jerked at the gun in his jeans.

He never came close to getting it out. Billy's round caught the man in the shoulder and spun him around and knocked him to the ground face up. Billy moved quickly to Stitch and stood towering over him to watch with glee as Stitch writhed in pain.

"I intentionally wounded you, Stitch," Billy grinned. "I wanted you to know that I'm more than just a woman killer. I wanted you to know that you died at the hands of a true bad-ass. A real by-God outlaw." Billy put the next bullet between the man's bulging eyeballs. Brain matter splattered the grass beneath and beyond the distorted head.

Billy rummaged through the trashy car and luckily came up with a stub of a pencil. He wrote the message on a hamburger wrapper and stuffed it down the front of the dead man's filthy T-shirt. He addressed it to "Whomever it may concern."

Chapter Eight

River stood in his workshop, staring at his handiwork. It wasn't far from being finished, and still he'd be damned if he knew what he'd do with it, or himself, once it was. The knock at the door startled him. No one ever bothered him in his place of refuge.

River begrudgingly walked to the locked door and mumbled, "Who is it?"

A noticeably uncomfortable and hesitant voice returned the answer. "It's me...Carrie."

River brought both hands up to rub at his whiskered, tired face. He simply did not know how to respond. On one hand, the woman was intruding. On the other, he did not want her to go away.

"River? Can we talk?"

River opened the door, stepped out, and quickly shut the door behind him. The spring night air felt soothing and smelled fragrant. The stars glowed brilliantly and the moonlight served to spotlight the wonderful face staring up at him.

"I hope you don't mind me interrupting...whatever you do in there," she practically whispered.

"It's just, uh, busy work, a project. You're not interrupting anything." It wasn't a lie, he hadn't been doing anything. Just staring. And remembering.

"I'll come to the point, River. I felt that you were avoiding me today, or us, I guess...both Andre and me, because of what happened yesterday. I fear that maybe you think we...or I, might fault how you reacted."

At first, the words were metered. Clearly, they had been practiced, rehearsed. When River didn't, couldn't, offer a response, Carrie's words lost their structure, became more spontaneous.

"I know you're embarrassed, although you have no reason to be. I wanted so much, all day, just to talk to you. To tell you...I know you're hurting...I heard you screaming last night...I talked to Thelma, and..."

River let out a moan. "Oh, my God," he exhaled while turning his eyes from Carrie's face to stare into the darkness.

"I think I understand," she blurted.

He turned back to her and asked point blank, "Do you think I'm a coward?"

"It doesn't matter to me, River," she exclaimed.

"Then you don't understand," River said gently. He could not fathom why this woman would care in the first place, but it seemed she did. No way in hell could he respond to that rudely.

"You can't understand," he continued. "Hell, I don't completely understand. But if you think I didn't fight that boy because I was afraid of what might have happened to me, then you're wrong. All of you are wrong."

"Will you explain to me what you were feeling, what you were thinking?" Carrie pleaded.

River responded with the one word that came to mind. "Why?"

"Because...I care."

"How could you?" There was just enough moonlight for River to see that the words stung. He had not meant for them to. "Please, I didn't mean that to be cruel. This, uh, talking stuff has never come easy for me, and I don't do a good job of expressing what I really mean sometimes. It's just that I don't understand why you, a woman I met two days ago, a woman of your, I guess, means...Hell, you're rich and famous and beautiful, and, well, I'm none of those things and I just can't see why or how you could care what's going on in my little world. Let me ask you something, Carrie. How much are you worth?"

The question clearly caught her by surprise. "What possible difference does that make, River? How does that impact right here and right now?"

"It makes all the difference in the world, because right here and right now, I'm only months away from a foreclosure on this ranch. I need twenty thousand dollars, and I'm sure that amount is a drop in the bucket to you, but to me...it's my whole world. And I don't have it and I don't have anyway to get it."

"I had no idea. I didn't mean to pry," Carrie stammered. "I'm sorry, River, I don't..."

"Please, Carrie," River interrupted, "I certainly didn't tell you that to play on your sympathies, and I'm damned sure not asking for a hand-out. I just wanted to make the point that you really and truly don't have a point of reference that will let you understand what's going on in my life. I mean, you tell me, what do we possibly have in common?"

The answer came immediately. 'Pain, River. I feel we both live with an injury that most other people never have to experience. I sense that you, like me, are stumbling beneath a burden that you simply need help in bearing. I guess I feel a ... kinship. I just thought maybe I could help you and that you might want to help me."

"Carrie, I would help you if I thought I really could, but as far as you helping me, well..." River paused a minute to clear his head and collect his thoughts. He did not in the least care to air his past and expose his pain to anyone. "...Well, to help me, you'd have to go back and change a lot of things I've done...and didn't do. To help me, you'd have to go back and help everyone I've hurt, and that's something you can't do "

"You think it's your fault that your brother died," Carrie said softly under her breath.

"I know it was my fault. Nothing can change that."

"Can I tell you something I've never told another living soul?" Carrie asked.

The pain in her eyes touched something in River that had not been touched in years. "I reckon so," he said softly.

"My mother died a terrible death when I was twelve. What I've never shared with anyone is that I could have saved her life, but I didn't. I let her die."

* * * *

Carrie didn't like Marvin Taylor. She hadn't liked him from the first day her mother brought him home with her. She'd even disliked him worse than the last man Rita Baker dragged home to stay with her and her daughter. Carrie wasn't even sure what the last man's name had been. There had been so many.

Even at twelve, Carrie had no problem identifying the flaw permeating Marvin Taylor's handsome face and mannerisms. At such a young age, she could already identify meanness and this man possessed the unabashed and unadulterated kind. Couldn't her mother see it as well? Or had she simply stopped caring? "The perfect man just isn't out there," Rita Baker had been fond of saying. Carrie believed it, especially in the nightclubs her mother both served drinks in and frequented during her off-hours.

Taylor did a good job of keeping his meanness tucked out of sight for the first week or so. Then, slowly but surely, it started to seep like puss from a boil. First to come were the criticisms and harsh words. Taylor liked to say the word "fuck" a lot. Rita didn't keep the house fucking clean enough. Didn't fix the right fucking foods the right ways. Stayed out too fucking late. Didn't bring enough fucking money home. Shortly after that, the name-calling began. Her mother, according to Taylor was a bitch and a whore. Once, right in front of Rita, Taylor called Carrie a fucking brat. Another time, when Rita wasn't there, Taylor asked Carrie if she was going to be a fucking slut just like her mother. That very same night he tried to touch Carrie. When she pulled away and started to cry, Taylor warned her, "Say one word, and you won't like what I'll do to you." Carrie had not said a word. She wasn't sure Rita would have done anything if she had. Besides, Carrie grew very fearful of Taylor. Deeply, terribly fearful of him.

Mere days after the bad words and name-calling and touching and threatening began, Carrie came home from school to find her mother crying. Rita Baker wore a busted bottom lip and her right eye showed signs of swelling. Taylor came home a few hours later and both he and her mother acted like nothing ever happened. Or would ever happen again. But it did. The very next night, Carrie watched as Marvin Taylor grabbed her mother by the throat and shook her like a rag doll. The fucking potatoes had not been fried to his fucking liking. When Carrie screamed she would call the police, Taylor turned his look of stark meanness on her.

"You ever call the police, you ever even think again of calling the police," he'd hissed, "and I'll give you scars you'll wear from now on."

Marvin and Rita made up after that. For two days. The third night after that, a scream woke Carrie in the middle of the night. She heard Taylor's blows striking her mother's body. She heard her mother's body colliding with the walls. She heard the lamp hit the floor and the mirror shattering. She heard Marvin Taylor jerk open her mother's closet door.

"No, Marvin! Please no, Marvin! Put that down! I didn't do anything," her mother cried pitifully.

"You been fucking around, you worthless whore!"

"No, no, no, please, God, no. Put...it...down..."

Her mother begun to hysterically babble. Carrie thought about the police. About the phone, it sat only feet from her bed. And, too, she thought about scars she would wear the rest of her life. Carrie could not force herself from her bed.

For several more minutes, time enough for the police to have gotten there, the battle in the next room waged on.

Then came another scream. It rose with the intensity of a siren and wailed on until abruptly and eternally quieted by an earth-shattering blast of the shotgun Rita Baker kept in her closet for protection. Carrie fought for her breath. Hot, stinging tears came without benefit of sound. Before she had too many terrible seconds of fearing Taylor would now come for her, the shotgun thundered again. All that followed was a sickening silence.

Carrie didn't know how she managed to lie in bed so long, or how she managed to finally get up, or why she entered that room.

The top of Marvin Taylor's head no longer existed. Her mother's face was mangled. Blood and worse coated the walls and ceilings and still more flowed from the gruesome remains. Carrie fell across her mother's body and held it while it twitched. She lay there until pulled away by the hands of strangers.

* * * *

"I could have called the police. I could have saved my mother."

Tears streamed down the woman's face. The terrible ending of the terrible memory came in torrents of gasping sobs. River brought a hand slowly up to wipe the tears gently from her face. He hoped the man who inflicted scars, currently burned in hell. River felt both pleased and relieved when Carrie didn't shy away from his touch.

"You were only twelve," were the only words that came clearly to his mind. They did not seem to help. Knowing nothing else to offer, he thought his memories might offer a diversion. He used the hand at her face to softly turn her head toward the structure that loomed in the darkness off to the right of them.

"Some of my bad memories live in there," he rasped.

"In the barn?" Carrie whispered.

River nodded. "In my dreams...my nightmares, voices call to me from there."

"Sky's?" she asked.

"Well, yes, he did in last night's dream."

"And others?"

"Yes. Others."

"Whose?"

River took a deep breath and dropped his hand from Carrie's face to take hold of her hand. He'd touched her first to ease her pain.

Now, he held onto her to help with his own. He didn't think he could begin. When he did, he felt as if he couldn't stop. He told her first about the Vietnamese and went directly from the jungle to the street where he'd gunned down Moose Boggs. River spared no details. Carrie never interrupted. Her face displayed no judgments. Her hand gripped his in support.

"And because of all that," River concluded with a heavy sigh, "I don't carry guns anymore. They're all locked away in the basement. Almost everything I used to be is down there. Hell, there's even a bulletproof vest I wore when I was a cop. Don't know why I even kept that silly thing. And because of what happened to Sky, I don't want anything to do with horses. I moved all of them to a little piece of land that Hank Sioux owns. He takes care of them for me.

"It ain't that I'm afraid of being shot, and I'm not afraid of being stomped to death by a horse, it's just because, well..." River paused to search for a way of putting into words something he'd never yet had a need to. Before he could, Carrie drew her own conclusions.

"Because you don't want to hurt anyone else," she spoke up. "And you gave up horses to punish yourself."

"I don't want anymore voices," River said with a shake of his head. For a second, he considered telling her about the dream he'd had the night before. But only for a split second.

* * * *

If Carrie ever felt closer to a man, she couldn't remember when. She felt sure she'd never met a finer one. The pain still loomed in his stunning eyes. She wanted, more than anything in the world, to help it go away.

"What happened to the boy was tragic, but you had no way of knowing. It was a war for Christ's sake. You were so young. With Boggs, you were trying to defend a woman's honor. It wasn't as if you'd gone looking for him with the intent of killing him."

River dropped his head. "And I've hurt others as well."

Carrie involuntarily tightened the grip she held on his hand, and he must have sensed her sudden dread.

"No," he said with a weak smile, "I've not killed anyone else. Messed up far too many old boys in bars and honky-tonks. I'm talking about women...and, well, others. I'm talking about broken promises. I'm talking about wives. I've had four. All good women. Much too good for me. I've made so many promises I never kept. Promises to love and protect until death do us...well, you know that tune. Anyway, I hurt them."

"How?"

"Oh, I never laid a hand on anyone of them. I never hit a woman. I never will. I hurt them with my ways. I, uh, well, I wasn't loyal. I guess you know what I mean."

Carrie had a good idea. Experiences taught her it was simply a way with men. It didn't demand explanation. It was life.

"And the others?" she asked to change the topic. "Who were the others you feel you've hurt?"

It took River several long seconds to respond. "You told me something you never told anyone else. I'll show you something I've never shown anyone else."

With that he turned and opened the door to the shop building. River led her in by the grip he still maintained on her hand.

An old table sat in the center of the shop. On top of it rested a grand and adorable Victorian doll house.

"It's almost finished," River declared.

"It's beautiful," Carrie exhaled without exaggeration.

"It was a promise. One of many not kept," River said in a voice painfully soft. "I have a daughter from my second marriage. Her name is Sandy. She always wanted a doll house. When she was five, I promised her I'd build her one. I never got around to it. I left her mother when she was seven. I've not seen her since, and don't even know where she's at. She's a grown woman now."

After moments of silence, Carrie spoke words coming from her heart. "You're a good man, River Yates."

"I don't think you'll ever convince me of that," he mumbled.

Carrie moved closer and wrapped an arm around his waist. "I can try."

River responded by draping his arm around her shoulders. Arm in arm they walked back to the house, cutting a wide swathe around the old red barn.

* * * *

Chief of Police Mike Simms grew close to wrapping up a long night of paperwork when the phone on his desk jangled.

"Wilburton Police Department," he responded with a yawn.

"This is Sergeant Danny Thompson with the Texas State Police," a gruff voice sounded. "Who am I speaking with?"

"I'm Mike Simms, the chief of police. What can I do for you Sergeant?" The late hour left Simms feeling no more cordial than the voice addressing him.

"Evening, Chief," the voice lightened. "I hate to bother you so late, but I'm hoping you can shed some light on a case we're working down here in God's country!"

Despite the hour and his fatigue, Simms chuckled. He'd be damned if Texans didn't hold a patent on arrogance. "I certainly will if I can."

"Well we got an abandoned Chevy truck down here with Oklahoma tags. It's registered to a Walter Bates there in Wilburton. We found a rather strange note in it signed by a Billy Shiloh."

Simms sat up straight in his chair. "I'm looking for Shiloh. He murdered his wife up here a few days back."

"Well, we got something in common then. We're looking for him, too. Besides the abandoned pick-up, we got us a dead body as well. One used-to-be piece of shit by the name of Stitch Hatley. Your boy, Shiloh, left a note on the body, too. Kind of a cocky son of a bitch ain't he?"

"He's an animal," Simms grumbled. "What do the notes say?"

Thompson paraphrased the one Shiloh left in Bates' truck, but read verbatim the one they found tucked in the dead man's clothing. "To Whom it May Concern," Thompson deadpanned, "This man challenged me to a gunfight, and I shot him down. Let all who reads this know that I am not a woman killer. That was an accident. Killing this man was no accident. Any lawman that gets in between me and Mexico will be shot just as dead." Thompson paused before concluding, "The ignorant bastard signed this one like he did the other one, 'the outlaw Billy Shiloh.'"

"Could he be in Mexico by now?" Simms asked.

"Well, we think he took Hatley's car. So, yeah, he could have made it by now."

"Do me a favor," Simms growled.

"Sure. What?"

"If you find him, and there's a gun fight, put a round in him for me."

"We'll make it two ..just for good measure."

"And keep me posted."

"Will do. You take care, Chief."

After hanging up, Mike Simms decided to stick around the office. Peaceful rest and relaxation at home seemed no longer an option.

* * * *

River walked Carrie to her bedroom door. They stood in the hall for the longest time in a jittery, twitching, fumbling sort of silence. River wanted to kiss her. Wanted to do so much more. He felt Carrie might be willing, and just for a moment, River almost forgot the vast distance separating his world from hers.

With a simple goodnight he left her at her door and went to his bedroom to find himself missing her. He tried to remember how long it had been since he held a woman's hand, or had a woman's arm around his waist. He tried to convince himself not kissing her, not doing more, had been the right decision. Carrie Deshazo was not the kind of woman his kind of man could simply wave good-bye to forever in a mere week and a half. Because he'd changed and because she was so very beautiful, River knew that if he had her once, he'd have to have her forever.

With these thoughts and emotions pinballing through his mind, River turned off the overhead light and moved to his bed. Like he had every single night since the death of his brother, River got on his knees beside the bed. And like he had every single night since the death of his brother, River repeated the very same words.

"Please forgive me, and let...all of them...forgive me. Bless Sandy. Please let her know I love her."

River started to his feet, paused a moment, and then knelt again. "And, please," he said with eyes closed tightly, "help the woman. Let her realize she was only twelve."

Chapter Nine

River got up even earlier than usual to do his morning chores, and went about them with a spring in his step. He hadn't had a spring in his step for the longest time. He wasn't ready to admit that Carrie made it possible, but he could admit that the time spent with her felt damned good. River avoided having breakfast with the two guests since they'd been at the ranch. But this morning he felt sociable and unusually hungry.

River walked in the back door to be assaulted by a sight that stopped him in his tracks. Andre sipped coffee at the table in the breakfast nook.

"Damn, man, that's one of my sister's robes!" River gasped.

"I think it brings out the green in my eyes, don't you?" Andre asked over the rim of his coffee cup.

"Why the hell are you wearing it?" River scowled.

"My jeans are dirty," Andre shrugged. "I only have the one pair, and Thelma's washing them for me. I need another pair. Do you think one of yours might fit me?"

"Sweet Jesus, Andre," River moaned, "men around these parts don't go borrowing other men's jeans."

"It's not as if I'm asking for a pair of your underwear."

"Thank God," River said under his breath as he got himself a cup of coffee. He took the chair furthest from Andre.

"I knew you were no coward," the robed man said with a sly wink as River settled into his chair.

"Oh, shit!" River groaned. "She told you?"

"Well, she wouldn't tell me much," Andre said with a girlie wave of his hand. "I tried to get her to tell all, but all Carrie would admit was that you didn't take that horrid Billy Shiloh to task because you didn't want his demise on your conscience. I can understand that."

"I don't want to talk about it, Andre," River winced.

"Guess where I spent my afternoon and evening?" Andre rebounded in a wink.

When River didn't, Andre provided the answer. "With the boys at the Silver Dollar Bar."

River just shook his head and sighed.

"Oh, I behaved myself. Didn't drop a single homosexual innuendo!"

River sighed again. This time out of relief.

"No, it was simply time spent amongst good ol' boys chewing the fat. Mostly about you."

River buried his head in his hands.

"About your police days and your rodeo days and your bounty hunting days. My Lord, River, it sounded like something out of an Old West saga! Please, Hank told me his version, but you must tell me about the time that judge in Dallas caught you in bed with his wife and her blind sister!'

River's head bounced up and an index finger shot to his lips. "Shhhhhhh, Andre! Damn, don't be so loud!" he hissed while craning his neck to see if the comment stirred any attention in the adjoining kitchen.

"Well? So?" Andre giggled.

"Hell, I didn't know she was blind," River whispered. "I just thought she might, well, you know, some people wear sunglasses indoors!"

"And did that judge actually take a shot at you?"

"No," River emphasized bluntly. "See, Andre, you can't believe everything you hear. Things get twisted in all the telling and retelling. He shot at me three times. Thank God the gun jammed before he could get off a fourth. Scared that poor blind girl half to death. She wouldn't let go of me. I was wrestling around to get free of her and get my pants on and that ol' judge was cussing me and cussing that gun and I was trying to tell him that I hadn't gotten around yet to even laying a finger on his wife."

River paused for a breath and another look into the kitchen. "Now, the only reason I told you all of that is to let you know that those three assholes in the bar don't know near what they think they know about me. You need to take every damn thing they tell you with a grain of salt."

"What about the time," Andre started, but then stopped. Thelma entered from the kitchen with a platter of pecan waffles and scrambled eggs.

"My, my," she smiled broadly, "you boys are sure chatty this morning."

"I'm not chatty," River said with a vigorous shake of his head. "He's chatty. Why the hell are you letting him wear your clothes?"

Thelma placed the platter in the middle of the table and then bent to pinch Andre's right cheek. "Isn't he simply adorable?" she beamed.

"Thelma has expressed a desire to turn me," Andre beamed back.

River's mouth fell open as he brought the heel of his hand up to slap his forehead. "You know, uh, well, that's about, uh..." the words just would not come. "Damn. I'm not even hungry anymore."

"Why not? What did I miss?"

The sound of Carrie's voice from the doorway affected River in ways he wished it couldn't.

"River doesn't want me doing his sister!" Andre burst into shrill laughter.

River jerked his head in the direction of the doorway to say something. Exactly what, he did not know. Maybe a rebuttal. Maybe to agree vehemently. But when his eyes fell on Carrie, it all became moot. Her hair was pulled back in a ponytail and she wore a form-fitting black T-shirt tucked into a pair of cut-off jeans. River's breath caught in his throat. He must have gawked.

"I was thinking," Carrie smiled slyly, "that I might be able to talk you into a ride on the back of your bike."

"And I'm thinking from the look on River's face," Andre interjected, "you just did."

* * * *

Carrie wanted to see the ranch. River couldn't have hand-crafted a more perfect morning for tooling around with a beautiful woman on the back of his old Harley. The dirt road that wound through the hills and trees and pastures of the ranch served up just enough bumps to keep Carrie's arms around his waist. River hoped the roar of the big twin cylinders drowned out the vibrant pounding of his heart.

The large pond on the back acres of the Working Y had always been one of River's favorite places on the ranch. The still, deep blue spring-fed waters now, as always, had a calming effect on River. He pulled the bike to a stop beneath a clump of oaks on the bank of the pond and killed the engine. A gentle breeze carried the fragrance of a nearby field of native flowers, and River breathed the sweetness deep into his lungs. He felt Carrie doing the same. River put down the kickstand, swung his leg over the broad gas tank and then helped Carrie off the bike.

"Oh, this is so wonderful," she sighed, taking in the sights of the peaceful water and distant mountains.

"I was hoping you would like it," River exhaled.

For the longest time, neither spoke a word. To his surprise, River began to feel comfortable in her presence.

"How many girls have you brought out here, River Yates?" Carrie ribbed.

"Would you believe none?"

"No."

"Good," he chuckled.

"Are you dating anyone special?" she asked bluntly.

"I'm not dating anyone. That's another thing I've pretty much given up."

"Why?"

"I thought we kind of covered that last night," he said shyly.

"Yes," she responded thoughtfully, "I guess we did."

There were seconds of silence as River considered the question on his mind. "I would guess you're seeing someone," he said, averting his eyes to the ground.

"I am," she said after a moment's hesitation, "although I don't know why."

"You're not in love?"

"Do you know what love is, River?"

"Well, I've thought a couple of times that I did."

Carrie chuckled at the response before responding. "Yes, me too."

"I mean, I know that I love my daughter, even though I haven't laid eyes on her in years. And I loved my mama and daddy, my brother, and I love Thelma, too. But I'm not sure I can give a definition of what love is between a man and a woman. You know what I'm saying?"

"Exactly," she nodded before adding, "boy, we are quite a pair."

"A pair of what?" River grinned.

"Now that does seem to be the question, doesn't it?" she laughed.

"Who's this man you're seeing?" River asked, while bending to pick up a rock.

"Clive Benz. I guess you know who he is," Carrie said, sounding almost embarrassed.

River certainly did and suddenly remembered just how far this woman lived out of his league. He tossed the rock into the water with a vengeance. "Is he really a tough guy?"

"By what I would imagine your standards of a tough guy are? Not even."

"Does he love you?"

"Oh, I believe he thinks he does. But I fear his concept of love is far more distorted than yours and mine."

"Damn, that's screwed up."

Carrie laughed again, and River tried not to adore the sound of it.

"What's it like being so famous and all?" River asked while surveying the ground at his feet for a rock flat enough to skim.

"From what I can gather, from Thelma and Andre, you're very famous around here. You know what it's like."

"Famous? Not hardly. Notorious maybe, but not famous. What's it like?"

"I liked it at first. You know, being recognized every place you go and having fans asking for your autograph. But, now, well, it's basically a pain in the ass."

River laughed this time.

"You have such a nice laugh."

River found his rock and now gave it a fling. It skipped four times before sinking to the depths of the lake. "So do you."

"Let's laugh some more then," she said gleefully. "Tell me, River, what is the funniest thing that has ever happened to you?"

* * × *

He did not like talking about himself, and it numbered among the things Carrie found so attractive about River Yates. Clive, on the other hand, could go on forever about himself. Clive Benz was and would always be Clive Benz's most favorite topic. The contrast felt gloriously refreshing.

"Come on," she prodded, "you've had plenty of time to think of something. What do you think is the funniest thing that has ever happened to you?"

"Well," he said as he kicked at the ground with the toe of his boot, "if you'd tell me the funniest thing that ever happened to you, then maybe I could think of something."

"I'll tell you the funniest thing I've ever seen. Of course, it wasn't very funny at the time," she giggled.

"Okay. What's that?"

Carrie laughed at the recent memory. "You getting tossed around by Bobo was, in retrospect, pretty damned hilarious!" Her words now came with torrents of laughter. "Just picture what I saw. I'm enjoying a peaceful afternoon when all of a sudden, I hear this commotion and look up to see this man running at breakneck speed across a pasture with this huge beast right on his ass! The next thing I know, you're flying through the air. Then you both disappear, and then your reappear in reverse order. Now, the cow...excuse me...steer is running and you're right on its tail with this big old stick!"

"Your version does sound funnier than it actually was," River commented dryly.

"All right, you do better. Tell me something funnier that's happened to you."

River thrust his hands deep into the pockets of his jeans and started gently rocking on the heels of his boots. "I'm sure I've seen a lot of damned funny things in my life, but at the moment, none come to mind. How about me just telling you the funniest thing I've ever done, or I guess actually, the dumbest thing I've ever done?"

"I'll settle for that," Carrie said as she found herself once again admiring the color and sincerity of his eyes.

"About ten years back, I was following the rodeo circuit up in Colorado. One night in Durango, I stepped out of my motel room and there in the parking lot right outside my door was this ol' boy with a big buckskin gelding. Now, that was one of those horses that just catches a cowboy's eye and won't let go of it. I mean, it was one of most beautiful horses I'd ever seen.

"Well, this cowboy is out there in the parking log drawing a big circle in chalk on the asphalt. I'd say this circle is about fifteen feet in diameter. So, I ask this guy what's he doing, and he says, 'I'm getting ready to make me some money.' I ask him how. He asks me if I got a hundred dollars on me. I was still pretty cocky back then, and as usual, I'd been drinking, which always just tended to make me cockier. 'Hell, I said, I got a bunch more than a hundred.' He asks me if I want to try to make a hundred more and I ask him what he's got in mind.

"He points to that fine young buckskin and says, 'That horse won't buck and when I put that horse in this little circle here, he won't come out of it.' And then he says to me, 'But I'll tell you what, I'll bet you a hundred dollars you can't sit on that horse in that circle for two minutes.'

"I say, 'He ain't going to buck?' And he says, 'Nope.' And I say, 'He ain't going to run out of that circle? And he says, 'Nope.' And I tell him he must be out of his mind, or drunker than I am, and I take him up on his bet. You see, Carrie, that circle wasn't even big enough for that horse to run around in, so I didn't see how in the hell I could lose that bet.

"He takes that horse and puts him right square-dabbed in the middle of that circle. The horse is all saddled up and everything, so I get up on him and take the reins in my hands. He's real calm and I can tell he's well broke. I don't have any concerns, I'm not worried. And the guy asks me if I'm ready and I tell him I am.

"Well, that cowboy brings his fingers up to his mouth and let's go with a whistle. What then happened was one of the damnedest things I've ever seen a horse do. The best way I can describe it, is that horse started chasing its tail just like a dog will do. And it was smooth, no bucking, but damn it was fast. And it got faster. Pretty soon I felt as if I knew what it was like to be right in the middle of and riding a tornado. Girl, I got so dizzy and that buckskin was moving so fast, I just couldn't stay in the saddle. I hit that pavement and rolled and tumbled a good twenty yards. Tore up my face and my hands and ruined a brand-new pair of Wrangler jeans. That cowboy was laughing his ass off."

And so did Carrie. River Yates had a talent for storytelling. "That was a pretty dumb thing to do. I mean there on the concrete and all," she laughed.

"Oh, that wasn't the dumb part," River said with an embarrassed grin. "After I handed that guy his hundred, I asked him how much he'd sell that horse for. He said, 'this horse makes me a lot of money.' I told him to just name his price. To make a long story even dumber, I wrote him a five-thousand dollar check for that buckskin."

"Is that a lot for a horse?" Carrie giggled.

"It was for that horse. Hell, all it was good for was chasing its tail. But, boy, he's a beauty. That guy had named him Twister. That's another name for a tornado. And a funny thing is, that horse has a white spot right between his eyes, and I'll be damned if it don't look like a twister."

"Do you still have him," Carrie assumed by his last words.

"Yup. He's one of the horses Hank is keeping for me."

"Don't you miss your horses, River?" Carrie asked.

The man seemed to deeply consider the question. Before answering, he turned and gave Carrie what she took to be an appreciative once over.

"I miss a lot of things I once had and did."

Carrie did not fail to notice the spark in his eyes.

* * * *

Billy Shiloh made it over halfway to where he'd intended all along to end up. Everything so far went as planned, and that called for a celebration.

He had the prostitute bent over the sagging bed of the filthy, dilapidating motel room. Boy oh boy, did he ever lay it to her. At first, she'd objected, saying she didn't participate in abnormal sex. But it only took a couple of well aimed blows to influence her. She wasn't crying, but she damned sure whimpered one hell of a lot. She wasn't much to look at, and her old ass drooped with mileage, but Billy could say one thing for the bitch, she could sure take a punch.

The faster and harder he thrust, the better he felt. Damned if he wasn't going to fool them all. Damned if he wasn't the craftiest outlaw of all times. Billy let out a rebel yell and slapped the old whore on the left cheek of her ass. The sound cracked like gunfire, and the woman let out a scream of pain. Billy grabbed a handful of her brittle hair and jerked her head as far back as it would go. He used the grip to intensify his pounding thrusts. The woman could only gasp and gurgle.

He could feel it coming on. Climbing, building, burning, almost there. At just the right second, he pulled out. He used the grip on her hair to spin her over on her back. Quickly, he straddled her waist, brought his hands up and folded them behind his head, and looked down at his erection just as it erupted.

Billy looked down into the trembling face of the prostitute. "Do you know how lucky you are?" he hissed.

The woman shook her head, her eyes averted from his face.

"You've just been fucked by Billy Shiloh, woman. Before I'm finished, a lot of people are going to be fucked by Billy Shiloh."

* * * *

Carrie's day had been delightful. She never enjoyed keeping company with a man like she did today. They spent their time riding and talking and laughing. There were moments they enjoyed nothing but comfortable silence, moments neither sensed a need for words.

Like now. Sitting on folding canvas chairs in the backyard, her with lemonade, him with beer. Both entranced on the deep orange of the setting sun and purples and pinks of the bracketing clouds. Each with their own thoughts.

Carrie decided to voice one of hers. "River, if you could have anything in the world you wanted, what would it be?"

"Damn, don't you ever have any simple questions?" he responded without taking his eyes off the glorious sunset.

She learned many things about him in the course of the day. One of which being that his gruffness served mostly as a front. She ignored it. "Would you like to know what I would want if I could have anything I wanted?"

He simply turned to her, looked deeply in her eyes and nodded his head. He didn't have to say it. It showed in his eyes. He cared about what she wanted.

"If I tell you, will you then tell me what you would want?"

"Well, I don't really ever..."

"Okay, it's a deal," she interrupted. "I'll tell you and then you tell me."

He just turned his eyes back to the horizon and slowly shook his head, but she knew he would listen. He'd proven a good listener. Something she was not use to, but quickly grew very fond of.

"If I could have anything in this whole wide world, I would choose ending every day with the tranquillity and happiness I'm feeling right now."

"That would be nice. Okay, I wish for the same thing."

"Oh no you don't. You're not getting off that easy. We had a deal."

"You had a deal," he grumbled.

But then, as she knew it would, the front crumbled.

"I'm too old to have what I want."

"Oh, come on, what is it?"

He took a deep breath and looked away. She also learned that this was his way when forced to talk about things of the heart.

"I would want," he started slowly, awkwardly, "a forever kind of relationship with a woman. And I would want kids. At least three."

He paused to look at and rub the rugged skin in the palm of his right hand with his left. "And I would never, ever do anything to mess it up."

"You're not too old for that," she responded softly.

"Yes I am. I'm too old to be raising children."

"There are men who father children up into their seventies."

River brought his eyes back up to look into hers. What they harbored did not resemble hope. The sad look stirred in Carrie a burning desire to make it go away.

* * * *

Billy thought it would be a nice touch for the history books:

The famed Billy Shiloh never gunned down an opponent without first giving the other man a chance to shoot first. Before his victims fell at the hand of his lightening fast draw, they all heard the same last words...

He'd thought it a cool effect how he'd let Stitch go for his gun first. It was the kind of thing Billy wanted to be known for, and someday, it'd look damned good in the movies about his life. He hadn't thought about the words until after he'd killed that frog-looking piece of shit in Texas. What he needed was a "saying." Something he spoke just before pulling the trigger. Something that would be repeated down through the years by history professors and such. Billy bounced his ideas off the whore.

"Okay, I'm ready again. Go ahead and bring the gun up and point it at me."

Of course, he'd unloaded the gun before giving it to her. She called herself Delight, and at first, Delight refused to help Billy with his saying. He'd tried slapping her around a little more. But it just seemed that with Delight, that the more you hit her, the more stubborn she'd become. Billy finally agreed to walk across the street to a liquor store to buy her a bottle of cheap whiskey. The cheap stuff didn't seem to bother ol' Delight. The more she drank, the more willing she became to help Billy with his saying.

"Come on, Delight, dammit, point the gun at me."

"Wish you'd give me a bullet," she slurred. "I'd shoot your mean ass!"

The more she drank, the nastier she grew. Now, she pointed the gun with enthusiasm.

"Okay, so now I've let you get the drop on me," Billy said as he spread his feet shoulder-width apart and brought his hands up parallel with the stained, crusty carpet. He cleared his throat.

"If you are going to point that gun at me, mister, you best..."

"I ain't no, mister," Delight belched.

"God dammit, Delight, this is play acting. You're playing like you're a fucking man."

"If I was a fuckin' man, I'd kick your fuckin' ass," she nodded as a matter of fact.

"Do you want to keep that bottle, bitch?" Billy yelled.

"Don't take my bottle...please," Delight said, suddenly sounding a hell of lot nicer.

"Okay, then, shut the fuck up. Where was I? Oh...you best be pulling the trigger. Because when I'm finished talking, I'm going to start shooting!"

By God, that captured it. Billy let out such a loud whoop that Delight practically dropped her bottle. "Get your ugly old ass back up on that bed," he grinned. "This puts me in the mood for another round!"

"Why are you so mean? Did your parents beat you when you was a kid?" Delight said as she ambled toward the bed.

"They never laid a hand on me." Billy beamed as he stripped off his underwear.

"Well, then maybe that's the problem," Delight said before falling back on the bed and spreading her legs.

* * * *

Carrie freshened up for dinner before Thelma knocked at her bedroom door.

"Carrie, you have a phone call, dear," Thelma said with a cordless phone in an outstretched hand. She left the phone with Carrie and hurried back down to her work in the kitchen.

"Hello," Carrie said, just knowing it would be Todd Wald.

"Hello, darling. How much are you missing me?" It wasn't.

The sound of the voice might have affected her differently ten or so hours earlier. Now, it simply annoyed her.

"Hello, Clive."

"I thought you would have run back to me by now, Carrie. Or, at the very least, called a couple of times."

Some men would say such things jokingly. Clive really had no sense of humor. "Sorry I haven't called. That is rude of me." Carrie thought about making an excuse, but didn't care to.

"Well, you're forgiven. And to prove it, I have a surprise for you. Next week, I'm coming out there to be with you!"

"Oh, Clive," came immediately to mind but she struggled to come up with the rest. "You, you, don't need to, uh, come out here...well, to be honest, I don't want..."

"I know, I know," Clive said with a laugh, "you don't want to interfere with my schedule. You don't want to put me out. Right?"

He didn't give Carrie the chance to respond.

"You can be so sweet. You are a doll. Well, Wednesday, I'll be there. Can't wait. Love you."

She had no say, Clive was coming. For long seconds, Carrie could only stand in place curling her toes and gritting her teeth while squeezing like hell the cordless in her hand. She considered calling him back, but then decided the arrogant son of a bitch could just come on out and, just maybe, learn a thing or two about what it meant to be a real man.

* * * *

Shortly after Delight finished her bottle, she passed out on the bed. Billy had waited for this to happen. It would be easier this way. It was time for him to go. He'd been doing his traveling at night, and it wasn't going to get anymore night than at the present moment.

He'd thought about not letting the prostitute know his true identity. The first part of his plan included letting the cops know his location while giving them glimpses of his activities. He'd meant to throw his name around during that part of the plan. Time had come that he needed to execute the second part of his plan, and this part required secrecy. He couldn't take the chance of some twenty-dollar whore telling the entire world that she'd fucked the one and only Billy Shiloh right here in this place, right here on this date. The cops might then figure out his true intentions.

Yes, she had to go. Yes, it would be better this way. Billy picked up one of the pillows from the bed. This way, there would be no screaming. He put the pillow over the bruised face and held it down tightly. Delight drank too much to put up much resistance. She only twitched and jerked for a minute, two at the most.

Immediately after he'd done the deed, Billy momentarily wished he hadn't. He wouldn't have minded just one more go-at-it with the whore. She'd been damned good, even though somewhat hard to look at. Billy strode from the room thankful he no longer needed to leave notes. People knowing Billy Shiloh had fucked well beneath his ability might cause some to think less of him.

* * * ×

It wasn't something Carrie decided on the spur of the moment. She gave it a lot of consideration. Whether right or wrong, she still didn't know. Did anyone ever really know? Before she could think of too many reasons not to, Carrie crawled out of her bed and pulled on her robe. She paused momentarily to look out the window at the lurking red barn in the distance. Carrie did not like the message the structure seemed to communicate. "You have no right to judge me," she murmured before slipping out of her room.

* * * *

River tried to sleep, but sleep would not come. Too many thoughts bounced around between his ears while too many emotions tore at his innards. River sat up at the sound of his door being pushed open. It didn't startle him. Instead, it filled him with hope. His heart nearly stopped when hope became reality.

Carrie came to his bed without a word. She let her gown fall to the floor. River raised the covers and welcomed the warmth of her naked body next to his. For a fleeing moment he wondered where it all could lead. His concern did not linger.

Chapter Ten

Walter Bates crawled into bed at nine. That had, what seemed like a lifetime ago instead of only ten days past, been his regular bedtime. But tonight, like the past ten nights, sleep would not mercifully overtake him. At eleven he decided to get up and go to his grocery store. Some things needed doing. Things that might take his mind off of his loss and his pain and his hatred.

Walter came in the back door of the closed market to find the light on in his office. No big surprise because the new stock boy would have been in there last and perhaps failed to turn it off before leaving. The surprise came when Walter walked into the office. Newspapers were strung on his desk and across the floor.

"What in hell..." he started to question out loud before being interrupted by the sound of the toilet flushing in the adjoining restroom. Before he had time to draw conclusions, Billy Shiloh stepped out of the restroom door.

"You," Walter Bates exclaimed in surprise that instantaneously erupted into rage. "You!"

* * * *

It was a good thing Billy just emptied his bowels. Coming out of the john to find Bates standing there startled the hell out of him. The old man lunged at him so suddenly that it momentarily stunned Billy. But when the hands fell upon his neck and the force of Bates' charge slammed him into the door behind him, Billy moved to action. First his right fist and then his left found the old man's exposed and soft stomach. The hands fell from his neck as Bates doubled over, gasping for air. The fight drained from Bates, but not from Billy. He brought a knee up hard into the lowered face, sending Bates backwards and then to the floor. For good measure, Billy planted two kicks in the downed man's ribs. Walter Bates cried out in pain and rolled onto his side, pulling his skinny legs up to his damaged stomach and chest.

"That was a very dumb thing to do, you stupid old fuck," Billy spat.

The response came in tortured gasps. "You're supposed to be in Mexico."

Shiloh threw back his head and laughed, "Yeah, pretty slick, huh? Guess I had all you fooled!"

He pulled up a chair close to Bates' head and plopped down on it. "Yes, sir, I left a trail just to double back on it. Hell, I never got close to Old Mexico. Now, you tell me that wasn't one hell of a smart plan!"

After Billy shot down the bullfrog-looking dude just north of Austin, Texas, he'd taken the man's car and turned it back toward Oklahoma. It took him three days to make a trip a man not having to be careful could make in less than ten hours. Billy kept to the back roads. He'd gotten rid of Stitch's old Dodge about three hours after he'd taken it by driving it off in a river. He didn't want the cops finding it and figuring out he'd doubled back. Billy stole three more cars along the way. In between cars, he'd done some walking because hitching rides seemed a little too risky. He just knew, by that time, that his face would have been in enough papers and on enough television screens to make him as recognizable as McDonalds' golden arches. He'd picked up that whore just north of the Oklahoma and Texas border, and now wondered how long it took before someone found her body. He'd been back in Wilburton for a little over twenty-four hours. Most of that time he'd spent sleeping like a baby in his cave.

"What are you doing here?" Bates managed to moan.

Billy laughed again, and nudged Bate's head roughly with the toe of his boot. "I bet you wished you'd changed all the locks now, don't you? But, hell, why would you, I mean me being down in Mexico and all?"

Billy paused a minute to consider why he came to the store, why he'd been searching through all them damned newspapers. The sour mood, the one he'd been in before the old man interrupted it, came rushing back in gushes of disappointment.

"Maybe you can tell me something, asshole," he started with a sad scowl. "Why in the hell aren't there any stories about me in all those papers? Here I am the most notorious outlaw to hail from these parts since Jesse James, and I can't find a single damned story about my crime spree!"

"Outlaw?" Bates mumbled through his busted lips and the blood streaming from his nose. "Is that the way you see yourself? Is that what you want to be...famous?"

"You damned straight," Billy grumbled. "At least as famous as that bitch actress staying in town." All the state papers had something to say about her being in Wilburton. The gossip column of the local paper even made accusations that her and River Yates were some kind of item. Billy was still puzzling over that bullshit.

Walter Bates rolled over on his back, but made no attempt to get up. "Well, you ain't nothing but trash," he rasped, "a petty, murdering thug. And you'll never be any more than just that."

Billy sprang from the chair and kicked it across the small office. "You better watch your mouth, you silly old fuck!" he bellowed.

"Why? You going to kill me, too? Go ahead, put me out of my misery..."

Billy started to do just that, but then Walter Bates gasped in enough air for a few more words.

"...but you better do it here and now, cause if I live, I'll pay good money to see you dead."

* * * *

Bates expected to die, and expected it to be slow and cruel, the way his only child died. He did not expect Shiloh to pick up the chair and sit back down in it. The terrible moments of following silence unnerved him. When would the next blow fall? What terrible things did the bastard contemplate? The waiting hurt more than his nose and lips and stomach and ribs. When Shiloh spoke, Bates flinched.

"A bounty? A reward? Now, that ain't a bad idea."

Shiloh started laughing, and Bates despised the sound of it.

"Matter of fact," Shiloh emphasized by slapping his thigh, "that's a damned good idea. If you put a reward on my head, just like they did the James' brothers and the Younger boys, that will damned sure get the attention of the news people. Damn sure will!

"Tell you what I'm going to do for you, Dad...Hey, I never did call you that, did I?"

There existed a time Walter would not have cared, might have even welcomed it. Hearing him use the word now turned Bates' already heaving stomach.

"Oh, well, guess it's a little late for it now," Shiloh chuckled. "Anyway, here's what I'm going to do for you. I'm going to let you live. I'm going to let you live so that you can tell the cops that I'm hiding up in the mountains, and so that you can put some money on my head and get some bounty hunters up there looking for me.

"And what's going to come from this is that you are going to live to see just how famous I become, and how wrong you were for saying that I never would be. I guess the only bad part about this new plan is that it sure seems to make that trip to Texas feel like a waste of time. I wanted the law to think I was in Mexico so they wouldn't be crawling all over them mountains, and here I am now wanting them to come crawling all over them mountains just to try and find me. I'll be double damned if life can't take some funny turns. Know what I mean, Dad?"

"Fuck you."

"Fuck me?" Shiloh snickered. "Damn, I ain't never heard you use the 'F' word. I guess that kind of shows just how pissed you are at me. And don't think for a minute that I don't understand, but still I think you ought to realize what happened to your daughter wasn't exactly all my fault. You see, that woman didn't know how to act like a woman. She didn't know how to treat a man like a man. In other words, she wasn't brought up right. And for that, don't you know, you got to take some of the blame."

Bates wanted on his feet and made a move to get up. Shiloh used the sole of his boot to shove him down and hold him in place.

"I guess you haven't noticed what I got strapped around my waist, or you'd said something by now." Shiloh chuckled.

Walter wasn't looking at him and didn't intend to, but out of the corner of his eye, he caught Shiloh making a slapping motion at this mid-section. It made a sound of flesh falling on...leather.

Bates jerked his head up and around to see if what he feared could be true. And it was. "No. Not those, you son of a bitch. You take those off!"

Shiloh hooked his thumbs into the upper edge of the hand-tooled leather gun belt and leaned back in the chair. "Ain't going to do that, Walter."

The black leather gun belt with its fancy hand-tooling and double holsters had been a prized possession for many years. Walter had it made in Dallas when he was a young man. But it wasn't as old or as precious as the guns the holsters held. The matching, mint condition Colt 45 Peacemakers belonged to his grandfather. Walter kept them on display in his office. To a collector, the revolvers would be worth several thousand dollars. To Walter they were priceless.

"Please, don't take them."

"I'm going to take them, Walter. But, just consider it another favor. Cause someday, you might get them back. And if you do, they'll be famous. Hell, you'll be able to tell people that these old guns were carried by the Outlaw Billy Shiloh."

"I'll see you dead, you bastard," Walter said as he fought back the tears. "I swear to God, I'll see you dead."

Shiloh laughed loud and long before saying, "Hey, you remember that time you let me wear them and I showed you just what I could do with them?"

Walter did. He'd been astonished at the quickness of the boy's draw, amazed at his accurate aim. The memory, as well as a realization, gave Bates a chill. If men went up in the mountains to find Shiloh, a lot of them would be carried back down.

Billy Shiloh pushed to his feet and stood for a moment with his hands resting on the ivory handles of the fine old Colts. "Well, it's been a pleasure seeing you, Walter. I'm glad we could catch up a while, but it's time for me to be heading out. Now, you be sure to tell them all where they can find me, and be sure you tell them I'll be ready if they do find me."

Shiloh walked to the door before he stopped and turned back to look down at Bates. "Tell me something, Walter, are the papers right? Is that old man Yates really fuckin' that actress woman?"

Walter knew they'd been seen around town together the past couple of days. About their personal business, he knew nothing and didn't care to comment. Besides, just the mentioning of River's name gave him something he hadn't felt in days. Hope. If any man could give him what he so desperately wanted, it would be River Yates.

* * * *

Carrie sat on the front porch sipping her second cup of coffee. Andre rested at her side. Both had been getting up much earlier than they were accustomed to. The Oklahoma sunrises proved just too wonderful to miss. River already toiled at his morning tasks, and Carrie missed him.

"May I pry?" Andre asked thoughtfully.

"Don't you always?" Carrie smiled.

"What's been bothering you the past couple of days?"

The question surprised Carrie. She hadn't thought it showed.

"Is it your new relationship?"

That was part of it. Four days passed since they first made love. It had been four days of tenderness and attention like she'd never known. Carrie didn't want it to end in seven more. She'd grown so close to River since their first night together. River showed her the town and its countryside, and rumors flourished of their relationship. They spent every night since the first in each other's arms. But it wasn't her concerns about the relationship she feared Andre detected.

"Clive is coming here Wednesday," she sighed.

"Oh...my...God," Andre gasped.

"Tell me about it," she smiled wearily.

"And you haven't told River," Andre assumed.

"No."

"When do you intend to?"

"I don't know."

"He knows about Clive?"

"Yes. I've told him that much."

"I would think the sooner you told him, the better. He needs time to prepare. I need time to prepare. I can't stand that prick!"

"I know," Carrie said under her breath.

"Why didn't you tell him not to come?"

"I tried. You know how he is. I've called twice since he told me, but he hasn't returned my calls. He's on location in Colorado. I didn't want to leave him a message. That doesn't seem right."

"So, what do you tell him when he gets here?"

Carrie had given it a lot of thought. Hours upon hours of thought. "That it's over."

"Although I find the man despicable, letting him come all the way down here to be dumped doesn't seem right either," Andre said before taking a sip of his coffee.

"I know that. What do you suggest I do?"

"I suggest you keep trying to reach him. Stop him from coming."

"He'll be home Tuesday before flying here Wednesday. I'll call him then."

"Good. That way you won't have to even mention it to River."

"Yes," Carrie nodded, "that would be nice."

* * * *

River twisted the last strand of barbed wire around the corner post and nailed it in place. He moved on, attaching the come-along in order to stretch the wire tightly to the next oak fence post. Carrie wanted to come with him, but he knew there would be no shade to protect her from the hot afternoon sun. It bothered him how much he missed being away from her. In just seven more days she would go back to her world and he would be stuck here in his. It would be like their time together never happened. A dream, both bitter and sweet.

River strained to tighten the wire when he heard the rumble of the approaching truck. He turned toward the sound, wiping at the sweat running from beneath his stained John Deere cap and into his eyes. He recognized the new Chevrolet immediately. It belonged to Walter Bates. River wondered why the older man seemed to have such difficulty climbing from the cab. A limp loomed obvious; Bates seemed to be in pain. It wasn't until he hobbled much closer that River noticed the puffed, bruised nose and busted lip.

"Howdy, Walter," River said with a slight wave of his hand and then added, "Damn, man, what train hit you?"

Maybe the old man didn't hear him, or maybe he just didn't want to talk about it. He offered his hand to River and River shook it. He'd always thought highly of Walter Bates. He acted nothing like most rich men River met over the years.

"Don't seem right, River," Bates said in greeting, "that a man should have to be repairing fence on a Sunday afternoon."

River thought it seemed less right that such a good man should go through what Bates suffered in recent days. But, he didn't want to bring that up. "You know how it is, Walter. Damned old cows don't care what day of the week it is when they decide to slip through a downed fence."

Bates just nodded his head thoughtfully before saying, "Your sis told me I could find you out here. Can I give you a hand?"

It proved the kind of man Walter Bates was – always willing to help. "No, thanks. I've about got this job whipped."

"I got to meet that Deshazo woman while I was up at your place. I've never been that close to a famous person," Bates said as he pulled the brim of his hat down to shade his eyes from the glaring sun.

The comment caused River to ponder the fact he now tended to overlook – the woman's stature. Although she could never in a hundred years be commonplace, he'd become comfortable in her presence, and grew quickly to consider her, simply, a wonderful and caring human being.

Bates brought an arthritic hand up to gently rub at the bruises on his face. "I, uh, told your sister and Miss Deshazo what I told everyone else I've run into today. I told them I took a nasty fall. People seem to have no trouble believing that I'm old enough to do that." Bates smiled, but it looked to be forced.

"But that ain't what happened, River. Billy Shiloh did this to me."

River wasn't sure he'd heard right. So, he repeated it. "Billy Shiloh did that to you? When, Walter? How?"

"Last night. In my grocery store. I'd gone down there to do a little work. I ain't sleeping so good nowadays. Anyway, I found him in my store. I tried to take care of him. Give him what he had coming. Kind of a stupid thing for an old man to attempt, don't you think, River?"

The thought of Billy Shiloh laying a hand to Walter Bates stirred an anger in River that he knew best not to let take seed. "I'd heard he's in Mexico," he responded, fighting to keep the anger at bay.

Bates turned to look at the not so distant San Bois Mountains. "He's not in Mexico, River. He's up there."

River followed the other man's gaze while slowly cracking the knuckles of both his hands. He would not dwell on the thoughts beckoning for action.

"He's suffering from delusions of grandeur, River. Sees himself as some notorious outlaw like the ones that hid up in those mountains over a century ago. He wants someone to try to come up there and find him, take him on...I want the same thing, River."

River turned away from the mountains. It grew too obvious why Walter Bates paid this visit. "Walter, you need to be telling Chief Simms this." River just knew he hadn't done that.

"I don't want the police in on this, River. They'll try to bring him in alive. I don't want that. Do you know what all he did to my little Cindy, River?"

"I don't want to know, Walter," River stammered.

"She gagged to death. Couldn't move because her back was broken and her hands were tied. After she was already dead that bastard..."

"Walter," River interrupted with both palms in the air, "I ain't going after him. I, uh, can't go after him."

"You're the only man that can, River. You've tracked men in those mountains before. You know those rocks and crevices like you know the back of your hand. You're the only one that's..."

"I ain't going to do it, Walter."

"…that's man enough to go up there and face him and kill him."

"I won't do that."

"River, you know I've never been one to get in a man's business, but I know about the money you owe on this ranch. If you go up in those mountains and find him and kill him, I'll pay you the twenty thousand you need to get out of debt."

The air seemed to grow hotter and heavier and terribly difficult to breathe. It angered River that Bates would dangle such a cruel carrot in front of his face. Without the twenty thousand, River would most assuredly lose the place his grandfather and father and Sky and Thelma, as well as he, toiled to build. Where would Thelma go? And how would he go on if such a large part of who he was and what he was became lost forever?

"River, I know you ain't afraid of Billy Shiloh. What is it that's happened to you?"

River looked up and into the tortured eyes that welled with tears and he quickly turned away.

"Walter, have you ever killed a man?"

"No, River. I haven't."

"Well, believe me…You don't ever want to."

* * * *

Thelma didn't like it. It just wasn't right.

"I get paid to do this. Actually, you are paying me to do this," she insisted.

Just like she had done after the past two days' meals, and over the same conversation, Carrie Deshazo just laughed, and shrugged her off.

"I would object to any guest doing this. Especially you," Thelma insisted.

"Why especially me?"

"Because of who you are, silly...Oh, my! See what this type of behavior breeds? Now I'm calling Carrie Deshazo silly," Thelma blushed.

"I can be just as silly as the next woman," Carrie giggled.

"Do you do this at home?"

"Of course not. I have a maid," Carrie responded with overly exaggerated arrogance.

"Exactly. And if you don't do the dishes and clean up the kitchen at home, you most definitely shouldn't be doing it here."

"I don't cherish the company of my maid. If I did, I'd help her as well."

Duly charmed and knowing she simply wasted her breath, Thelma gave in once again to the absurdity.

Carrie placed a stack of soiled dinner dishes on the counter and then paused to pull back the curtain on a window overlooking the front porch.

"The way those two interact," Carrie said with an amused shake of her head, "truly astounds me."

Thelma took a second to glance out the window. "Or how, you should say, they don't interact."

River and Andre sat side by side on the front porch as they had several evenings during the past week. An occasional word might be passed, but mostly they just sat silently staring across the pasture while sipping the Scotch Andre kindly shared with River.

"True," Carrie said before turning back to the work, "they don't say much. I guess what astounds me is that they don't feel like they need to say much."

"Men are strange animals," Thelma agreed.

"River has been awfully quiet since he came back from fixing that fence," Carrie mused, "even quieter than usual. Do you think seeing Mr. Bates upset him? He seems upset to me. Maybe it has something to do with that poor girl's terrible death."

"Well, as I'm sure you're well aware of by now, River is a deep thinker, and much more sensitive than most would realize. I'm sure being around Walter Bates would upset him."

Thelma agreed he did seem disturbed. She'd already drawn her conclusions on what disturbed him. She didn't think, overall, that Walter or Cindy Bates weighed on his mind too heavily.

"This afternoon aside," Thelma started in an attempt to gently broach what she thought to be the problem, "I haven't seen River acting like he has the past couple of days for the longest time. He is so much enjoying the time spent with you, Carrie. It's good to see him smile and hear him laugh. You know, he's smitten with you."

"Yes, as I am with him."

The words were so obviously heart-spoken that Thelma considered stopping and not saying another word, but a deep concern wouldn't let her. "Do you think it possible, Carrie," she asked delicately, "that what could be upsetting River tonight is the thought of your impending departure?"

The lovely woman's posture as well as her expression noticeably drooped. "I suppose so."

"I don't mean to interfere," Thelma said apologetically, "it's just that I'm concerned what your leaving will do to him."

"I am too, Thelma. And I'm almost equally concerned about what it will do to me."

"Oh, you dear thing," Thelma said, taking Carrie's hands into her own, "You know, on a brighter side, long-distance relationships are fairly common in this day of modern travel."

"I guess so. I'm just not sure either of us are long distance type of people. Thelma, I have to ask. Please answer honestly. Do you consider me careless for letting it come to this?"

Thelma's answer came quick and absolute, "No. Not at all. He is smiling. He is laughing. It is better for him to have known this joy for just a matter of days...if that is what it comes to...than to have not known it at all. And, I think more importantly, I've not heard him cry out once since you two have been sleeping together."

Carrie blushed a second time, this time to a deep, dark red. "Oh, you know."

"His bedroom is next to mine," Thelma giggled. "Of course, I know...silly. My God, you two do carry on like a couple of teenagers!"

Thelma feared Carrie might turn completely purple.

* * * *

River returned to the fence he'd repaired the day before, and it had been torn down again. What in the hell, or maybe who in the hell did it?

"Peek-a-boo...I-see-you!"

The words came from over his shoulder in an icy whisper.

First River thought to spin around, but then wanted to run, but he did neither.

"I got'cha old man!"

The voice rang colder and deader than anything that ever called to him from the barn in his nightmares.

"What do you want, Shiloh?" He'd wanted his words to sound as steely as the ones coming from behind him. They didn't.

"I want you, Yates. You wouldn't come after me. So, I've come for you."

"I didn't want to kill you." River's words, for some reason, sounded hollow.

"Is that what it is, old man? You didn't want to kill me? Oh, I don't think so. I think we both know why you don't want to come after me. Don't we?"

River heard the hammer cock behind him, and he wished, more than he'd ever wished anything, to have a gun. With a gun in hand this very second, he would turn and fire and fire and fire again because...

It didn't happen like it was supposed to. He heard the shot and then he started forward, his knees buckling. He should have fallen first, and then if able, he should have heard the shot. Maybe Shiloh missed. Maybe stark fear projected him forward. For a brief moment there seemed hope, but then he looked down.

The bullet had exited through the front of his shirt.

Billy Shiloh laughed.

River reached down to hold his intestines in his hands.

And he began to scream.

* * * *

"River! River!" Carrie spoke gently while holding him and rocking him and trying to awaken him.

River came to with a start and bolted upright.

"He was right, oh, dear God, he was right," he gasped.

"You had a dream, River. Just a dream," Carrie said, taking him back in her arms.

"No! It was more! He was right. What's keeping me from going after him ain't because I don't want to kill him."

"Who, River? Who were you dreaming about?"

"Bates offered a bounty on him But I said no. Didn't want to kill again. But, but, that's not what I'm afraid of."

"Mr. Bates offered you money to go after Billy Shiloh?"

"Yes. Yes," River nodded. "I didn't think I could kill him, but now I know I could. He's done so much evil. But, I can't because I'm afraid, Carrie, I'm afraid!"

"Of what, River?"

"I didn't think I was. Never thought I would be again, because I just really didn't care, but, now.. now there's you and I don't want...I'm afraid...to die, Carrie."

"Oh, River, River," she said as she tightened her arms around him even more and started kissing his face, "you are not going to die."

"Now, I *am* a coward," he said flatly.

"No, River. Not wanting to die doesn't make you a coward. It makes you normal."

"I'm not going after him because I'm afraid he'll kill me. That makes me a coward."

"But you also don't want to go after him because you really don't want to kill again. That's still part of it, isn't River?"

"Yes, but, mainly I don't..."

"It doesn't matter. And if you're just afraid of dying because of what I mean to you, well, I can't think of a grander compliment. You're anything but a coward, River Yates."

* * * *

River let Carrie talk him into going down to the kitchen for coffee. Thelma already had coffee brewing.

"I heard the commotion," she said sheepishly. "I thought we all might could use a cup."

River didn't feel like talking. He'd said enough already. But Carrie told Thelma that Bates offered River a reward for Billy Shiloh, and the two women started assaulting him with questions. River told them what really happened to Walter Bates' face. He told them Shiloh was hiding in the mountains.

"You are not going after him, River," Thelma said sternly.

"I don't intend to," he mumbled, not about to say another word on why.

"If Walter Bates is too foolish to call the police, then we'll call them ourselves," Thelma declared.

Carrie seconded the motion.

"If the police go up there, Shiloh will kill some of them. Maybe a bunch of them," River offered.

"Well...well, that just comes with the job of being a police officer," Thelma said without conviction. "Better them than you."

"Thelma," River exhaled and shook his head regrettably, because she did have a right to know, "Bates offered me twenty thousand for Shiloh. Dead of course. That money would pay off our note. We wouldn't have to worry about it anymore."

"You don't have to worry about that anymore anyway," Carrie inserted.

Thelma arched her eyebrows, pursed her lips and turned quickly toward the coffeepot.

"Carrie, what are you talking about? Thelma, what's going on?"

"It's not a handout," Carrie blurted.

"And it's not a loan," Thelma jumped in.

"It's an investment. For me," Carrie quickly added.

"One of you tell me what's going on, because I don't think I'm going to like it."

Thelma moved shoulder to shoulder with Carrie. They looked a little surer of themselves that way.

"You don't have to like it, River. It's a done deal. We discussed it earlier tonight and we've shaken on it and we're having the papers drawn up tomorrow."

Carrie reached out and took River by the hand. "I love this place, River. Really and truly love it. I simply cannot imagine it being in the hands of someone else. I'm purchasing ten percent of the bed and breakfast business for an initial investment of twenty thousand dollars. Now, if that makes you angry, then you'll just have to be angry. And if I have to come here often to check on my investment, well, you can just ignore me. Play like I'm not here."

River thought of a lot of things to say and not to say. Finally, the right words came to mind. "How often might you be coming to check on your investment?"

"Very often."

"Well," he forced himself to grumble, "sounds like you ladies have made a deal. Don't guess I have any right to try and interfere."

Chapter Eleven

River left half an hour earlier to feed his steer. When Carrie grew tired of waiting, she walked down to the shed looking for him. She found him leaning against the corral staring at the mountains on the horizon. He'd been in a quiet, brooding mood all day. She didn't have to ask what held his thoughts. When she walked up beside him, he nodded and made an attempt to smile, but didn't say anything.

"You can't get him out of your mind, can you?" she asked, placing her arm around his waist.

He looked back to the mountains and waited a few seconds before responding. "He's not going to just sit up there and hide out. He's a predator. He'll need to attack someone sooner or later."

"You still think we shouldn't notify the police?"

"I don't know."

"You're still contemplating going after him, aren't you?" she asked apprehensively.

River took a deep breath. "You ever been terribly torn up inside with conflicting thoughts?"

"Sure. But never with anything of this magnitude."

"He won't be taken alive. And I don't want to kill him. And I don't want him to kill me. And I don't want to stand by and do nothing and let him kill someone else. Not a single option sits right with me."

"Why would you even think it's your place to do anything?"

"Because of something Bates said. He thinks I'm the only man who can take Shiloh."

"Is that what you think?"

He turned back to stare down at her. The look in his eyes stabbed at her heart. Haunting seemed the best description she could give.

"I don't know."

Carrie didn't like the conversation, and didn't even know why she'd brought it up. She never liked things she couldn't understand, like the things that motivated men to do what they did. And what they didn't. She wanted to change the topic. She wanted his mind off of it. Now.

"Do you know why I came to Oklahoma?"

"I can't imagine," he sighed.

"Well, mostly for the rest. Just to get away for a while, but I did so on the insistence of my agent. He wants me to portray Belle Starr in a movie he's all hot about."

River turned his back to the mountains and leaned back on the rail fence. Her diversion appeared to work.

"Hell, you could never play the part of Belle Starr," he stated as fact.

"And why is that?" she asked playfully.

"I've seen pictures of her. She was a damned ugly woman."

"Is that a compliment?" she laughed.

"Not for ol' Belle, it ain't," he answered with a smirk.

"Well, I didn't want to do the movie at first. And, I don't really want to now, but just being here, seeing the country, I've kind of, as you would say, kicked the idea around a little. And do you know what I've been thinking?"

"A man sure wastes a lot of time if he tries to figure out what a woman's thinking," he said with a shake of his head.

Carrie nudged him in the ribs. "I'll tell you then. I've been thinking about what a fine character you'd make in a western. Have you ever given any thought to acting?"

The look he gave her painted total discomfort. "Hell no. I couldn't act my way out of a paper bag."

"Oh, but you have such a, well, presence. The way you look, the way you carry yourself. I can just picture you as a lawman."

"I've been a lawman," he fidgeted, "and I wasn't any good at it."

"Did Belle Starr every carry on with any lawmen?" she teased.

"I hear Belle carried on with a lot of ol' boys. But I don't know about any lawman in particular."

Carrie loved his shy way of grinning about anything of a sexual nature. "Still, you ought to give it some thought. If you were to try for a part, I'd consider doing the movie."

"Guess you won't be doing the movie then."

"Most of it would be filmed right here. I'd be here at least a month or two," she said seductively.

River pulled her into his arms and kissed her long and passionately. When he finished, he whispered in her ear, "I'm not good at acting."

* * * *

When Walter Bates pulled into his drive, he realized he'd spent far too much time going over the books at his hardware store. He'd been foolish not leaving there hours ago to come home. He should have returned before sundown to prevent entering a dark house.

Why, he admonished himself, had he not thought of this possibility before now? Maybe he could blame advanced age. His mind wasn't near as sharp nowadays. Or, maybe, he didn't think to return home in daylight because he'd always tried to be a good man and never, until now, possessed an enemy. The simple truth being that a man such as himself couldn't naturally anticipate the actions of a demented mind. Not, that is, until coming face to face with something as obvious as a dark and foreboding house.

Walter did have a gun with him. But that did little to soothe the anxiety striking him like a punch to the gut. A gun in his hands would be of little use against the uncanny skills of Billy Shiloh.

Bates stepped out of his car on legs feeling hollow. He could not still the hand gripping the nine-millimeter. He thought about checking the perimeter of the house for signs of intrusion and then felt stupid for even considering it. Shiloh had keys. Tomorrow, if there turned out to be one, Walter would get the locks changed on everything he owned.

"Are you in here?' Bates hollered out as he cautiously stepped through the front door. Of course, there came no answer. "I have a gun!" he shouted, feeling pathetic and impotent.

Walter searched his house room by room. Upstairs and down. Nothing looked out of place or disturbed. The old man did not sense any presence other than his own. Eventually his nerves calmed and it became easier to breathe.

As he got ready for bed, Walter promised he would not go through this again. Tomorrow he would go back to River Yates, and he would double the price he'd offered on Shiloh's head. If that didn't work, he'd triple it.

Walter placed the gun on his nightstand and turned back the covers on his bed. He'd intentionally left lights on throughout the house. Upstairs and down. As he crawled beneath the sheets he considered the bible lying beside the nine-millimeter. Traditionally he read passages every night before turning in. He could not bring himself to pick it up this night because the thought of murder filled his heart. The rules he'd lived by for a long life suddenly seemed forsaken. He tried to force the thought out of his mind when the bedroom's closet door sprang open.

Walter grabbed for the gun.

"Don't even," the voice hissed from the shadows of the closet.

And he didn't. Billy Shiloh stepped from the closet with a sadistic grin. Walter felt his blood both chill and boil.

"I'm really pissed at you," Shiloh spat. The old Colts still rested in their holsters on Shiloh's hips. "I waited, and prepared, and waited some more, and the cops never came. You wasted my time, Walter. You didn't do what I told you to do."

"I'm not sending the cops after you. I don't want you brought back alive," Bates said through gritted teeth.

"Then tonight you'll die," Shiloh said without feeling.

Walter Bates did not want to die. Not now. Not with Shiloh still living. "I went to River Yates," he blurted. "I offered him money to kill you."

Shiloh tilted his head like a curious dog. A smile slowly crept across the hard face. "Well, now," he said thoughtfully, "that ain't a bad idea. What'd he say?"

"He said he wouldn't do it. But I plan on offering him more money. I'll give everything I own to see you dead."

* * * *

"That bastard's afraid of me. He won't come. Not for any amount of money," Billy thought out loud. Something, a fleeting thought, scurried across his mind. Later he would dwell on it.

"He says he doesn't want to kill again. But, every man has his price," Bates insisted. His voice quivered and his old body quaked.

The thought came again and this time it stuck. Every man did have his price. Billy suddenly knew what River's would be. It came to him in an instant what would bring Yates up to the mountains – to die. Killing River Yates, as Billy knew all along, would bring him the notoriety he so wanted.

"I ain't going to kill you tonight," he said to the cowering old man. "I ain't got the time. I got some planning to do. You go back to Yates, and you offer him whatever the hell you want. I don't care, but you give him a message from me. Tell him he has no choice. You tell him he can come after me, or I'll get him to come after me. And tell him he ain't going to like how I do that. He ain't going to like it a damned little bit."

* * * *

This morning Thelma only put up token resistance to Carrie helping in the kitchen. They were putting the final touches on the clean up when they heard a car pull up in the front drive. Thelma went to the nearest window.

"Oh, my," she exclaimed, "a limousine."

Carrie's heart suddenly raced. It was only Tuesday morning. Surely it couldn't be. She hurried to the window. What surely couldn't be certainly was. She beat a path to the front door. Thelma stayed at the window. Carrie made it out the door before hearing Thelma's shrill announcement.

"Good Lord! That's Clive Benz."

Carrie hadn't thought it necessary to warn Thelma of the possibility of an additional guest. Today she'd planned to call Clive and tell him not to come. Carrie hurried out to the car, to say what, she did not know.

Clive clearly mistook Carrie's rush to get to the sleek black Lincoln. He bounded to meet her.

"It's Tuesday, Clive! Not Wednesday!" she gasped.

"I knew you would be surprised!" he beamed as he quickly closed in on the few feet separating them.

"I don't want..." made it out of her mouth before Clive grabbed her up in his arms and swung her merrily about the front yard of the Robbers' Roost Bed and Breakfast.

* * * *

River hadn't picked flowers for a woman since – well, he wasn't sure he'd ever picked flowers for a woman. At his age and picking flowers for a woman for the first time. It wasn't something he'd want the boys at the Silver Dollar knowing about. He did, however, take consolation in the fact he didn't know the names of the flowers he'd picked. To him they were just purple ones and red ones and the tiny yellow ones that grew wild in the fields around the ranch. He'd taken his time gathering the ones he thought she would like the best.

River walked around the corner of the house when he glimpsed the rear end of the Lincoln and heard joyous male laughter. Two more steps gave him a clear view of Carrie being swirled around in the arms of another man. They didn't see him, and he didn't want them to. He quickly turned and started back in the opposite direction. River recognized the man from the movies. The flowers in his hands might as well been weeds, and maybe they were. River didn't know a hell of a lot about such things.

** * * **

"Put me down!" It was the third time Carrie said the words. This time she all but screamed them.

Clive Benz finally did as she said. The smile on his face spiraled down from joy to shock and finally bottomed out at embarrassment.

"What's wrong? You don't seem very excited to see me," he pouted. No action hero could pout as well as Clive Benz.

"I was going to call you today," Carrie shook her head. "I didn't want you to come."

"Why? What's going on, Carrie?"

"Oh, Clive, you didn't give me a chance on the phone. You just said you were coming, and..."

"Are you breaking it off, Carrie?"

The look on his face looked incredulous. It seemed to emphasize that no woman in her right mind would dump Clive Benz. The look motivated her to go on.

"Yes, Clive. It's over. Hell, it's been over for the longest time. You know that as well as I do."

"It's not as good as it was at first, but...*You're* breaking up with *me*?" He stomped his right foot once with each of his five last words.

"Would you feel better if I let you break up with me?" Carrie wasn't being snide. She simply knew Clive all too well.

"Well, no woman has ever tossed me out," he mumbled thoughtfully.

"I wouldn't mind the media thinking it was your idea," Carrie inserted.

Clive Benz shook his head vigorously as if to clear his mind. "Hey, that's not what's important here. What kind of man do you think I am?"

Carrie knew exactly what kind of man he was, but didn't get a chance to say so.

"What's important," he quickly added, "is that I love...wait a minute," he scowled, "are you dumping me for another man?"

"I'm afraid so," she winced.

"I'm going to whip his ass!" Clive announced a little too dramatically.

"I don't think so."

"And why not?"

"He'd tear you limb from limb."

"Really?" Clive asked timidly.

"Really."

"I know karate," he said with little enthusiasm.

"He'd maul you, Clive."

"Oh. Are you sure about this?"

"Yes. I'm pretty sure he'd tear you apart."

"No, not that!" Clive whined. "Are you sure you don't love me and we can't work this out?"

Carrie reached up and patted the much too pretty face. "Yes, Clive, I'm certain. I'm sorry."

"All right. I'll go along with this, but I'm not leaving. I'll spend the night. Give you some time to reconsider."

"I don't need time to reconsider. Besides, the man, his name is River, lives here, Clive. It would simply be too awkward. Please, Clive, just..."

"I'm staying."

Carrie could do no more than just shrug her shoulders, "Have it your way."

"I will."

* * * *

"Were these for me?"

River spun around at the sound of the voice behind him. Damn if the woman didn't move like an Indian. Carrie held the flowers he'd tossed aside. River had been standing behind his shop building, staring out across the pasture, thinking. He hoped the awful pain he felt didn't show on his face.

"How'd you know I was out here?" he asked, avoiding her question.

"Andre was watching from his window. He saw you toss these on the ground."

There were too many sets of eyeballs on the damned ranch nowadays, River thought as he pawed at the ground with his boot.

"They're beautiful," Carrie smiled shyly. "I'm guessing you picked them for me, but then saw Clive spinning me around in the front yard."

"I feel like a damned fool," River mumbled before turning to gaze again at the pasture.

"Why?"

It wasn't something he cared to talk about, but his options were limited. "Only a fool would let himself think and feel the way I do. I mean, hell, I really believed that..." he paused and shook his head, "...well, that I really had a chance of having a woman like you."

"River, turn around and look at me," Carrie said emphatically.

Slowly, begrudgingly, he did so. The radiant smile surprised him.

"River, are you falling in love with me?"

He practically choked. It took him more than a few seconds to recover. Even then his voice did not want to cooperate. "I, uh, thought you didn't believe in love."

"I never said that. If I remember correctly, I just agreed with you. I said I wasn't sure I know what love is."

"Oh, yeah, right," he stammered.

"But I think I do now."

It hit like a fist in his gut, but without the pain. Like a good fist to the gut, if such a thing existed. He felt like picking Carrie up and swinging her around, but that had already been done. So, instead, he simply pulled her into his arms.

"Me too."

* * * *

"My, my, but haven't things taken a complicated turn!" Andre squealed as River stepped up on the front porch.

"Where's he at?" River asked, barely above a whisper. He wasn't any too anxious to be bumping into Clive Benz. He'd seen the movies. The son of a bitch had muscles that had muscles.

"Probably up looking at himself in the mirror, but he's not what I'm talking about. Clive Benz is no complication. He's a twit," Andre said with a flip of his hand. "No, when I speak of complications, I'm speaking of the other," he giggled and rolled his eyes.

"Other what?"

"Love, sweet boy, love!" Andre sang out gleefully.

"Good God Almighty, does that woman tell you everything?"

"But of course. I'm her closest girlfriend!"

River had no verbal response. He just sighed and shook his head.

"So, now, where will this newfound love lead?" For the first time in the conversation, Andre took a serious tone.

River plopped into the chair next to Andre before admitting a great concern. "I have no idea."

"I wouldn't want her hurt."

The tone sounded fatherly – in a feminine sort of way.

"Me either. It's the last thing on this earth that I want."

Andre brought a shot glass up to his lips. Until now River hadn't paid enough attention to even see it in the man's hand. A quick glance revealed the bottle sitting between the two chairs.

"Starting a little early today, aren't you?"

"Clive Benz is here."

"Yeah," River said with a solemn nod of his head. "Care if I take a hit or two from the bottle?"

"Please, help yourself."

A hit or two spawned a hit or two more, and Andre kept pace. Neither man found anything else they needed to say. Andre seemed to settle into deep thought as River's head began to spin.

It wasn't because of the Scotch, but all the changes. It seemed as if someone grabbed his world out of its mundane orbit and started dribbling it like a basketball. In just a little over ten days' time River picked up a dangerous new enemy, fell in love with a big-time Hollywood star, and, to top it all off, grew unusually comfortable in keeping company with a homosexual who acted anything but subtle. Life, it seemed to River, should have been called something else. Something harder to pronounce and spelled with many more than just four letters.

* * * *

The front door squeaked open and someone stepped out of the house while River closely examined the fingertips of both his hands. Some of his fingers felt tingly. The others were numb. It took his eyes longer to focus than usual when River looked from his fingers to the figure standing a few feet away. Because of the height of the blurry figure he thought it either Carrie or Thelma. Andre set him straight.

"Clive Benz," the words came out of Andre's mouth as if they tasted really bad.

"Andre Norman," Benz replied icily.

River pushed to his feet and took a single step that put him within hand-shaking distance of Benz. It occurred to River that he now stood face to face with one of America's most famous bad-asses, whose woman he'd stolen, and River felt only mildly nervous. He contributed this to the Scotch. But, then again, it could have been because the man stood at least a foot shorter than River.

"Mr. Benz," River said with his shaking hand extended, "I'm River Yates."

River thought the man would insist he drop the mister stuff. He didn't. For a second or two, River wasn't real sure Benz intended to shake his hand. He just stood there and looked at River the way a cat might look if it accidentally stepped in dog shit. When he did take hold of River's hand, the actor's grip was brief and uncomfortably infirm. Not at all what River expected from a man who went hand to hand with a squad of VC in a war movie River watched a couple of years ago.

"You're much older than I expected," Benz said with nostrils flaring, like he smelled something foul.

River could ignore the jab at his age. Hell, he was old. But that thing Benz did with his nose kind of pissed River off.

"Yeah, and you look a lot bigger in the movies."

"Touché!" Andre exploded with a giggle.

"You stay out of this!" Benz blurted with the tone of a spoiled child.

"I should have prepared you, River," Andre said, ignoring the warning. "Clive is very sensitive about his height, and well…"

"I'm warning you, Norman," Benz said through gritted teeth.

"…well, according to Carrie," Andre said with a devilish expression, "he's sensitive about size in general!"

Clive Benz turned a deep red and bellowed his response. "Faggot!"

"Pussy!" Andre squealed back.

It appeared to River that Benz might spring on the still-seated Andre. He quickly stepped between the two men.

"Mr. Benz, you're a guest here. I shouldn't have said that," River said sincerely.

Benz puffed up like a king cobra. He made apparent attempts to regain his composure. When he spoke, his voice came out calm, confident.

"River Yates, I intend to win her back."

River earnestly considered the declaration before nodding his head and responding, "You'd be a fool not to try."

* * * *

River didn't mind one damned bit having his lunch interrupted. The atmosphere around the table matched the consistency of peanut butter. He sat on one side of Carrie with Clive Benz seated on the other side. He knew for sure there must have been another time in his long life he'd been more uncomfortable. He just couldn't remember when. The knock at the door couldn't have come at a better time.

Thelma tried, but River wouldn't hear of her getting up and going to the door. He all but sprinted from the dining room.

River's relief at being away from the table subsided the moment he opened the door to find Walter Bates. He could tell by the look on the drawn face that Bates wasn't there with anything good to say. The men exchanged solemn greetings and River invited Bates in.

"No, why don't you come out here, River. You know, out of earshot," Bates practically whispered.

River pulled the door shut behind him and motioned for Walter to have a seat on one of the porch chairs.

"No, thanks. I'd feel better saying what I got to say on my feet," Bates said, averting his eyes from River's. "I'd planned all along to come out here and double the price I offered for Shiloh. And if you didn't take that, I planned on tripling it."

Sixty thousand dollars. The sum staggered River. The logic baffled him. "Now, Walter, you're the businessman, but that damn sure doesn't seem to me the way to drive a bargain. You know, just jumping right up forty thousand to your bottom dollar."

"I said that's what I planned on doing, but that was before, well, I'll get to that. But, now, I'm not here to talk you into it. I'm here to apologize, and give you a warning."

Walter Bates wore a tortured look. He clearly felt awfully bad about something.

"What's going on, Walter?"

"I could have lived, I think, with paying you what you agreed would be a fair price for risking your life. That is, of course, if you got him instead of him getting you. I don't think I could have lived with sending you to your death. But I might have already done that anyway."

Bates told how Billy Shiloh paid him another surprise visit. "I was crazy with hate, River. But I was scared, too. Just a foolish old frightened man. I told him I had offered you money. And it pleased him. It sparked some evil thought in his head. I could see it in his eyes.

"He told me you don't have a choice, River. He said for me to tell you that you either come for him on your own, or he'll get you to come after him. He's planning something awful, River. I don't know what. But I do know he's out to kill you."

River suddenly felt trapped – and angry. A little at himself. A little at Bates. And a whole lot at Billy Shiloh.

"I feel terrible about this and I apologize for sticking you in the middle of it. I've been thinking, River, that maybe you should just, well, leave. Get out of here."

"Run?" River asked under his breath.

"If that's what you want to call it, I wouldn't fault you for it."

"Don't sound like he's going to let me do that, Walter."

"If it's any consolation, River, my offer of sixty thousand still stands."

It wasn't.

* * * *

At the sound of the man's voice at the front door, Thelma announced, "Walter Bates."

Carrie's heart began to race. Up to this point Thelma acted giddily enamored with her newest guest, and Carrie couldn't blame her. After all, Thelma knew only the movie version of Clive. But with Bates' arrival the ever-diligent host turned her attention to her plate and picked aimlessly at her food. Andre, at Thelma's mentioning of

Bates' name, even ceased with the snide comments he'd directed at Clive. River had been gone for several minutes, and little was being said over the splendid lunch of leftover lasagna and a salad with romaine lettuce fresh from Thelma's garden.

Carrie's pulse quickened even more when she heard the front door finally being opened and then closed. River walked through the dining room without saying a word. He did not appear to be in a hurry, but his pace seemed deliberate. Carrie heard a door opening in the kitchen.

"That's the door to the basement," Thelma exclaimed anxiously.

Carrie knew the significance of the statement. She remembered River's words. "His guns are down there," she moaned.

"Guns?" Clive asked. "What's going on here?"

No one bothered to answer him. No one said another word. Carrie guessed Thelma and Andre waited anxiously as she did to hear the door in the kitchen open and close again.

A few minutes later it did, and River stepped into the dining room wearing two large holstered handguns. He'd tucked one in a western-styled holster and gun belt strapped around his waist. The other dangled menacingly beneath his left armpit in a shoulder holster. In each hand he held a rifle. The one in his right hand bore a scope.

"Looks like Billy Shiloh is coming for me," he said in a voice so void of emotion that it made Carrie shiver. "I fear we could all be in danger."

"Who is Billy Shiloh?" Clive piped and quickly followed up with, "Someone tell me what's going on here."

Andre provided an answer. "My dear cinema hero, you may soon learn what real action is all about."

Chapter Twelve

It was so dark he didn't know for a split second if his eyes were open or shut. He didn't know immediately if he awoke or still slept, and thereby just dreamed he heard the noise. The cloudy haze of sleep suddenly vanished and Walter Bates knew his eyes were open and staring into the darkness to see only familiar shapes and the usual faint shadows. He needed to breathe deeply, but didn't dare, because this time he knew he did not dream the noise he just heard for a second time. The floorboards creaked at the foot of his bed.

Reasoning blamed the noise on imagination. It couldn't be anything else – or *anyone* else. He'd changed every single lock out earlier in the day. He'd checked everything before going to bed. Every room. Every closet. Everything. It couldn't be him. Then the floor creaked again, and Walter stared hard into the darkness. At the foot of his bed, he could just make out the shadowy outline of a man.

"How?" Walter moaned. "How did you get in?"

No response came for the longest time. During that period nothing sounded but the thumping of an old man's heart. The figure simply stood like a ghost at the foot of Walter's bed. For just the merest of moments, Walter Bates let himself think that it might be Cindy coming back to be with him, to watch over him, to never...

"What does it matter how I got in?" The words coming from the darkness sounded dead cold.

"But I had the locks changed."

"I know you did. Had the ignition on your truck rekeyed, too. That was a mistake, Walter. You should have waited just one more day. You see, I was going to borrow your truck tonight, and your stock trailer. I'd had them back by morning, and you'd never even known I'd had them. But you had to go and change the locks, and that went and changed everything. Get up, Walter. Get dressed."

In their last two encounters, Shiloh used a condescending, taunting, and cruel tone of voice. Tonight, it was chillingly mean.

"I did what you told me to do. I told River what you said." Bates wanted to change the tone of Shiloh's voice. Soften it.

Shiloh turned on the overhead and the room exploded with light. "I ain't got much time, and I got no patience tonight. Get your ass dressed," he hissed.

Walter rolled over to crawl from bed and his eyes fell on the nine-millimeter resting on the nightstand. The thought racing through his mind could not have been more ludicrous. Shiloh wore the old Colts he'd stolen from Walter – his grandfather's guns, and Walter knew he had as much a chance of grabbing his gun and shooting Shiloh as he did whipping the man with his bare hands. Walter stopped his mind from dwelling on resistance and thought instead about survival. He dressed as quickly as could in the same clothes he'd taken off just a little over an hour earlier. It was only eleven now, but seemed much later.

"Okay, where are the keys to your pickup?" Shiloh asked, once Walter finished dressing.

"Downstairs."

"Let's go get them."

Walter started toward the bedroom door when Shiloh placed a palm in the middle of his chest.

"Turn around and make that bed up before we go downstairs."

"What? Why?"

"You always make your bed up when you get out of it, don't you?"

"Yes. But this isn't like I'm leaving for the day. I plan on coming back to it whenever you get finished with me."

"Make the fucking bed, old man."

* * * *

Carrie and River simply held each other tightly upon first getting into bed. They held to give comfort as well as to take. Their initial kiss served only to soothe. With the kiss came the need to escape as well as the route to take. What started gently and tenderly turned tumultuous and escalated in mere heartbeats from love making to something so much more carnal. Almost savage. What began as a breeze ended like a tornado. It left in its path tangled hair, moist sheets, and a realization for River that everything might have stepped aside for the past few minutes, but none of it went away.

Carrie started on top. River ended there. Worried that he might be too heavy, he shifted most the weight of his upper body to his elbows without breaking contact. Her breasts still heaved against his chest as he remained inside her.

"I love you," he whispered in her ear.

"I love you, too," she returned.

"But you have to go. All of you have to go. You have got to get out of here as soon as possible."

Carrie kissed him and then said, "We've already been over this, River. I'm staying."

And so were the rest of them. They refused to listen to him. Even that haughty actor, saying he would stay just to make sure Carrie would be safe. So far River found nothing about the guy that he could like. River and Carrie had been anything but quiet during their lovemaking. River found satisfaction in thinking Benz might have heard them.

"I can't even go looking for Shiloh with all you staying here. I couldn't leave you here alone. If you don't go, we'll all just have to stay here. We'll be like sitting ducks."

"I don't want you to go looking for him, River. Besides, where would you begin to look?"

River rolled off of her but pulled her close into his side. "I don't really know. But looking would be better than just sitting. If I had a known starting point, I could track him."

Carrie turned to look him in the eyes. "You are a real mountain man, aren't you? I mean being able to track a man and all. That impresses me."

"Oh, I ain't all that good at it, but I've tracked a few up in those hills. My grandfather taught me. He was good."

"Why don't we all just leave?" she whispered.

Carrie and Thelma offered that solution earlier. Then and now, the option did not appeal to River. Out and out running just wasn't something he wanted to do. But, too, he didn't want to be responsible for the lives – and maybe the deaths of four others.

With nothing left to say, River exhaled long and hard. Just minutes earlier he'd been virile, impressing even himself with his stamina. He'd performed like the man he used to be. The man that wouldn't have given a second thought about protecting someone from the likes of Billy Shiloh.

Now, he didn't feel so virile. Tomorrow he would take the four people staying in the house his grandfather built, and leave the Working Y Ranch. It would be an act of impotency.

* * * *

Walter Bates stared out the passenger window into a night as hopelessly dark as his mood. He didn't know where they were going. He hadn't asked. Bates didn't want Shiloh to talk. The sound of the bastard's voice sickened him. Looking at Shiloh enraged him. When he looked out the window, all Bates felt was fear. A fear so intense that it nearly suffocated, but still, suffocating felt better than feeling a rage he fell powerless to enact.

Shiloh sat behind the wheel humming. Being in the truck with the horse trailer in tow seemed to lighten his disposition. The last time Bates forced himself to look at the murderer the glow of the dash lights illuminated a smug look. The old man was curious as to what the younger one was up to, but didn't dare ask. Not only did Bates not want to hear the voice, he didn't want to give the asshole satisfaction of telling Bates it wasn't any of his fucking business.

Shiloh kept to the back roads while heading north into the foothills of the San Bois Mountains. The woods on both sides of the dirt road grew thick and tangled. Once they had hitched up the stock trailer and taken off, Bates expected Shiloh to head toward River Yates' ranch, but he hadn't. He drove in the opposite direction.

Suddenly, Shiloh hit the brakes. Bates' truck came to a stop on a short concrete bridge that spanned a narrow but deep ravine. Shiloh's humming evolved into a whistle, a lively little tune that Bates did not recognize. Shiloh reached in front of Bates and grabbed a flashlight out of the glove box.

"Let's go for a walk, Walter," Shiloh grinned broadly.

Bates assumed since they hitched the horse trailer, they were going somewhere to pick up a horse, or maybe even two. But there would be no horses out here. This area consisted of thick forest with no pasture in sight. Shiloh stopped at a place both dense and remote.

"Where we walking to, Billy?"

"We goin' down under this bridge, Walter," Billy's grin broadened even more.

Hopefully Shiloh had something under the bridge he wanted to haul away – something he'd stolen and stashed there. That's why he'd gotten the horse trailer instead of one of the flatbed trailers. He surely intended to conceal something in the enclosed stock trailer. Walter wanted to believe this. He wanted to believe it with all of his heart. But he couldn't.

"You are going to kill me down under the bridge, aren't you, Billy?"

"Yeah," Billy chuckled, "your time has come, old friend. I would have went ahead and done it in the comfort of your own home, but I need at least one full day before anyone finds your body. No one should find you here for a week or two. Maybe longer."

Walter Bates began to tremble a little from fear, but mostly from hate and anger. "Since you plan to kill me, I'm not going to make it easy on you. I'm not going to walk down there. You'll just have to kill me here and then go through the work of carrying my body down there."

Billy Shiloh threw back his head and laughed. "Now I kind of figured you'd take that attitude, and me killing you up here is damned sure one of your options. But, now let me say," he smiled showing nearly ever tooth in his head, "dying down under this bridge can be a fast thing. Sudden, you know. But up here..."

The smile faded, and the look in Shiloh's eyes grew demonic, "...up here, dying is going to be a terrible thing for you, old man. Slow. Painful. A fuckin' nightmare."

Billy Shiloh already caused Walter Bates enough pain for three lifetimes. Walter didn't want any more. He'd always held a theory that being dead was no big deal, but the dying part could be a real bitch. Bates opened the door and stepped out. Neither man said another thing until they were underneath the bridge.

Shiloh directed the flashlight's beam to the underside of the bridge. The light reflecting off the concrete lit the confined area with a hazy glow. He held the flashlight in his right hand. He dropped his left one to rest on the butt of the Colt on his left hip.

"Tell me, Walter, are you afraid of dying?"

"At the point of death, a man only has to fear meeting his maker. I'm at peace with mine. Just get it over with, Billy."

Shiloh pulled the Colt from its holster and started twirling it around his index finger with the skill of a wild-west show cowboy.

"Well, now, that is good, Walter. I don't really want this to be hard on you." Billy spun the revolver smoothly into the holster and jerked it back out and started twirling it again in a quick, fluid motion. "And, you know, dying at the hands of this century's most famous outlaw will guarantee you a place in history."

"You really believe that don't you, Billy? I mean that part about you being a famous outlaw?" Bates did not want to prolong his torment, but he could not let this absurdity go unchallenged.

"Sure do, Mr. Bates. I am the Jesse James of the new millennium. I'll go down in history just like Jesse and his brother, and the Younger and Dalton boys. Yes sir, I guess you could say I'm Billy the Kid all over again." With that Shiloh holstered the Colt once again and started slowly popping the knuckles of his left hand with his thumb.

Bates started shaking his head slowly. "Those men are folk heroes. They became legends because the common people back then could relate to some of the reasons they were outlaws to begin with. And the people found some merit in their stealing and killing.

"But with you, boy," Bates said as he brought up an index finger to point at Shiloh's face, "the people will never relate. Your only claim to fame is women killing. No, you'll never be remembered as another Billy the Kid. You'll simply be Billy the fool."

Bates seen the left hand move so quickly it seemed a blur. There followed a sensation of his right foot being crushed by an incredible amount of weight. The flash and deafening roar seemed to come after that, as Bates crumbled. He hit the ground before fully realizing Shiloh practically blew his foot off.

"I ain't no fool," Shiloh said in a voice both low and mean. "You're the fool. Your daughter was a fool. You know what I made her do right before I broke her back?"

"You're scum, Shiloh," Bates moaned through gritted death. "God will have a special punishment for you."

The elbow on Bates' right arm just seemed to disintegrate into a mess of blood and mangled flesh. He initially felt no pain. Then there existed nothing but pain. Searing, nauseating, engulfing. Bates' vision began to blur.

"I made her suck my dick, old man," Shiloh snarled. "I made her swallow my load. Then I broke her fucking back."

Bates heard the words, and they stung, but he didn't concentrate on them. He tried to focus on the two wavering shapes moving up behind Shiloh. Help had come.

Yet, Shiloh didn't know it. He continued to say words meant to rip and tear, but they lost their effect on Bates. Suddenly, but faintly at first, there came other voices. Bates allowed himself a sigh of relief. The pain began to ebb.

Bates felt the barrel of the gun being pressed to the top of his head. He heard Shiloh laughing. Bates tried to laugh, too. The joke was on Shiloh. He didn't know they had come. With the arm that still worked, he reached for them.

"I missed you both so much," Bates gurgled.

First came darkness. Like being submerged in motor oil. Then, hand in hand, in the light, Walter Bates and his family left Billy Shiloh forever.

* * * *

Shiloh sunk into a foul mood. Having to go miles out of his way to dump the old man off under the bridge put him behind schedule. On top of that, the ancient bastard's head splattered. Billy now wore chunks of Bates in his hair and all over his clothes. If all that wasn't bad enough, Walter Bates did not die the way Shiloh wanted him to. He didn't show fear and he didn't beg for his life. The silly son of a bitch died with a smile on his face and mumbling something Shiloh had not understood, but it sounded happy. Killing just wasn't fun when the one you killed didn't seem to mind it.

Had he made it where he wanted to be when he wanted to be there, it would have been so much easier. Hell, he could have pulled right up to the corral, loaded up the horses and tack and been gone. A light now burned in the little house the Indian lived in, and the house sat just a hundred or so feet from the corral. Shiloh suddenly felt pressured to quietly retrieve the tack and horses and move them out to the road and the awaiting trailer. If the Indian heard him, Shiloh would kill him, and that would further fuck up his plans. He needed Hank Sioux alive. Him being alive worked as a key part of a plan Shiloh considered nothing if not brilliant.

Shiloh planned to break into the tack room in the barn, but it wasn't locked. First, he carried the two best looking saddles out to the truck. Next, he went back for bridles. He counted five horses to choose from. Shiloh picked the two appearing most capable of meeting his needs – a large, stout mare and a sleek gelding that looked in the darkness to be the color of honey. Both took easily to the halters and let themselves quietly be led to and loaded into the stock trailer.

With the animals and gear loaded, only one more task required completion under the cover of darkness. He had to get the horses in place, hobbled and hidden. When he went back to them tomorrow he would be in a hurry, but only needed to saddle them and haul ass.

Shiloh drove off from the Sioux place in a hell of a lot better mood than he'd arrived. He even threw back his head and laughed, thinking it funny that a man with a ranch as big as River Yates' would keep his horses at another man's place. When Yates realized what Shiloh had done with Yates' very own horses it would add insult to injury. It served the bastard right, Shiloh reasoned. A man ought to keep his fucking horses on his own fucking ranch.

When the horses were in place, Shiloh would only have to return the truck and trailer to Bates' house. He would lock the truck in the barn. A passerby would assume Bates wasn't at home. And they'd be right. While there, Shiloh thought, he might as well take a shower. He'd also get a charge or two of the old man's clean clothes. One thing proved sure, Walter Bates no longer needed them.

Chapter Thirteen

Hank Sioux stood in the back room when he heard the front door of the Silver Dollar open and then shut. He glanced at his watch. It was too early for any of the three regulars so he hurried to the front. New customers were few and far between, and Hank didn't want to make them wait. It wasn't good for business. When he came through the door behind the bar, he froze in place. Billy Shiloh sat at the bar.

"I heard you were in Mexico, Billy," Sioux said with a catch in his voice. He didn't know why Shiloh came to his bar, but it couldn't be for any good reason.

"What else you hearing, Hank?" Shiloh grinned.

Hank heard he'd gunned down some man in Texas, but he didn't think bringing it up was too good of an idea. "I don't get just a whole lot of customers coming and going, Billy. I don't hear much of anything."

"I had a gun fight down in Texas," Billy said proudly. "You ain't heard nothing about that?"

"Can't say that I have." Hank didn't want Shiloh catching him in a lie. No telling what his type might do.

Shiloh looked disappointed. Maybe even a little bit pissed off.

"Why do you call this place the Silver Dollar Bar? Hell, you ain't got no silver dollars in here," Shiloh said testily.

"I named it in honor of my daddy. He was killed in the Silver Dollar Bar in Oklahoma City," Hank said uneasily.

Shiloh stood up. Hank saw the two guns strapped around his waist, and took a deep breath and held it.

"You ever heard that saying, 'like father like son?'" Shiloh asked with a nasty snarl.

"I don't have no beef with you, Billy. I don't want no trouble," Hank exhaled.

Shiloh put his hands on the butts of the two big revolvers. "Does that mean you don't want to die in a bar of the same name that your old man died in?"

"That's exactly what it means," Hank nodded, his stomach twisting into a knot.

"Then I'd suggest you do exactly what I say. I ain't got no problem with shooting a fuckin' Indian dead right here and right now."

Hank Sioux didn't want to die right here or any other place anytime too soon.

* * * *

They discussed leaving all day long, but no decisions were reached about where to go or how long to stay there. River suggested that all from California simply go back to California, and that Thelma go stay with some relatives in Tulsa. No one bought into his suggestion. Thelma and Carrie seemed convinced that police protection was called for. River could not warm to the idea. They all still sat at the dining room table discussing and disagreeing when the phone started ringing. Thelma got up to answer it and brought back the cordless to River.

"It's Hank Sioux," she said nonchalantly.

"Yeah, Hank? What's going on," River sighed.

"Billy Shiloh is here, River. He's got me at gunpoint."

River stood up so fast that his chair toppled over backwards. "What the hell's he doing there?"

All eyes turned to River. Thelma gasped.

"He says he'll kill me, River, if you don't get down here right away. He's holding me hostage."

River wanted it to be a joke. He could tell by the sound of his old friend's voice that it wasn't. "Let me talk to him, Hank."

River heard Hank relay the order, and heard a mumbled response in the background.

"He says what he has to say to you he'll only say face to face. I don't think he's in any mood for chit-chat, River. I'm damned sorry but..."

River heard more words from the background. Angry ones. Then he heard Hank say, "Okay. Okay."

"River, he says you can come armed, but if the police show up, I'm a dead man. I hate it, River, but you best get down here."

Then the phone went dead. River laid the receiver on the table.

"What's going on, River?" Carrie asked.

"He's got Hank. He'll kill him if I don't get down there."

"You're not going!" she nearly screamed.

Thelma took Carrie in her arms. Thelma's eyes filled with tears. "He's going, sweetheart," the sister sobbed. "I know he's going."

"I don't have a choice," River said softly.

"You do have a choice," Carrie stormed, pulling away from Thelma. "What kind of ridiculous place and bullshit is this? My God, River, you can call the police!" Now she cried along with Thelma.

"He'll kill him for sure if I do. I'm going," River said as he started for the stairs to go up and get his guns.

"Then I'm going, too," Carrie said as she hurried after him.

River stopped, turned and embraced her. "No, you're not, Carrie. You stay here with Thelma." He'd said it with authority, and Carrie stiffened in his arms.

"Take her," he said to Andre.

"I insist on accompanying you," Andre responded.

"I wouldn't mind having you at my side, Andre, but I'd feel a lot better knowing you were here to take care of the women."

"What about me?" Clive Benz said indignantly.

"Yeah, he can take care of you, too," River said under his breath.

"No, I mean..."

River didn't stick around to hear what he meant. He hurried up the stairs and to his guns while Andre tried to move Carrie to a nearby couch.

* * * *

Hank Sioux lived through divorce, robbery, tax court and a good swindling or two. About everything that could be taken from a man had, at one time or another, been taken from him. But through it all, he'd always managed to hang on to his pride and dignity. Now, he'd let a man take even that from him without a single blow being thrown. Hank felt ashamed. He wanted his pride and dignity back.

"I didn't like doing that," he announced within seconds of Shiloh pushing the disconnect button on the bar phone. "River Yates is the best friend I've ever had, and I let myself be used as bait to get him into your trap."

"Yup," Shiloh chuckled, "that's pretty much the way I see it, too. And, you make pretty damned good bait, chief."

"I'm no chief...white trash!"

Shiloh's cocky grin turned to a grimace. "Get your ass from behind that bar and over on this side with me."

"Why?"

"'Cause I'm going to give you a fighting chance."

"So you planned all along to kill me before River gets here, so you can ambush him when he does."

"I don't need to ambush that old fuck. I'll be taking him on face to face. Now, do you want a fighting chance or not?"

"A fighting chance is better than no chance at all," Hank grumbled as he moved around the corner of the bar and stepped up to face Shiloh.

"Good," Shiloh nodded. "now you're about to hear my saying."

"Your what?"

"My saying."

"What's a saying?"

"It's the words I'll be known for down through history. The words I say to a man just before I gun him down."

"Son," Hank said with a sad shake of his head, "you're ate the fuck up!"

Shiloh pulled the revolver from the holster on his left hip, placed it on the bar and slid it toward Hank.

"Pick it up, asshole," he snarled.

"I've heard how fast you are. I guess the minute I touch it you'll put a bullet or two in me," Hank said as he eyed the fine old firearm.

"No. I said I'd give you a fighting chance. You pick that thing up and go ahead and point it at me."

Hank wondered what kind of bad dope the boy smoked, but he picked the gun up, and pointed it at Shiloh, but felt no sense of relief in doing so. It was a double action, and would have to be cocked. Hank felt certain, from what he'd heard of the boy's skills, that Shiloh could pull, cock, and shoot in the time it took Hank to simply pull back the hammer.

Billy Shiloh cleared his throat. "If you are going to point that gun at me, mister, then..."

"Just a second," Hank Sioux said as he showed the palm of his hand not holding a gun. "Is this the saying part?"

"Yeah, fuck dummy," Shiloh said with great agitation, "this is it. Now shut the fuck up and get ready to cock that thing and pull that trigger if you think you can."

Shiloh cleared his throat again. "If you are going to point that gun at me, mister, then you best be pulling the trigger. Because when I'm finished talking, I'm going to start shooting...I'm finished talking."

Hank Sioux thought Shiloh's right hand moved and thought about thumbing back the hammer, but by then, he was already shot.

* * * *

River parked his truck a block away from the Silver Dollar Bar. His palms were sweaty from the tense grip he'd maintained on the old truck's steering wheel. From where he sat he could see the front of the bar. There were no cars parked there. He adjusted his denim jacket to conceal his shoulder holster and then crawled out of the cab.

He made his way quickly but carefully to the back of the bar. There were no cars there either. Not even Hank's truck. That wasn't right. He quietly tried the back door. It was locked. He considered that a good sign. Shiloh expected him to come in the front door. He reached up to the overhang of the roof and found the key Hank used to let himself in his bar. River crept in the back door with gun in hand. He paused after stepping in to listen. He heard nothing. He waited and counted to thirty. Still he heard no sound whatsoever. The absence of noise bothered him. In a crouch, he worked his way to the door leading to the business side of the bar. The lights in the lounge were on, but nothing moved. Again, he waited and counted. He observed no movement, saw nothing at all. Standing erect with his gun arm extended, he stepped through the door. A quick glance revealed the Silver Dollar apparently empty. Then he heard the groan and saw the form lying on the floor next to the front door. He hurried around the bar.

"Hank? Oh, God, Hank, what'd he do to you?" River asked as he holstered his .45 and dropped to his knees beside his fallen friend.

"The son of a bitch shot me in the leg, River. Intentionally shot me in the fucking leg," Hank moaned.

The big Indian had lost blood. Lots of it. "Where's he at, Hank?"

"Outside. Waiting for you. He left me alive to tell his damned saying."

"His what?"

"His saying. That boy's as goofy as a goat with a hard-on," Hank gasped.

"He ain't outside," River said as he pulled off his jacket to wrap around Sioux's badly bleeding leg.

"He said he'd be out there waiting for you. Told me he'd kill me if I tried to come out. I crawled over here to the door to listen. When you pulled up, I was going to try to get out and warn you."

"How did you get here, Hank?"

"My truck."

"It ain't out there."

"He must have taken it, but where would he…"

"Oh, dear God," River bellowed, "The ranch! He's headed for the ranch!" River jumped up and bolted for the phone to find it pulled from the wall and flung to the floor.

"Shit! He broke the phone. I can't even call them, Hank."

Hank took a deep breath before moaning. "We're probably the only two fucking idiots in a ten-mile radius who don't own cell-phone."

"Never felt a need for one of the damned things," River groaned, "until now."

"Go, River. Get to 'em," Hank grunted through clenched teeth.

"I can't leave you here, Hank. You're bleeding badly. You got to have help."

"Stop on your way. Send help. Don't worry about me."

It did seem the only solution. River ran to the front door.

"River!" Hank cried before he made it outside, "the saying. He'll use it on you. I got to tell you the saying."

River stayed just long enough to hear it.

* * * *

The four of them could not stay idle in the house so they moved to the porch. Benz took a chair and did not move. Thelma and Andre rotated between sitting and pacing. Carrie couldn't sit. She couldn't stand still. She felt as if electric currents surged through her arms and legs. She wanted to cry. She wanted to scream. She wanted River back. She felt angry with him for going. She didn't understand. The whole, stinking mess seemed so absurd. This was America. Nearly new millennium. Not the old west. Had these people all lost their minds?

"We can't just stay here!" she said emphatically.

"And we can't do anything else," Andre responded.

"He's been gone over an hour," she all but sobbed.

"It takes nearly a half hour to get into town," Thelma reminded her.

Carrie glanced down at the older woman. Her eyes were swollen from crying. "But why hasn't he called?"

No one offered an answer.

Carrie walked to the end of the porch, and suddenly, from around the corner of the house, right in front of her, a man leading two horses stepped into view. She could have reached out and touched him.

"Well, howdy folks!"

Carrie didn't immediately recognize him, but then Thelma let out a shriek. Movement broke out behind her. Everyone scurried. Then Billy Shiloh suddenly produced a gun.

"Now, everyone just stay put," Shiloh said calmly, "and nobody will have to catch a bullet."

"Who the hell are you?" Benz shouted.

"This is the infamous shit Billy Shiloh," Andre hissed.

"Why hello, faggot!" Shiloh beamed.

"Where is River? What have you done to him?" Carrie screeched.

"Well now, pretty miss actor woman," Shiloh started while seeming to study her curiously, "I haven't seen him. But I hope he's back in town looking for me. I'm surprised you're still in these parts. I hadn't counted on you being here," he concluded thoughtfully.

Then he turned the same curious glance on Benz. "And you, you're someone famous too, aren't you?"

"I'm Clive Benz."

"Clive Benz," Shiloh mulled, "Clive Benz. I know that name."

"He was Crusher Jones in the asinine series of Back to Nam movies," Andre inserted dryly. "Movies on a level, I'm sure, Mr. Shiloh, that would match your cinematic sophistication."

Benz shot Andre an acidic look, and Carrie breathed a sigh of relief because Shiloh obviously didn't know he'd just been insulted.

"Hey! Okay! I know who you are. I've seen you on lots of stuff. Hell, you're a badass, aren't you?"

Benz cleared his throat and dropped his gaze to his feet. "I'm an actor," he said softly.

"No, no, no," Shiloh laughed, "I've seen you doing all that fancy karate fighting. I've seen all those big muscles. Damn, if I had time, we'd do a little sparring. You know, go at it. Get it on. See who's the toughest."

Carrie thought Benz looked relieved that Shiloh seemed to be on a schedule.

"All right, folks, tell you what. Why don't you all just move right down here in the yard so as I can keep a better eye on you." He emphasized the request with a wave of the huge gun. "Get on down here. I got business to conduct."

"Billy, what do you want with us?" Thelma asked nervously as she shuffled off the porch with the rest of them.

"Mrs. Mayhue, I'm awfully glad you asked that. For you, in particular, I got good news and I got bad news. The bad news is, I came here to take you away with me."

Thelma gasped and brought a hand up to her throat. Carrie thought Thelma looked faint. She hurried to Thelma's side and put an arm around her waist.

"Now hold it," Billy chuckled, "don't go getting all upset, because the good news is I've decided I ain't going to take you."

Carrie felt Thelma relax, but only a tad.

"You see," Shiloh continued, "I could have stuck around and taken River right there in town, but..."

"Why River?" Carrie interrupted. "Why are you after him? He's done nothing to you."

"That's a fair question, good lookin'," Shiloh nodded. "You not being from around here and all, you wouldn't know just how famous that old man is. Ever since I was a little boy, I heard all these stories about River Yates. How tough he was. How strong he was. How good with a gun. I heard all kind of stories about him whipping this old boy and shooting some other old boy. I even watched him beat an uncle of mine like a drum, and for no good reason. Yeah, he's a hell of a hero around these parts."

Billy Shiloh paused a second and made a face as if trying to concentrate. "The best way I can explain it is...do you know any history?"

Carrie stared at him, coldly. "I know some."

"We'll you've heard of Jesse James, right?"

Carrie didn't want to answer, but Shiloh waited.

"Yes. Yes, of course I have. Everyone has heard of Jesse James."

"Okay. Well ol' Jesse always had men seeking him out, wanting to gun him down. You know why?"

"I don't care."

"Yes, you do," Shiloh said with a taunting laugh. "It was because he was so famous. You see, the man who could take on Jesse, and kill him, would be just as famous as Jesse himself. Maybe even more famous. Get the picture, miss hot shit Hollywood woman?"

"You think killing River will make you famous?" Carrie asked incredulously.

"I know it will," Shiloh nodded emphatically. "It will make me more famous than you or even that muscled up karate man back behind you."

"You're an animal. A ridiculous, pathetic little..."

"Shut up, bitch!" Shiloh thundered while taking a quick step that put him dangerously close to Carrie.

At the same instance Andre sprang in front of her and Thelma. Shiloh thrust the barrel of his gun into Andre's chest. Both women screamed.

"Is this how you want to die, you old queer?" Shiloh said through gritted teeth.

"I won't let you harm these women," Andre replied without a hint of fear.

"Taking a bullet would be quicker than AIDS," Shiloh taunted.

"Just leave these women alone," Andre shot back.

Shiloh took a step back and studied Andre for the longest moment. "You got guts. I respect that. But get in my way again, and I'll hurt you. Badly. Now, where was I? Oh, yeah, anyway, I could have shot ol' has-been River right there in town, but that just don't make for a good story.

"No, I want him to come up in those mountains after me. Just like the lawmen used to go up there looking for outlaws a hundred years ago. But, there's a problem. River ain't going to come up there for me all on his own. He needs some motivation. That's why, Mrs. Mayhue, I was going to take you. But damn, wouldn't it make me just more famous if I was to..." Shiloh pointed a finger at Carrie, "...take you!"

The contents of Carrie's stomach suddenly wanted out. Andre moved for Shiloh again. This time the gun crashed down on the top of his head, and Andre tumbled to the ground and did not move. Before Carrie could even scream, Shiloh grabbed her by the hair and jammed the gun beneath her chin.

"You seem to think a lot of that pervert," Shiloh whispered into her ear.

She could smell his breath. It smelled foul.

"So, from this point on, if you don't do exactly like I say, I'll start shooting little pieces off his body. Do you understand?"

Carrie could only nod her head. Terror seized her tongue.

"Good. Now crawl up on that horse. The dark one. The buckskin is mine."

"You can't take her!"

They were the first words Clive Benz said since confessing to be no more than an actor.

"Are you going to stop me, Mr. badass movie man?" Shiloh growled.

When Benz didn't respond, Shiloh put the pistol in a holster on his right hip. For the first time Carrie realized he had another one just like it on the opposite side.

"I've put my gun away. You going to stop me now?"

Benz still said nothing and made no attempt to move a muscle.

"I'll be damned. You're just a goddamned coward, aren't you?" Shiloh laughed.

When Benz didn't answer, Shiloh screamed, "Aren't you a fuckin' coward?"

Benz slowly started nodding his head. "Yes. Yes, I'm very frightened."

Billy Shiloh walked up to within inches of Benz. And spit on him. The saliva clung to the handsome face, and Benz just let it stay there.

Shiloh turned and started for the big buckskin. "Get on that fuckin' horse," he bellowed at Carrie.

With Andre lying at her feet and having witnessed the cruel degradation of a man she once loved, Carrie felt almost as much anger as she did fear. Her anger gave her the ability to speak.

"I've never ridden a horse."

"You're not going to ride this one. You're just going to put your fine ass in that saddle and hang on to the saddle horn. I'll have the reins and will be pulling you along behind me."

Carrie wanted to cry. Once again, she wanted to scream, but she feared what the man would do to Andre and Thelma and Clive. Also, she didn't want to give Shiloh the satisfaction of hearing her cry or scream. She pulled herself up onto the big horse before Thelma spoke.

"Those are River's horses and his saddles, too. He won that one in a rodeo in South Dakota."

Carrie looked to see Thelma pointing at the saddle on the other horse.

"You're right," Shiloh grinned as he swung up on the butterscotch colored horse. "And you tell him if he wants them back, he'd better hurry his ass up and come and try to take them back. And you tell him this, Thelma Mayhue, tell him I better not see any cops. If I see cops, his woman dies."

"Thelma," Carrie cried, "you tell River not to come. You tell him to send the police."

Shiloh held the reins to her horse now and they were turning away. Carrie rotated in the saddle. "Thelma, tell him I said he doesn't need anyone else calling to him from the barn."

Thelma gave her a questioning look.

"Tell him that, Thelma. Just tell him no more voices. Let the police do this!"

Then her horse started trotting, and Carrie turned her attention to simply hanging on.

* * * *

River slammed on the brakes and the old truck slid to a stop just feet from the front porch. He jumped from the cab and ran around the front of the ancient Chevy. Thelma and Benz ran to meet him. Andre sat slumped in a chair on the porch. River didn't see Carrie and his guts clenched.

"Carrie!" he bellowed. "Thelma, where's Carrie?"

"He took her, River! He took her away on horseback!"

River spun and brought both fists down hard on the truck's hood.

"How long ago? Which direction?"

Thelma pointed north. "They've been gone about fifteen minutes. Andre tried to stop him. Shiloh pistol whipped him." She started sobbing.

River looked at Benz, and Benz looked away. River held his questions as well as his accusations. No time for that, not now. Now he had to act. He needed a horse. Shiloh would be going places the truck could not follow.

Tony Jones was his nearest neighbor, and Tony kept good horses. "Thelma, take the truck and get to the Jones' place. Borrow

207

his trailer and have him load up a horse and saddle. Get back here as fast as you can. I'll go put my gear together."

Andre pushed out of the chair. "Get two, Thelma. I'm going with River."

Before River could object, Benz stepped in front of him.

"Get me one, too. Please, I've got to go."

Shame blazed in the man's eyes and his words. River bounded up on the porch and said over his shoulder, "If you two want to follow, I don't have time to stop you. Just don't get in my way."

Chapter Fourteen

Thelma explained the situation while Tony Jones saddled and loaded his best three horses. Jones was a good man, and could be trusted to keep his mouth shut so word didn't get to the police. He even offered to ride along with River. Thelma told him River already had more help than he wanted, and Tony Jones understood. He knew River well.

Now Thelma checked the time as she pulled into her drive. She'd been gone just a little over an hour. It took twice as long to get back from Tony's place than it had getting there. It took all the old truck possessed to pull the big stock trailer with three horses, but it managed the stress and strain. Thelma just hoped she could do the same.

River stood waiting in the front yard. He wore a black duster that fell almost to his ankles and a cowboy hat Thelma hadn't seen on him in years. It had been his rodeo hat. His lucky one. The felt Stetson had once been white, but sweat and dust and age turned it a color she could not explain. River pulled the brim pulled down low on his forehead. His eyes hid in its shadow. Thelma could see the buckle of a gun belt around his waist and the bulge of his forty-five under his left arm. River looked noticeably thicker in the torso.

Maybe the duster fit a little tighter nowadays, or maybe, Thelma thought, seeing her brother the way he used to dress just seemed to make him look bigger and stronger. The scoped rifle rested in a scabbard and lay across a bedroll and saddlebags at River's feet. Andre and Clive were nowhere to be seen.

By the time Thelma could get out of the truck and to the back of the trailer, River already backed the first horse out.

"It's all my damned fault," he said with a shake of his head as he cleared the horse from the trailer. "I should have put my foot down. I should have made you all leave early this morning."

"It's not your fault, River," Thelma insisted as she moved around him to pull out the second horse. "It's Billy Shiloh's fault. His and nobody else's."

"But Shiloh took her to get at me, Thelma. My God, that makes me responsible. If I'd gone after him when Bates wanted me to, he'd not had to come and get her. That makes it my fault. If he hurts her, I don't know how I'll live with myself."

The tone in his voice brought tears to Thelma's eyes yet again. She turned in the cramped trailer to look at him. She found River staring in the direction of the mountains with his shoulders drooping.

"River, you've seemed for the longest now to be carrying the weight of the world on your shoulders. Don't you think that's heavy enough? Don't add to it," Thelma pleaded.

River pricked her heart with tormented eyes. "You know, Thelma, if you ever hurt a single human being your whole life long, I wouldn't know who it'd be. You married one man and made him a good wife. You taught school and had an impact on the lives of all those children. You've done good in your life. You've served a good purpose."

River turned back to the mountains. "I've done no good," he seemed to say to the far horizon. "I've accomplished nothing other than hurting the ones I loved. My life's had no purpose."

Thelma backed the second horse out so she could stand closer to her brother. "River, you have a purpose now."

He looked at her questioningly with maybe the slightest glimmer of hope.

"Go save your girl, River. That's your purpose," Thelma smiled while reaching to pat his face.

The slamming of the front screen door diverted their attention in that direction. Andre hurried toward them with a bedroll under one arm and a twelve-gauge shotgun across the opposite shoulder.

"Which horse is mine, River?"

"Andre," River said with a look of deep concern, "can you ride?"

"Like Dale Evans," Andre winked with confidence.

"What about him?" River said, nodding in the direction of the front porch where Benz fumbled with his bedroll and another shotgun.

"Just point out the difference between the horse's head and ass and I think he'll manage," Andre scowled.

"Well, okay," River said uncertainly. "Go ahead and take your pick, Andre. They're all fine horses."

Thelma just backed the last horse from the trailer – a paint with beautiful markings. Andre pointed it out and moved to claim it. River nodded Benz toward a sorrel mare. Thelma thought it the more docile of the three. River tied his saddlebags, bedroll and rifle to the saddle of the remaining horse, a spirited Appaloosa.

Andre pulled himself effortlessly into the saddle. He looked at ease on the paint. Thelma could tell he'd ridden before. She could not say the same for Clive Benz. River held the man's shotgun while he struggled up and onto the horse. Thelma could tell River had qualms about handing the shotgun up to the man, but he did it anyway.

Thelma struggled with conflicting views on seeing River once again on horseback. It brought back good memories of a different kind of man, but thinking what might lie in store frightened her beyond words.

"Thelma, you pack a bag and get out of here," River said. "Leave me a note telling me where you'll be. I'll get hold of you when it's over. If you don't hear from me in forty-eight hours, call the police. Tell them everything."

The mentioning of police reminded Thelma of Carrie's last words.

"River, I almost forgot. Carrie told me to tell you not to come. She said for you to send the police. She said something about the barn and no more voices. It didn't make sense."

It seemed to make sense to River.

"You two wait here," he said under his breath.

River turned the Appaloosa and nudged it toward the old red barn. He rode the gelding up to the double doors, and sat motionless in the saddle for several long seconds before reaching to unlatch the doors. He threw both open wide without ever getting out of the saddle. Horse and rider then disappeared into the shadows within the ancient structure.

* * * *

Dust particles shimmered in the sunlight sifting through the plank walls. It smelled of old hay, and brought sorrowful memories from the past. He'd played here as a boy and worked here as a man, and River didn't want to be here now. Still, he reined the horse to the place where he'd found his brother's body. River pictured in his mind the way the blood had spread beneath Sky's still form like a purple blanket. He removed his hat and slumped in the saddle, remembering the last dream he'd had about Sky.

"You said there would be more voices."

His words echoed in the stillness.

"I'm awfully afraid you could be right."

He turned the horse slowly in place, circling, staring into the shadows.

"I didn't want any of you to die," he called loudly.

He stopped the horse when he once again faced the stall Sky died in, and then said more softly, "And I don't want anymore voices...especially hers."

River put his hat back on his head and moved the gelding toward the door. When he reached the rectangle of sunlight falling on the hard-packed floor through the entrance, he stopped and twisted in the saddle to stare back into the dark recesses of the barn, and his past, and his nightmares.

"Come to think about it, it won't be her. I won't let it be Carrie. It will be him or me. So, either way it goes, you boys best make room for one sorry son of a bitch."

* * * *

He knew his mind should be on River Yates. Sure, Yates looked old and acted cowardly, but there were all those stories and that living-legend bullshit. Maybe the old bastard still concealed a surprise or two up his sleeve, and Billy didn't want no damned surprises. Try as he might though, he just couldn't concentrate on Yates and his plans to kill the man. He could only blame the woman on the horse behind him.

She was the most gorgeous thing he'd ever seen. Every few minutes he'd catch himself looking over his shoulder just to get a glimpse of her. She looked better in person than she did in the movies, and Billy couldn't get one burning thought out of his mind. He'd seen her tits and her ass on the big screen, and he'd seen none finer. Just the memory alone was enough to keep him erect. He looked back to steal another peak and this time their eyes met.

"Where are you taking me?" Carrie huffed.

Billy gave her the smile. The one he'd used to win more than one girl over. Cindy always called it his bedroom smile. He knew even this woman, eventually, wouldn't be able to escape it.

"You been to see Robber's Cave yet?" Billy responded.

"I've been there," the woman said dryly.

She wasn't acting scared anymore, and that was okay with Billy. That meant she might have grown comfortable with him.

"Outlaws made that place famous, you know. It's where they hid out from the law," Billy said over his shoulder. "Well, I got my own cave. A secret cave. That's where we're going. It'll take us about four hours to get there at this pace."

"River will catch us before then," she said defiantly.

Billy laughed joyously. He liked her spunk. Cindy never had spunk. That proved one of her faults. A woman with spunk out of bed had to have spunk in bed. Billy reached between his legs and stoked his erection.

"Oh, no he won't. See, I know where I'm going. We'll keep traveling after dark. Yates is having to track us. He'll have to stop for the night. A man can't track in the dark."

Carrie didn't say anything else, and Billy turned back to his thoughts. It'd be around noon tomorrow before the old man found the cave. That would give Billy the rest of the evening, all night and most of the morning alone with the woman. A whole lot could happen between a man and a woman in that length of time. One way or another.

* * * *

A secret cave – Carrie concentrated on the words. It kept her mind off other things, like the way Shiloh kept looking at her. If she thought about the way he smiled, the look in his eyes, she'd most assuredly lose her mind.

River knew the mountains. She'd heard it from him, and she'd heard it from others. If there existed another cave up in the mountains, River would know about it. Carrie believed that and clung to River's ability to track.

Soon they hit a marshy area, wet and muddy. To their right grew a clump of trees. Carrie knew she would not get a better chance to initiate a plan she'd formed over Shiloh's confession about the cave. It was now or never.

"I have to pee," she called out to Shiloh.

He stopped and turned in the saddle to look at her.

"Well," he grinned, "this is a good a place as any. Jump on off and get at it."

"Right here? In front of you?"

"Why sure. Hell, woman, I saw everything you have in that one movie. The whole damned world did," he leered.

"I can't, Billy..." she hated using the name. It felt filthy on her tongue, but it leant the familiarity she needed to be persuasive. "...I need some privacy. Let me walk over to those trees. Please?"

Shiloh studied her for a long second or two. "You wouldn't be planning on running, now would you?"

"I'm not stupid, Billy. I know I can't outrun a man on a horse. I just have to pee. Badly. I'm hurting. All I want is a little privacy."

Shiloh finally nodded his approval. "But you hurry it up now. We ain't got all day."

Carrie made a production of slowly getting off the horse as if actually in pain. She made sure her feet hit the ground hard, making a deep indention in the soft ground. Limping and rubbing at legs she wanted to look stiff, she started around her horse and made about ten feet before tripping and falling heavily to the ground.

"What the hell's wrong with you?" Shiloh asked.

"I'm not used to riding. My legs went to sleep on me," Carrie lied. She scuffed the ground thoroughly in getting to her feet. Shiloh did not appear suspicious. Only amused.

It looked like at least fifty yards to the trees and undergrowth. Carrie picked a place from which she could not see Shiloh and hoped he couldn't see her. After going through the motions of pulling down her jeans and panties, Carrie squatted and quickly started pulling tufts of grass and weeds to make a good-sized bare spot on the ground.

* * * *

Billy kept his eyes on the spot where she'd squatted down. Hell, he kept telling himself, what else could she be doing but pissing? And after about the time it would take, she popped back up. He watched as Carrie started back in his direction. He no longer felt suspicious of her motives. The woman was just damned good to look at. Carrie walked only a few yards out of the brush when she suddenly threw up her arms and started screaming.

Billy thought it might look good if he rode hard acting like he gave a shit. He spurred his horse and galloped both horses to where she jumped up and down while screaming bloody murder.

"Snake! I saw a snake!"

Billy didn't see a snake and said so.

"Well, there was one," she said indignantly. "A huge one."

Billy climbed out of the saddle and moved close to the woman, who took a step backwards.

"Ain't one around now. You probably scared the poor thing to death with all that commotion."

When Carrie didn't say anything, Billy reached for his zipper.

"What are you doing?" Carrie asked as she took another step away from him.

"Now it's my turn."

Carrie winced as Billy pulled his penis out of his jeans.

"Just goin' to piss," he grinned.

Carrie quickly turned her head, but Billy knew she'd gotten a good look. Although she acted all disgusted, he knew she liked what she'd seen. What woman wouldn't? Later, he'd show her more. A lot more.

* * * *

Shiloh intentionally left an easy trail to follow, and River rode hard to follow it. Andre kept up with him, but Benz fell back behind them. River didn't give a shit if he kept up or not.

"Can we catch up with them tonight?" Andre asked.

River looked to the west. The sun was setting fast.

"Only if he intends for us to," River said with a shake of his head.

"Are you thinking ambush?"

"I'm thinking a lot of things, Andre." At least a million thoughts assaulted his mind for each mile they'd traveled.

"Do you have a plan, River?"

"I plan on finding them. After that, I plan on playing the cards dealt."

It was that simple, and that complicated. Shiloh would deal the cards.

"How you holding up, Andre?"

"My head hurts, but I'm okay."

"You should go back."

"I love her too, River."

River glanced over at the man riding beside him. Andre's look remained determined. A week and a half earlier River would have summed Andre up with a few ugly words. Now the words, the demeaning generalizations, humbled River. Andre Norman showed to be more of a man than most River associated with over the years.

An hour later, River reined his horse to a stop. The sun now sunk below the tree line. The trail grew too dim to follow. Shiloh had weaved in and around the pockets of dense forest, and River couldn't afford a wrong turn. Benz fell too far back to be seen.

"We'll spend the night here," River grumbled.

He could tell Andre wanted to object, but didn't. They weren't offered a better alternative.

River dismounted and removed his saddlebags and bedroll. Andre followed his lead.

"Should we remove the saddles?" Andre asked.

"I'd like to, but better not. Don't know what surprises might lay in store."

River took two pop-top cans of pork and beans from his saddlebags and handed one to Andre.

"Do you think Benz gave up the chase?" River asked.

"I put nothing past that man," Andre hissed.

River gave him a plastic spoon. "How come you don't like him?"

"He's a cad. I don't know of anyone that truly ever liked him."

"Carrie evidently did," River said, not really wanting to pry, but doing so anyway.

"No. I think she desperately tried, but soon accepted the relationship for what it was, a Hollywood thing. Nothing more. Nothing less."

"What happened back at the house with Shiloh and him?"

"Shiloh demeaned the pathetic bastard. Spit on him, actually. Clive did nothing but quake."

The words caused conflicting emotions. River despised Benz for not trying something, anything, to stop Shiloh from taking Carrie, but he pitied the man for not being able to act.

"What is that?" Andre said, pointing in the direction they'd come from.

River turned and saw the faint bouncing glow through the trees way back behind them. It took a minute or two for him to identify what they saw.

"It's a flashlight beam. Benz has got a flashlight," River said.

"I didn't think to bring a flashlight. Did you?"

"Well, no, I didn't think about bringing one. But, even if I had, I wouldn't have brought it. No one tracks by flashlight beam," River concluded.

"Clive Benz evidently does," Andre mumbled.

River scowled, but didn't say anything. Both men stood silently beside their horses watching the beam of light slowly work its way up to them.

"Why'd you stop? Did you find something?" Benz asked excitedly.

"Yeah, we found something," River replied dryly. "A good place to spend the night."

"You're stopping? All night long?" Benz asked as if he thought River lost his mind.

"You can't track at night, and you can't see..."

"I'm tracking just fine," Clive loudly talked over River, "and I've never tracked in my life. A fucking blind man could follow this trail!"

"You didn't let me finish," River said evenly. "We're not only tracking here, but we're also keeping an eye out for Shiloh. It's hard enough to spot a man in this timber in broad daylight, much less at night. And if he's hiding and waiting, that little ray of light aimed at the trail ain't going to find him. All it's going to do is better point you out to him."

"Listen, if you two pussies are afraid of the dark, then you stay," Clive barked. "But I'm going on."

"How dare you!" Andre screeched. "After how you let that man castrate you earlier today you have the nerve to call us pussies!"

"It was different then. He was armed. I wasn't. Now I have a gun. Now we're evenly matched."

"No," River said shaking his head, "that shotgun doesn't make you a match for Billy Shiloh. He could be hiding in the dark, and you'll be lighting yourself up. But I'm afraid even if you went up against him in the best of conditions, you wouldn't have a chance."

"And I guess you would?" Benz shouted angrily.

River took a few deep breaths to force himself to take no offense at the words, and then he sighed the truth.

"Probably not."

For long seconds no one spoke. When Benz did, there showed no trace of anger. "I can't stay here all night. I have to go. I have to do it now."

"A man has to do what a man has to do," River nodded his understanding.

Benz shone his light back on the ground and moved his horse on down the trail. River thought the man sat just a little taller in the saddle. At the very least, he wasn't as afraid of the horse as he had been at the start.

* * * *

River and Andre silently stared in the direction Benz traveled until the woods and distance swallowed up the last traces of his light.

"We should have stopped him," Andre said reluctantly.

"Don't know how we could have," River answered.

"We could have taken his light from him."

The words painted a funny mental image, but River didn't laugh. Carrie was out in the dark. With a madman. Not really hungry, but knowing he should eat, River popped the top on his can of beans. He worked on his second mouthful before Andre blurted out a fact.

"He's coming back!"

This time the beam of light bounced and danced about frantically. Benz apparently approached at a trot.

"Load your stuff up," River said as he quickly gathered up his saddlebags and bedroll and started securing them to his horse.

River mounted the Appaloosa just as Benz made it into shouting range.

"Yates! Get on your horse! I have to show you something!"

River galloped toward the sound of the voice and jittery beam of light. He could hear Andre close behind. They closed in on Benz in a matter of seconds.

"What did you find, Benz?" River asked as he pulled back hard on the reins to stop and hold the big horse in place. The Appaloosa pawed at the ground with its front hooves signaling to River that it enjoyed the sprint and stood ready for more of the same.

"The tracks," Benz huffed, "they're doing some funny shit up ahead. I don't know what happened, but it doesn't look good."

"Lead us back there," River ordered.

"You take the light," Benz said as he thrust it toward River. "You'll get us there quicker."

River took the flashlight and struggled to keep his horse from bolting into the night.

Chapter Fifteen

River had no problem identifying the spot that excited Benz. The tracks indeed gave evidence of funny shit. The flashlight's beam now weakened to barely a glow, but it didn't take much light to tell how badly the ground had been disturbed.

River jumped off his horse and drew a few conclusions by the time Andre and Benz made it up to the wet, muddy piece of ground.

"This is it. You found it," Benz exclaimed. "What do you think happened here, Yates?"

River looked up from the ground he studied. He calmed himself before speaking. The story he translated from the scarred earth nearly turned his stomach. "Looks like Carrie jumped off here and tried to run away."

"That doesn't make sense, River," Andre said. "If she tried to escape from him, why didn't she do it on horseback? If she did try to run away on foot, why would she do it in this open area?"

"I don't know, Andre. It doesn't make sense to me either," River agreed as he turned and paced off about ten feet. "But right here, it looks like she fell down, had a hard time getting back up, and then took off again."

River could picture it in his mind, but tried not to. Instead, he concentrated on something else that didn't make sense. "Right here, alongside Carrie's footprints," River said up to Andre and Benz, "is running hoof prints. It looks to me that for some reason Shiloh let Carrie get quite a way's off before he ran after her."

"The cruel bastard probably just taunted her," Andre said. "You know, kind of like a cat plays with a mouse."

River damned sure didn't want to picture that. "Bring my horse," he said over his shoulder as he started following the prints on foot. Thoughts of where and how they might end tormented him.

River followed the prints up to a copse of oaks and pines and puzzled over what he observed.

"Carrie ran into this thicket," he mumbled to himself more than to the two mounted men, "and Shiloh got off his horse here, but he didn't go in after her, and she came back out of the thicket and got back on her horse again."

Andre offered a quick. "I would guess she ran in there to hide? Maybe? And Shiloh simply coaxed her out with threats and probably at gunpoint as well."

"Could be," River said as he followed Carrie's footprints into the trees. Seconds later he found where she cleared a place about a yard in diameter underneath the trees. The flashlight had just enough power to allow River to make out the letters scratched in the dirt.

"Secret cave," he read out loud.

"Did you say something, Yates?" Benz called from outside the thicket.

River walked out of the trees and looked up at the two men on horseback. "Secret cave. She wrote that on the ground."

"Secret cave?" Andre echoed.

"Why?" Benz joined in. "What did she mean by that?"

"I can only guess that that's where he's taking her. To a secret cave," River deducted.

"Do you have any idea where that might be, River?" Andre asked hopefully.

"There's dozens of holes in these hills that people call caves, but I only know of one real, true cave. I used to play there as a kid," River said.

"Can you lead us there? In the dark?" Benz asked. The flashlight in River's hand now barely glowed.

"I can get us there, and in just a few hours, but if they're not there, we'll have to backtrack to here and start again. We'll lose a hell of a lot of time."

"River, are the tracks leading in the direction of the cave you're thinking of?" Andre asked.

Andre posed a good question that sparked enthusiasm in River. "Yeah, Andre, yeah they are. I mean, you know, in the general direction. But if I was riding across country from my ranch to the cave I have in mind, I'd pretty much be going right this way."

"Then that cinches it," Benz said forcefully. "Take us to that cave, Yates."

As if Benz had not spoken, Andre asked, "Do you think it could be a trick, River?"

"That's always that possibility," River sighed, "but I don't know that we have any better choice."

"I say we go now," Andre nodded with confidence.

"Well, then let's do it," River said as he swung up and into his saddle.

"That's what I said a couple of wasted minutes ago," Benz grumbled.

River turned in his saddle to stare at Benz. After a few silent seconds he extended the dead flashlight toward the man.

"I'm glad you brought that along. Smart thinking," River said softly.

Clive Benz cleared his throat and responded with a muffled, "Thanks."

* * * *

"Billy, I don't want to go in there."

The words came out of trembling lips and Carrie hated it. She didn't want her fear to show. But she didn't want to go in the cave, either. Shiloh looked close to losing what little patience he'd shown.

"Why the fuck are you so scared of going in a goddamned cave?" he blurted.

"It's a dark hole in the ground where things no doubt creep and crawl. I don't like places where things creep and crawl."

Above all else, Carrie didn't want to be in a dark hole in the ground with Billy Shiloh.

"Okay, well I'll just tell you your choices here, miss used-to-having-her-own-spoiled-fucking-way. You can either take your fine ass down in the cave with me so I can keep an eye on you. Or, I'll tie you up damned good and strap you to a tree and let you spend the rest of the night out here alone.

"And you want to talk about creeping and crawling things," Shiloh cackled, "up here, in these mountains at night, all kinds of things creep and crawl. Snakes, wild dogs and mean feral hogs. Hell, some people say there's still some bear and a few big cats up here. I tend to believe them, although I ain't never seen any myself."

The thought of trying to break and run crossed Carrie's mind as it had so many times since being abducted by Shiloh. Throughout the afternoon and evening, she contemplated turning her horse and bolting away. But she knew as a novice rider she would have no chance escaping from an accomplished equestrian, and she feared what Shiloh would do to her once he did catch her. Now, on foot, in the dark mountains and woods, she held no better hopes of gaining freedom.

"I'll go in the cave," she said without efforts to conceal her fear or loathing.

"I knew you had to have some brains to go with that hot body."

The stars and quarter moon threw off just enough light for Carrie to make out the two pistols Shiloh wore like some kind of matinee cowboy from the thirties. When she wasn't entertaining the fantasy of flight, she played with the idea of fight. Too many times, like at that very moment, she'd entertained the ridiculous thought of lunging for one of the big guns and turning it on Shiloh. The idea grew even more ludicrous after Shiloh demonstrated his skill in handling the revolvers.

They had stopped at a fast-running stream just before nightfall. The water coming down from the mountains looked clear and inviting. Shiloh squatted on one knee to drink from cupped hands. In doing so he turned his back on Carrie, exposing the guns to her reach. As he bent forward, Carrie spotted a third handgun partially concealed in the small of Shiloh's back. She eyed the guns for long seconds before noticing Shiloh had cut his eyes to stare back at her. Before she could even think to take a step backwards, Shiloh spun around and to his feet. The pistols from the holsters were in his hands, cocked and planted firmly beneath her jaws. Shiloh didn't say a word. He didn't have to. It frightened Carrie deeply, but not for herself. She now couldn't shake from her mind that River would be going up against this man and his terribly fast hands. She didn't want to believe it, but Carrie couldn't imagine in her wildest dreams how any man could be faster than Billy Shiloh.

So, knowing she could neither run nor overcome, Carrie reluctantly bent and crawled into the opening of what she hoped was not truly a secret place.

* * * *

"No. I won't let you," Benz said stubbornly. "You'd tell everyone, and it would end up in the tabloids. I'd be ruined forever."

River and Andre moved excruciatingly slow just so Benz could keep up. River climbed off his horse to stretch his legs while Andre presented his solution to the dilemma. The night grew too dark for River to see their faces, but he could tell Andre's next words were directed to him.

"Then let's just leave his self-centered, egotistical ass completely behind. Maybe a bear will fucking eat him," Andre concluded.

"There's no bears out here. Isn't that right, Yates?"

River had only one problem with running off and leaving Benz. Every time the man fell behind, he'd start to scream, "Hey! Where are you guys? Hey! Slow down! Wait up!" The way noises carried in the mountains in the dead of night, Shiloh would hear them coming from ten miles away.

"You know, Benz, Andre's idea ain't a bad one. And he won't tell a soul. Will you, Andre?"

Andre didn't respond. "Please, Andre, tell the man you'll keep your mouth shut."

228

"Oh, all right," Andre spat begrudgingly. "It will be a secret I carry to my grave."

Clive Benz gave no response. But when they started out once again heading higher into the dark mountains, they moved at a much faster pace. Traveling like this, River believed they would reach the cave before sunup. River glanced back over his shoulder but could only make out the forms of the two men on horseback. He was glad the figures blended with the inky darkness. River liked Clive Benz in every movie he'd ever seen him in. No matter what a prick the guy turned out to be in real life, River found it unsettling that the action hero relinquished the reins to his horse to be led through the dark by Andre Norman. It was just the sort of thing a man really didn't care to see.

* * * *

Being in the cave turned out even worse than Carrie imagined it would be. It felt damp, and she did not like the smell. The two lanterns Shiloh lit in what he called his living room cast eerie shadows on the slimy looking walls and served to make the blackness beyond their range extremely foreboding. Worst of all, it put her too close to Shiloh. And because he remained careful to stay between her and the mouth of the cave, Carrie had no place to run except into the sinister depths of the earth.

Shiloh offered what he had to eat: beef jerky, canned peaches, or crackers and Vienna sausages. Carrie declined but asked for a bottle of water. He gave her one of the many he stockpiled in the cave. He'd thrown a blanket on the ground between the two lanterns and told her it was where she'd sleep. He tossed one right in front of the opening for himself. He had been chatty since entering the cave.

Friendly. Leering. For the last few minutes he'd busied himself with some crackers and beef jerky.

"Guess you're wondering what'll happen next," he said after finishing off a final cracker and washing it down with bottled water.

"Of course I am."

"Well, it's all really up to that man of yours. He is your man, right? Yates?"

"He is my man."

"I don't understand that, but...oh well. Anyway, it's all up to Yates. You think he'll show up?"

"I know he will show up."

"I'm not so sure, him turning coward and all, but if..."

"He's no coward," Carrie said, trying hard to keep her voice calm, "he just doesn't want to kill you."

"Well, he won't have to worry about that," Shiloh laughed menacingly. "But, anyway, let me tell you what's going to happen. If he comes, I expect him here sometime before noon. But he might fool me and make better time. So, about sunup, I'll be waiting on the trail down below the cave. If he's alone, I'll call him out, and give him a chance to go for his gun first. Then I'll put a single bullet right between his eyes. I'll do that to make it easy for you.

"But, if he brings help," Shiloh said, as he moved to his blanket and sat down on it cross-legged, "or if anything else happens that I haven't planned for, then I'll make sure his death is one hell of a nightmare."

"And what will you do with me when you go to wait for him? Tie me up and leave me in here?" Carrie knew there could be no good answer.

"I got you here for two purposes. One is to get ol' River up here. The second is so you can see what happens. Then you, being all-important and shit, the whole world will know. So, when I go to wait on him, you'll go with me. If we ain't grown friendlier by then, then I'll tie your hands and feet and gag you."

"You're expecting us to grow friendlier?" Carrie asked.

"Can't never tell what can happen between a man and a woman...all alone...in a place like this."

The look in his eyes made Carrie's skin crawl. She thought it best to simply act as if she didn't hear his last comment. "I'm tired. I need some rest," she said while sinking to her blanket.

Carrie rolled onto her side facing Shiloh. She was tired. She did need rest. But she had no intentions of closing her eyes. Not even after he fell asleep.

* * * *

Carrie didn't realize she'd fallen asleep until she started to dream. She certainly had to be dreaming. River couldn't have found his way to her so quickly. It simply couldn't be that he was really there with her, in the cave, kissing her neck, caressing her breasts through her clothing, moving his lips up to hers. He had missed her. She could feel his want as a hunger...rough... demanding...obscene.

Carrie opened her eyes. Shiloh was on top of her. She went for his face with the nails of both hands, but Shiloh caught her by the wrists and pinned her arms back behind her head. In doing so, he scooted up to straddle her waist. He'd stripped off his clothing and his erection pointed at her face. It seemed to pulsate.

"You like that. I can tell," Shiloh panted. "You wanted it when you saw it earlier and you want it now. You don't have to fight it."

"Get off of me!" Carrie screamed.

"It's gone too far, baby. I won't stop now. I'm gonna fuck you every way a man can fuck a woman and then I'm going to fuck you some more. You be a good girl and don't fight me, and I won't even tell Yates about it before I kill him."

"You bastard!" Carrie screamed while struggling against the grasp on her wrists.

In spite of her efforts, Shiloh easily moved one of his hands into position to hold both of her wrists. He used his free hand to rip open her shirt. After freeing one breast from her bra Shiloh bent to take it in his mouth. Carrie felt the heat of his penis on her bare stomach. Disgusted and frightened to near hysterics, she could take no more.

"River will be here sooner than you think!" she cried. "He could be here any second. You are a fool and I tricked you!"

Shiloh stopped with his open mouth mere inches from her breast. He raised only his eyes. They stared threateningly from the upper edges of the sockets. "You tricked me? How?"

"You'll find out soon enough. Any minute River could be standing at your back. He could be here and..."

Shiloh brought his free hand to her throat and squeezed hard enough to cut off her words. While Carrie gasped for her next breath, Shiloh turned and looked over his shoulder to the mouth of the cave. When he looked back his face twisted with anger.

"How?"

At first, he squeezed harder and then let up so Carrie could speak. Her words came as she found the breath to say them.

"When I went...into the woods to pee...I wrote a message on the ground."

"What did it say?"

"Secret cave."

"He don't know about this place."

Carrie took several deep breaths. "He's been in these mountains all of his life. He'll know about this cave."

Shiloh seemed to ponder her words for an eternity. When he spoke, he did so without emotion.

"I trusted you. You fucked me. It could have been fun. Now it won't be."

Shiloh took the hand from her throat and slowly brought it up over his head. Carrie watched his fingers clench into a fist. She closed her eyes right before it collided with her face. Carrie did not cry out, and if he hit her more than three times, she never knew it.

* * * *

What River expected to be Shiloh's secret cave was now less than half a mile away. With Andre pulling Benz along behind him they'd made even better time than River thought they would.

"Let's take a break here," River said as he slowly lifted himself from the saddle. Everything on him that could hurt did hurt. He'd been too long out of the saddle.

"The cave is practically straight up from this point. It's pretty rough terrain up there," River said once the other two men climbed from their horses and moved close to his side. River had plenty of time to make his plans. He knew what he wanted to do and how.

"Benz, I want you to stay here and hold the horses. Andre and I will go in from here on foot."

"You want to leave me behind?" Benz objected.

"I want to sneak in from here and I need you to stay with the horses."

"We're surrounded by trees. Why can't we just tie them up?"

"They'll be quieter with someone here with them."

"Then Norman needs to stay with them. I'm going up with you."

River knew it would come to this. "Here's the deal, Benz. I need one man to stay with the horses. The other man will go up with me. No offense, but I'll feel better up there with Andre at my side."

"I don't know who in the hell put you in charge," Benz said angrily, "but they didn't put you in charge of me. I'm going up to that cave and there is not a damned thing you can do about it."

Benz's resistance did not surprise River. He'd anticipated the response and knew how to deal with it. "Andre?"

"Yes, River?"

The man had not come close to complaining, but at last light River noticed the wound on his head seeping and growing even more swollen. Although it too dark for him to see Andre's head now, he knew the night's rough ride couldn't have helped it any.

"Do you feel like walking up there, Andre?"

"I may be a butterfly by nature, but I'm a hawk at heart. I'm ready when you are."

"Okay. Good deal. Now, would you mind taking these horses and moving them out of the way. I don't want one of them stomping on Benz when he hits the ground."

"What are you talking about?" Benz erupted.

"I'm getting ready to whip your ass," River said nonchalantly.

"I have a right to go up there," Benz insisted in a softer tone than he used seconds earlier.

"No. The only right you have at this point and time is the right to do what I tell you to do. This ain't a movie. Real lives are at stake here. Five real lives. You can bet your ass that before this day's over, at least one of the five is going to be dead, and it ain't going to be from you fucking things up. So, you make the choice. You stay voluntarily with hurt feelings, or you stay involuntarily with a hurt everything else."

"What do I do, just sit here and wait until you get back?" Benz stammered.

"If you hear firing, then you bring the horses as quick as you can. If you don't hear firing, then you just sit here and wait until I get back."

River gave Benz several seconds to respond. When he didn't, he turned to Andre. "Let's go see if she's up there."

Chapter Sixteen

River moved slowly and tried to make as little noise as possible. Every few minutes he'd stop and listen. He didn't expect Shiloh to be making any noises at four a.m., but maybe his horses would be, giving River advance notice that this was actually Shiloh's destination. Every time River would stop, Andre would be right there. The older man moved like a ghost in the deep woods. River felt good having him in his company, and equally as glad he'd left Benz behind.

River couldn't remember the last time he'd been in these parts of the San Bois Mountains, but believed it at least twenty years, maybe thirty. He literally felt his way through the dark. When he sensed they were close he stopped and motioned for Andre to come closer.

"I don't know exactly where the cave is," he whispered. "I remember that the opening was very small. Sometimes that made it hard to find even in daylight. Of course, it could be larger now, or even smaller. I don't know what the years have done to it, and Shiloh could have it well hidden, camouflaged. So, stay alert. I'll need help finding it."

As it turned out, he didn't. In less than a hundred feet the ground leveled off, and they found themselves on a large ledge on the side of the mountain. From here they could see a vague glow thirty or so yards to their front. It showed as a faint spot radiating from a hole in the side of the mountain about the size of a manhole cover. River fell to the pine needle strewn ground knowing Andre would do the same. River pulled the .45 from his shoulder holster and saw Andre had his shotgun trained on the glow. From flat on his belly, River carefully surveyed what lay ahead.

It had to be a trap. River had more than enough time while in the saddle to take inventory of his enemy's strengths and weaknesses and compare them to his own. River could come up with only one clear advantage he had over Shiloh...smarts. From all indications, Billy Shiloh seemed less than bright, but not even Shiloh could be stupid or careless enough to so blatantly expose his "secret" place of hiding.

River concentrated on the light. Because it didn't fluctuate or waver, he believed it to be a gas or propane lantern. If he remembered right, just inside the opening was a small, tight area. He didn't think the lantern rested in that space or it would be much brighter. That meant the light probably came from the first big open space down deeper in the cave. If this was true, and anyone moved around in that area, the light would reflect the movement. Because it didn't reveal movement meant anyone down there either kept still, possibly sleeping, or they were back behind the source of light – awake and just waiting.

Knowing nothing else to do, River pushed to his feet, crouched low and started toward the light. When River went to the left of the opening, Andre took the right side. River pressed his back to the sandstone of the mountain and listened while trying to calm his nerves. He heard no noises coming from the cave. After a deep breath he bobbed his head to steal a quick glance into the opening. Lower this time, he stole another quick peek. River didn't see anything that bothered him and he didn't draw gunfire so he inched his head over the rim of the sandstone and looked long and carefully into the cave.

The tight area just inside the mouth looked okay. To see more, he'd need to enter the opening. River motioned for Andre to stay in place and then started into the cave – Colt .45 first. River wasn't sure he took a breath or his heart even beat until he made it safely into the tiny chamber. He scraped his belt buckle on the sandstone going in. The noise stirred no action from further in the cave.

River could see a little of the bigger chamber from his position, but very little of it. What he could see revealed nothing. He had to go deeper and positioned himself to crawl in headfirst. The very second his head became completely exposed to the lower chamber, River saw what awaited him, and instantly his insides felt like coming outside.

* * * *

"I should have kicked his ass," Clive said out loud to nobody but himself. "I have a black belt in Tae Kwon Do. I don't have to take that shit," he added while tightening the grip on his shotgun. It was darker than hell and Clive had never been overly fond of darkness. He continually turned in tight circles. He wished he could see all around him at the same time. He wished he'd been brave enough to take on River Yates.

All alone, in the dark, in the woods, Clive reluctantly admitted the truth – *I am a coward.* The only real fight he'd ever been in happened in his senior year of high school. The boy that bloodied his nose, and busted his lip, and sent him home crying was only a freshman three inches shorter and at least twenty pounds lighter than Clive.

He had his back to the horses when one of them snorted. Clive nearly jumped out of his boots while whirling around to level the shotgun on the horses. All three of them looked at him. He could see the disdain in their eyes.

"Fuck you. All of you," he hissed.

From behind Clive a hand fell across his mouth and something cold and hard suddenly became thrust forcibly to his left temple.

"You should have stayed at home, movie bad-ass," a mean voice whispered in his right ear.

Clive pissed his pants and dropped his shotgun. His knees buckled, and Shiloh let him fall to the ground.

"I'll go back home. I'll leave now," Clive heard himself whimper.

"Too late. Too bad."

"Oh, God! Don't hurt me!" Benz sobbed.

"Don't hurt me!" Shiloh mimicked before reaching down and grabbing Clive Benz by the hair of his head.

* * * *

Carrie was dead. River felt sure of it. She lay there so still, so broken. He'd taken one step into the large chamber and couldn't take another. He hadn't stopped to think that Shiloh could be lurking in the shadows. He didn't care. It didn't matter now. Then Carrie moaned.

River shouted for Andre while running the few feet to Carrie. He collapsed on his knees at her side and gently called her name. He wanted to hold her in his arms, but feared doing additional damage.

Blood dried on her face and matted in her hair. It looked like it came mostly from her nose, but both her upper and lower lips were busted as well. Both eyes swelled badly and already started to bruise, but Carrie opened the left and then the right. River exhaled a breath he had no idea how long he'd held.

"Oh, dear, dear God in heaven!" Andre shrieked from back behind River. He squatted on the other side of Carrie. Andre's eyes pooled with tears.

Carrie moved both hands, awkwardly at first, to the tops of her jeans. She patted the material as if looking for something and both hands stopped at the button and zipper. Then her hands moved to find River's face. He could tell she tried to smile.

"They're buttoned...zipped...I don't think he raped me," her voice rasped.

River took her hands in his. "I was so scared. I thought you were dead."

"I think he only hit me in the face. I think I can stand," Carrie said as she started to sit up.

"No!" Andre said while gently pushing her back on the blanket. "Rest a minute while I clean you up. Let us have a look at you before you get up." Andre then stood and moved for a stack of bottled water a few feet away.

"I knew you'd find me. I knew you'd get here," Carrie said to River.

"I'm so sorry I didn't get here sooner. I'm so sorry I got you into this. If only I'd done things..."

Carrie put a hand to his mouth, blocking his words. "I don't blame you. I just love you."

"And I love you," River said, feeling his throat tighten.

His fear started to subside while another emotion rushed to take its place. "Carrie, do you know where Shiloh is?"

"No."

River bent and gently kissed her on the forehead and then pushed to his feet. "Andre, I'm going out to fire a couple of shots to get Benz up here. Take care of her."

"You know I will, River."

River would get the three of them out of here, and if he didn't encounter Shiloh while doing so...then he would come back. Billy Shiloh crossed a line he shouldn't have crossed, and River intended to make him pay for it.

* * * *

"He's not here? He left us?"

River just nodded a response to Andre's questions. Clive Benz had left. Worse by far, he took the horses with him.

River had fired his two shots and waited for Benz to come up while Andre cleaned Carrie's face and hair. All Benz would had to do was follow the rocky trail straight to the cave. River doubted that even Benz could have gotten lost doing that. And even if he had, he knew for sure Benz would have screamed loud enough to be heard all over the mountain.

Benz could have reached their location in twenty minutes even at the pace he rode. After forty minutes of waiting, River, Carrie, and Andre started down the mountain. Carrie seemed confident that she could make the hike. River could tell she was in pain and weakened by her ordeal, but she made the trek without a great deal of difficulty.

Darkness still ruled, but it wouldn't do so for long. The sun would be up in an hour. With light, River could check for tracks and answers to the question – where did Benz go?

"He wouldn't just leave. Not even Clive Benz would do that," Carrie said.

"He would have been afraid to," Andre added.

River confirmed what they all thought.

"Then Shiloh must have got him."

And none of them said anything else until the sun came up.

* * * *

The tracks confirmed it. Shiloh captured Benz and the horses. There appeared no signs of struggle. That surprised no one. Unfortunately, the tracks led north. River planned to take the trails and pathways north to the small community of Kinta – the closest place to go for help. River feared Shiloh would now be waiting someplace between them and the town.

"Do we have options?" Andre asked, after River explained the dilemma.

"We can go east and intersect Highway 2, drop down south to Robbers' Cave State Park. That would be the next closest place to go for help, but it would add another ten or fifteen miles to our walk."

Carrie moaned, then looked embarrassed for doing so.

"I could hide you two out here," River started, "and I could take the quickest route..."

"No," Carrie said adamantly. "I don't want to be separated from you again. We go together. And I say we go east. Away from Shiloh. I'm up to ten or fifteen extra miles."

River nodded his head. He did not prefer leaving her behind. "We will keep off the trails and, in the trees, staying out of any open areas. It will be harder for Shiloh to find or see us."

He didn't explain the importance of moving under the cover and concealment of the forest. He didn't want to add to her burden of fear and worry. For the time being, anyway, Carrie did not need to know what else Shiloh seized along with Benz and the horses.

* * * *

Shiloh tied two horses up about a mile away from the cave before the sun came up – the mare the woman rode and a paint Yates left with the fool down below the cave. Shiloh presently rode the big buckskin gelding – the one with the unusual looking white patch of hair between the eyes. He took the Appaloosa that had been with Yates and secured him far from the other two. Shiloh now watched this horse from a great distance away. The Appaloosa looked the best of the three horses Yates brought into the mountains. Therefore, it would be the best one to use to fuck with Yates' mind.

Billy hadn't known where to tie the Appaloosa until Yates, his bitch, and the fag started to move. Billy watched that from a good distance away, too. Fucking Yates proved so predictable. He'd seen the tracks Billy left going north, so Yates went east, just like Billy wanted him to. They would have a longer distance to travel this way, giving Shiloh more time to terrorize them.

Billy trained his attention on the Appaloosa, but heard the muffled, "huuuhhhhmmmmmmmm, huuuhhhhmmmmmmmm," coming from behind him.

"What you need, Mr. Benz?" Billy called over his shoulder without taking his eye from the scope on the rifle that Yates kindly brought on the excursion. The scope allowed Billy to watch Yates and his party from a distance just after sunup, and it allowed him to stage the Appaloosa so far away

"Huuuhhhhmmmmmmuuuu, ooooohhhhhhhh," Benz said this time.

Billy had some time. On horseback, using the trails, he'd gotten quickly far out in front of Yates. The Appaloosa stood tied on the east bank of a good-sized creek adjacent to the only low water crossing area in miles. Where Yates would want to cross the creek. Billy laid the rifle aside and pushed up from his prone position. He ambled back to the two horses and Benz.

"You comfortable?" he snickered at Benz.

Benz raised his head and shook it emphatically. Shiloh couldn't help but laughing. When Billy captured Benz, he'd made him take off his socks. He then made the actor lie across the saddle on the sorrel mare Benz rode into the mountains. Billy ran a rope beneath the mare's belly and tied Benz's ankles to his wrists. Billy balled up Benz's socks and stuck them in the man's mouth as a gag. He'd used another piece of rope around Benz's head to hold the socks in place. The man had been that way for a long time now. He looked absolutely miserable. Shiloh laughed again.

"Guess you're wanting something?" Shiloh asked.

Benz's head bobbed up and down.

"Well, I got food and I got water, but not enough for you."

The head shook left and right.

"Not hungry or thirsty?" Shiloh said, while he thought for a few seconds. "Oh, I bet you have to use the restroom."

Yes. Yes. Benz nodded.

"Piss?"

No. Benz shook.

"Shit?"

Yes. Oh, yes. Benz nodded with a vengeance.

"Well, go ahead," Billy snickered as he went back to the rifle.

River Yates would be crossing the creek soon. Shiloh didn't want to miss it.

* * * *

River went first. The water ran only knee deep. Once on the other side of the creek, he crouched below the crest of the bank and motioned for Carrie and Andre. They splashed into the water at the same time, helping each other across. When they reached River, he had them sit and catch their breath. The crest of the bank on both sides reached high enough to offer some cover.

"How you two doing?" River asked.

Both said okay. River didn't believe it. Andre rubbed at his head with every few steps he'd taken and the wound showed signs of infection. Carrie's lips still seeped blood and the lids of her right eye had swollen shut. Again, like he did two or three times already, River asked if Andre wanted him to take the heavy twelve-gauge shotgun off his hands.

"No, River. And stop fussing over me. I might take it the wrong way!"

River shook his head and grinned.

When Carrie and Andre said they were ready, the three of them scrambled up the bank and started in a jog toward the tree line. They were almost there when Andre stopped to point and shout, "River, look! Your horse!"

River's heart raced at the sight. "Don't stop! It's a trap!" he shouted as he grabbed Carrie and Andre and sprinted for the trees, all but dragging them behind him.

The San Bois were scattered with large boulders. One jutted up from the ground just inside the dense line of pines. River maneuvered Carrie and Andre around and behind it.

"He knew we would cross there, damnit! He's in front of us and watching us!" River bellowed.

"But the horse isn't tied up, River. It's just standing there," Andre said. "Maybe it got away."

"And happened right into our path? I don't think so, Andre," River said as he peeked around the boulder and at the horse. The horse stood in thick grass up to its knees.

"He's hobbled the horse," River said, "and stuck him there in that tall grass so you can't see the hobbles."

"If he knew we were going to cross back there," Carrie said while still breathing hard, "then why wasn't he shooting at us?"

"Good question," River replied, "but I don't have a good answer."

Andre turned his back to the boulder and scanned the area to their rear. "As far as that goes," he said, "if he knew we were going to cross there, and his intention is to ambush us, then he could have easily have done it from a dozen different vantage points, including this boulder. I don't think ambush is his intention. Maybe sneaking up on us right now is though. River, I want to go get that horse."

"Andre, why risk anything for one horse?" River asked with a shake of his head. "One horse will not do the three of us any good."

"It would, River," Andre disagreed amiably. "I could ride for help. You could stay and protect Carrie."

River paused to think. Why hadn't Shiloh fired upon them? Clearly, he concluded, because he hadn't wanted to. Shiloh had something else in mind, and River felt pretty sure it wasn't shooting him down from a distance. Shiloh wanted a showdown – blazing pistols at ten paces and all that bullshit. But, River feared Shiloh would have no qualms in putting a bullet in Andre from a hundred yards away. There existed only one way to find out what Shiloh had up his sleeve.

"I'll try to go check out the horse," River said.

"No!" Carrie cried. "Why do either of you have to go? Why don't we stay right here?"

"For how long, Carrie?" River asked softly. The time arrived for him to tell her something he'd spared her from knowing. "Carrie, my rifle with the scope was with my horse. Shiloh has it now. If he wanted to, he could sit way back and pin us down here at this rock. Evidently, he doesn't want to. I think he wants to kill me up close and personal. He's playing some kind of game with that horse. I'm pretty sure it doesn't involve sniping at me."

"You don't know that for sure," she moaned.

"Sweetheart, right now, there isn't much I do know for sure."

* * * *

Carrie reached for River, and they hugged. He gently kissed her on her split and hurting lips. River sweated profusely. Carrie could tell by his determined demeanor that it wasn't from nerves. His sweat resulted from the duster he wore. She suggested earlier that he take it off, but River gave no response. Carrie could see the gun belt around his waist and knew he had the shoulder holster under his arm. Maybe River didn't want Shiloh knowing what guns he bore. It seemed the only reason River wouldn't shed the damned steaming black coat.

"Why do you think he's wearing that duster?" Carrie asked Andre, after River stepped around the boulder and started for the horse.

Andre positioned himself so he could scan the area in front of River through the shotgun sights. "I do believe it's a cowboy thing, dear. He certainly looks dashing!"

Carrie's thoughts turned from the duster to the shotgun Andre pointed. It proved easier to dwell on things like dusters and shotguns than topics like, "What had Shiloh done to Clive?" or "What was

Shiloh getting ready to do to River?" Yes, dusters and shotguns were just better for whiling away the nightmarish moments.

"It's a long way from here to the horse. Is a shotgun effective at this range? Won't it scatter?"

"Not if it's loaded with slugs," Andre smiled.

"Slugs? What is a slug?"

"Just a huge, practically blunt chunk of lead. If Shiloh should step out of those woods, I could cut him in two pieces with one of them."

Carrie studied her friend for a few seconds. One would have thought Andre very much out of his element here in the woods, with a firearm, being hunted by a madman. But that did not at all seem to be the case. It brought a question to mind.

"Could you grow accustomed to this manly bullshit, Andre? The boots, the guns, and horses, the excitement?"

"Are you asking if I'll find it difficult returning to blatant femininity?" Andre smiled.

"I guess so."

"Sweetheart, when I get home, if I get home, the only thing I intend to wear for a month thereafter are kimonos and my furry slippers!"

Carrie averted her eyes to look at Andre a few times in the short exchange, but turned her undivided attention on River. He'd drawn less than twenty yards from the Appaloosa, and still moved in the steady, ambling gate he'd started out in.

"He's almost there," she said in a whisper.

"So far, so good," Andre agreed.

River walked directly up to the horse, patted its neck for a few seconds and then squatted in the tall grass. Carrie could only see the very top of his hat. In less than a minute River stood, faced Carrie and

Andre and held up a length of rope for them to see. The horse had been hobbled. River turned back to the horse and once again reached to pet it.

Suddenly a tremendous splash of red gushed as the gelding's head all but disintegrated. The sharp crack of the single shot sounded a second later while the pink mist still glistened in the air. River, covered in blood and gore, stumbled backwards as the horse collapsed and sunk out of sight into the tall grass.

Carrie, screaming, tried to run to River, but Andre grabbed her and would not let her leave the safety of the boulder. Her screams turned to sobs as she looked at River as he stood looking down at the horse. After what seemed the longest time, River turned and solemnly started toward the creek. He did not hurry. He did not look back. River used the water from the creek to rid himself of the horse's blood, bone and brain.

Carrie's thinking, at the moment, questioned what kind of man would come back to her from the creek and that insane act of cruelty. On his way back to the boulder, River did not run across the open area. He did not scurry back to his place of safety with his tail tucked between his legs. But, coming back, he stood just a little less tall than he did going out. The look on his face could not be attributed to just one or even a couple of emotions. Sadness, rage, fear and confusion vied for expression in the arch of his brows and the stormy depths of his eyes. His jaw was set, but his lips seemed to have just the slightest tremor. The second River stepped behind the boulder Carrie grabbed him and hugged him with all her might.

"Are you okay?" she whispered in his ear.

"Yeah, sure," he said with quick nods of his head.

"What do we do now?" Andre asked.

River gently, if not hesitantly, pulled out of Carrie's arms. "We go on. We cover as much ground as he'll let us."

"Shouldn't we stay here?" Carrie asked, "behind this rock where we are safe?"

"We're not safe here, baby," River shook his head. "Anytime he wants, Shiloh can circle us. No, he wants us to move on. It's part of his sick game, and right now, we have to play his game."

"But if we could hide out until dark, and move then, wouldn't it be safer? Wouldn't we have better chances of escaping?" Carrie asked.

"Sure we would, but Shiloh won't let that happen, Carrie. No, this will all be over by dark. One way or another."

Chapter Seventeen

A bullet struck at about the same instance the shot sounded, meaning that it had been fired from close range.

River had kept to the trees and thick foliage. Using the cover and concealment wasn't much of an advantage, but they had nothing else. River estimated they'd made it about five miles since the awful ordeal with the horse. All the way, he'd felt Shiloh watching.

This shot didn't surprise River. He'd been expecting one at anytime, but it did rattle him. It severed a branch four inches in diameter just feet from River's face. Carrie screamed. So did Andre. All three went to the ground.

"Hey, Yates!" The voice sounded from the north. Shiloh had crossed their path and was now on the other side of them.

"What do you want, Shiloh?" River hollered back.

"Want to know if we're having fun yet!"

Then River heard Shiloh's laughter. River guessed him to be at least fifty yards away.

"Carrie, Andre, stay down a minute," River said before pushing to his feet. He scanned the rugged terrain to the north and saw nothing but trees and rocks.

"Shiloh! Why don't you show yourself? Come on out. Let's get this thing over."

"Too easy, old man. Time for easy is over. Blame your bitch for that. That little trick of hers changed everything. Ever watched a cat torment a mouse, Yates?"

River swallowed hard trying to force down his anger. He couldn't afford to reveal his emotions to Shiloh. "What did you do with Benz?"

"I cut his throat. Watched him bleed."

"Oh, shit," River said under his breath. He heard Carrie moan and Andre sigh wearily.

"Just kidding!" Shiloh then cackled.

"Fucking bastard," River grumbled through clenched teeth.

"He's with me, Yates. And right now, he's okay. But who knows, you just might start finding pieces of him in your path. Now, that would be fun, wouldn't it? Hey, what did you think about how that horse's head came apart? Huh? Popped like a balloon, didn't it?"

River offered no response other than clenching his hands into fists.

"Yates! One more thing for now. Something to look forward to. Here before too much longer, I'm going to shoot your pet queer!"

River looked down at Andre who responded by waving the middle finger of his left hand high in the air.

A few seconds later, Shiloh called again. He sounded further away.

"Yates! Best get to moving. Don't let me get bored with this. If I get bored, I plan on taking little nicks and chunks out of that Hollywood slut."

River Yates dropped his head and closed his eyes. It took several deep breaths before he found the strength to take another step.

* * * *

Benz screamed again. They would hear him now every ten minutes or so. What Shiloh did to him fell only to imagination. They did not discuss it out loud. Benz sounded as if in great agony. His cries both chilled the skin and boiled the blood. Carrie would grip her ears and shake her head each time he started to wail. River would try to pinpoint where the screams came from while trying to ignore the fact that a man was being tortured. He couldn't afford to dwell on it. He could not allow his anger or his fear to get out of hand.

They were between screams when River spotted the two large boulders up ahead and to their left. Both rocks were almost six feet tall and stood side by side with about a yard in between. They were almost as long as they were tall and offered just enough space for three people to squeeze into. Inside the space they would be safe from two of the four directions from which Shiloh could fire. River saw it as an opportunity for a break with a little peace of mind.

More space existed between the rocks than what it looked like from the outside – providing plenty of room for the three of them to collapse to the ground. For the first few minutes they simply rested. No one spoke a word.

Andre broke the silence. "Every step I take I wonder if it won't be the last. I keep waiting to feel the pain, but then I think of Korea. I saw men die that I am certain never knew what hit them. That would be nice, but I don't think Billy Shiloh will have the decency to afford me that luxury."

River didn't think so, either, but he couldn't say so. Still something needed to be said, and River tried to come up with it when something all together different came to mind. He sat crossed legged and slumped, but the thought prompted River to sit up straight and he almost smiled. Hope could do that to a man.

"These rocks, they made me think of something," he said with an energy he hadn't felt since leaving the ranch almost twenty-four hours earlier.

Carrie seemed to sense his enthusiasm. "What? A good plan, River?"

"Not really a plan, but a destination. One of the reasons this country was popular with outlaws and cowboys was because of its natural corrals. All over these mountains there are places where rock is formed and shaped in near circles and semicircles that provide natural fencing for horses and good protection at the same time.

"These rocks here," River said as he reached and patted the rough sandstone, "made me remember such a place, and it ain't far from here. The old-timers call it Satan's Crown because of its shape. It looks like a crown, a rough one. There's only one way in and one way out. The opening is only about forty or fifty feet wide and a man would play hell climbing over the steep and jagged rocks. Inside is about half the size of a football field. If Shiloh wanted to attack us there, he'd have to come in and get us. He'd be a sitting duck."

Andre pushed to his feet. "Can we get there, River?"

"We'd have to change our course just a little. We'd just have to hope Shiloh don't figure out what we're doing, where we're going. It'd take us about an hour and a half to get there."

"I wonder what I could do to stay alive that long?" Andre seemed to be wistfully thinking out loud.

"Well, I've had something in mind every since Shiloh said he was going to shoot you, but there hasn't been a good place to make it happen," River said as he took a second to look out both ends of the rocks.

"Carrie, would you stand up and try to block that end," River said, pointing to the narrower of the two openings. "And Andre, you block the other one. Just in case Shiloh is looking."

When they were in place, River stood and quickly started stripping off his duster.

* * * *

River Yates thought he was so damned smart. Thought he knew these trees and rocks like the back of his hand. Billy couldn't help but laugh. He'd been laughing for the past hour. He'd started when Yates first veered off course, drifting to the southeast. The fool didn't know his location or his destination. Had he continued heading east, he and his little party would have hit the state park and people and...well, no they wouldn't have, because Billy would have stopped them long before that. Anyway, in the direction they currently headed, there wasn't anything for miles. Nobody or nothing that could help them get...

"Wait a minute," Shiloh mumbled out loud. The thought flashed across his mind like a yellow highway caution sign.

It seemed possible Yates might have a destination in mind and knew exactly where he intended to go. Maybe he knew of a house stuck off someplace in this neck of the woods. Billy wasn't as familiar with this part of the mountain range as he was further east so he had to think hard and try to remember. Finally, he relaxed. No, he concluded, there wasn't a house anyplace close to here. Yates had to be lost, and Billy laughed again.

Then his thoughts turned to shooting the faggot. At the moment, Billy stood close enough that when he looked through the scope he could see deep into the eyes of his prey. There'd been several times he'd almost pulled the trigger on the prissy writer. But each time, just like now, Billy would make the mistake of looking first into Andre's eyes. The homo's intense dread and fear kept Billy from killing Andre. Because when Billy would see that, it just made him want to see more. Billy kind of related it to torturing cats as a mere kid. The more the cat fretted and worried, the more fun it provided Billy.

Billy shifted the scope from Andre to Carrie. He looked a few seconds at her face. It wasn't so pretty anymore, and Billy chuckled. He slowly worked the scope down, pausing a second on her tits before concentrating on her ass. He should have fucked her. It wasn't the condition of her face that stopped him. Hell, if he'd known he had so much time before River reached the cave he would have fucked her. If he'd known he had time and didn't have to keep looking up and wondering about being surprised, Billy's dick wouldn't have gone limp and refused to stand back up again.

It hadn't been Billy's fault he couldn't keep his dick hard, but still, thinking about it depressed him. Billy wanted to stay happy. He decided to make Clive Benz scream some more.

Plenty of time existed. Yates and his traveling circus pulled ahead of him, but from Billy's vantage point he possessed a clear view of them for a couple of hundred yards more. He wouldn't have to move for another ten minutes.

"Hey, Clive, scream for me," Billy grinned.

He'd set the actor upright in his saddle and tied his hands to the saddle horn. Benz screamed better that way. The whole thing just really cracked Billy up. He could say one thing for his prisoner, the man was a pro.

Benz took a deep breath, threw back his head and started to scream. Billy would swear someone put a torch to the man's balls or stuck barbed wire up his ass fast only to pull it out slowly. Billy would be damned if the man couldn't act.

Billy came up with the idea of unnerving his victims by torturing Benz so they'd hear him screaming. Billy pretty much settled on cutting a finger off every mile or so. He could hang them in the trees in hopes of Yates finding them. That would give Billy a double bang for his buck. Then he'd told Benz of his idea, and the man started to beg and plead and offered to do anything if only Billy wouldn't hurt him.

"Damn, Clive," Billy explained, "but I need you to scream."

Benz immediately let out a scream. He certainly proved to be a pro. Benz truly acted his ass off while Billy laughed his off. This time was no exception. While Benz wailed, Billy slapped his thighs and held his stomach and gasped for air.

"Hey, Clive," Billy said after Benz finished screaming, "you haven't forgotten our deal, have you?"

"No, Billy," Benz said, shaking his head earnestly and clearing his throat. Screaming seemed to take a toll on his vocal cords. "You can count on me, Billy, I'll tell your story to the world."

"All right," Billy grinned, "and I haven't forgotten my part, either. Since you are going to make me famous, I won't hurt you, and I'll never tell a single soul what a pussy you've been."

Benz dropped his head and slumped in the saddle. He would stay that way until Billy called upon him to perform. Benz didn't seem to be just a real happy sort of guy.

With the screaming out of the way, Billy picked the rifle up again and starting scanning through the scope for Yates. The forest thinned here and it wouldn't take much to find them. It took Billy less than a minute to spot them and when he did his pulse quickened.

"What the fuck?" he questioned.

The woman now led the group in an all out run. Andre raced a few yards behind her while Yates brought up the rear. All of them ran like hell. Billy's mind raced with them. What the fuck were they running for – or running to?

He quickly scanned the area in front of them. Just more of the same. More pine trees, more rock formations, more – Satan's Crown.

"Motherfucker!" he bellowed.

Billy jerked the scope back to find the girl. It took just a second, but a second too late. Carrie disappeared through the narrow opening. Shiloh lost her as a target.

He jerked the scope to place Andre in his sights. Billy had maybe two seconds to get off a shot – one more than he needed. He gently squeezed the trigger. The rifle's powerful recoil caused Billy to momentarily lose sight of Andre. Billy got him back in the crosshairs just in time to see Andre hit the ground and tumble. He rolled to a stop only steps from the entrance to Satan's Crown.

In the next heartbeat Yates grabbed the fallen man and tugged him toward the entrance. They were six feet from safety. Billy had only seconds to make a decision. Was this the way he wanted to kill River Yates? From a distance? With a scoped rifle? Is this how Billy wanted it to go down in history?

"God-fucking-damn!" Billy thundered, while stomping and kicking at the ground.

He let River Yates escape into Satan's Crown, and in the process, he'd paid little attention to the condition of the writer, but Billy knew for sure he'd seen blood and lots of it.

Chapter Eighteen

Clive cringed and closed his eyes. This time Shiloh actually shot at one of them. He just knew the madman wasn't shooting at a horse, and it wasn't harassing fire. He'd grown certain Shiloh always hit what he aimed to hit. He wondered which of the three Shiloh killed.

Clive thought about asking, but only for a hint of a second. Shiloh presently acted near crazy. On second thought, Shiloh always acted crazy. At the moment, he acted insane. Stomping, kicking, throwing anything he could find to throw. Spittle flew from him mouth and foamed around his lips as he screeched obscenities. Clive wanted to know who he'd shot, but more than that, he wanted to remain outside the focus of Shiloh's attention. But he didn't.

"What the fuck you looking at?" Shiloh screamed through gritted teeth, his face contorted with rage.

Clive tried to reply, but only stammered. It seemed to piss Shiloh off even more. He ran to his horse, the big buckskin, and grabbed a lariat from the saddle and then threw a loop around the neck of Clive's horse.

"What are you doing, Billy?" Clive stuttered.

"Have you ever been on a bucking horse, Clive?" Shiloh grinned madly.

"You promised me you wouldn't hurt me!"

"I ain't going to hurt you," Shiloh said while tying the opposite end of the rope to a tree, "but the horse might sure enough kill your pansy ass!"

Shiloh stepped back, drew one of his revolvers and pointed it at the ground beneath Clive's horse.

"Hang on boy!" he screamed gleefully.

"No! Let me help! I'll do anything!" Clive cried as Shiloh pulled back the hammer.

"How can you fucking help? You're fucking worthless as a man. You ain't got no balls!"

"But I have brains. Whatever's gone wrong, tell me. I can help you with a plan. We can work it out together, Billy."

Shiloh lowered the gun, giving Clive a chance to catch his breath.

"Those motherfuckers tricked me. Any plans I make will be plans that leave all of them dead and rotting. You going to help me with those kinds of plans?"

Clive's head nodded involuntarily. "Sure, Billy. Whatever it takes, Billy."

"Man, you are one cowardly, sorry bastard," Shiloh muttered before a smile crept across his face.

Clive would let the man think whatever the man wished to think.

* * * *

"How do I know you'll come back?"

This seemed the only flaw Billy could see in Benz's plan.

"Billy, is there a water source inside those rocks?"

"No."

"Well, they might have some water on them, and a little food. But they won't be able to stay in there long with what they have. They are going to have to come out. So would I. Sooner or later, I'd have to come out. And I know you could sit way back and pick me off when I do, that is if I disappointed you."

"Okay. Just as long as you know I'll kill you if you fuck me," Shiloh said with a mean squint of his eyes for effect.

"I know that, Billy."

"So, let me see if I got this right. You'll go in there and try to make a deal with Yates. Telling him that if he will come on out and face off with me, then I'll see to it that the woman gets safely back to the ranch.

"And if he don't agree, you'll tell him that when it gets dark, I'll scale those walls, hide in a crevice, wait until first light, and then shoot him and her both."

"That's the plan," Benz nodded proudly.

Billy hankered to get it over with. He didn't want to climb those rocks. It would be tougher than hell, and he didn't want to sit all night waiting until sunup. He'd just about eaten what food he'd brought with him. What remained wouldn't fill his stomach. Additionally, he could feel exhaustion creeping in.

"Now, on that damned woman, I might really let her live. I don't know yet, but I do know this. I'm going to fuck her. You got a problem with that?"

"Not a bit," Clive Benz smiled.

Still, it just did not sit right with Billy. "Why the fuck would you do this? Those are your friends. No man could be that cowardly."

"Friends? Benz spat. "I've despised that faggot from the first day I met him, and he hates my guts. Carrie dumped me for another man, and didn't have the decency to tell me until I showed up in this Godforsaken place so she could rub it in my face. River Yates? He took her away from me. He left me below that cave, probably hoping you'd find me…and kill me. As far as I'm concerned, Billy, they all deserve whatever you decide to do with them."

Try as he might, Billy couldn't help but start liking this guy.

* * * *

Like him or not, Billy still didn't feel comfortable putting all his eggs in one such flimsy basket. When Clive rode out, Billy moved too.

Billy always heard Yates was a hell of a shot. He'd studied the little group enough through the scope to know all Yates carried with him were handguns and a shotgun. Only the shotgun truly worried Billy. If River loaded slugs, and indeed could shoot really well, he could pick a man off at three hundred yards. Billy moved way back.

He positioned himself with a straighter shot into the mouth of Satan's Crown. Now as he peered at that opening through the scope, Billy feared he might have moved back too far. He couldn't adjust the scope to get a perfectly clear view of the opening. All looked fuzzy. He hadn't exceeded the effective range of the high-powered rifle, he just couldn't see really well from this far back.

Benz said it would take him at least thirty minutes to seal the deal, and tried to convince Billy not to worry if he took longer. Benz had ridden into Satan's Crown twenty minutes ago and Billy already grew worried.

Thirty more minutes after that, Billy became livid. Benz had been in there almost an hour, and Billy felt pretty goddamned sure he wasn't coming out. Billy got tricked three times in twenty-four hours. The people tricking him would soon start paying. The bitch would make the first installment.

Billy gritted his teeth and fought off the urge to stand and kick and stomp some more ground. Instead, he kept his head pressed to the eyepiece of the scope. If anything moved, he didn't want to miss it.

Man, oh man, did it move. The horse looked as if it were spit out of the mouth of Satan's Crown. Billy couldn't see much with the scope but he could make out the rider's cowboy hat pulled low and the black duster flying in the wind like Zorro's cape. Yates certainly planned to ride for help, leaving the others barricaded with the weapons. This time he left Billy no choice, as well as a very difficult shot to make.

Billy took a deep breath, let half of it out and held the other half as he slowly squeezed the trigger. The recoil again took its toll and for a second or two Billy lost sight of his target. Two precious seconds passed before Billy knew he missed. The first shot proved difficult. If Billy possessed time to get off another, it would be near impossible to make. Yates quickly moved out of range toward the thick timber.

Billy didn't have time to do it right the second time. He took a blurred sight picture, didn't bother with his breathing and jerked the trigger. He got his eye back on the scope just in time to see the horse and rider bolt into the deep woods and out of sight.

* * * *

It started like River said it would. He'd known Shiloh wouldn't pursue a lone rider with a significant head start. Instead, Shiloh would thunder into the rock corral at full speed to pick off what he would consider the weak and helpless, whether they were armed or not. Carrie sat well hidden in a crevice three feet wide that ran back several yards into the rock. She didn't see Shiloh ride in. She heard him. She also heard the gunfire erupt from up above and to the right of her hiding place and she heard Shiloh return fire. Then all went wrong.

Carrie counted the shots – one fired at Shiloh, and he returned a round. A second shot at him prompted two of Shiloh's in return. Then the firing from up and to her right stopped. Shiloh fired a third and then a fourth time, and still, no more friendly fire offered a response. Carrie slipped a peak from her hiding place, and felt the scream growing from somewhere deep within her core. It worked its way to her lips as she scurried on her hands and knees.

"Noooooooooooo!" Carrie wailed.

Billy Shiloh sat still on his horse and laughed hysterically.

* * * *

River was the best choice to ride for help – being the most accomplished rider, and knowing the mountains. All agreed they certainly needed help. They didn't know exactly Shiloh's position, but knew he could watch them with the scoped rifle. He only had to wait them out – which wouldn't take long because they had no food or water.

They also agreed the moment River rode out and got away, Shiloh would not give a second thought to storming the rock formation. He wouldn't fear coming right in on top of Carrie and Clive. Benz told River that Shiloh saw the blood on Andre and figured Andre very badly hurt if not already dead. What Shiloh would do when he got within the walls was anyone's guess as well as everyone's chief concern.

After yet more hashing over their possibilities, Benz initially impressed River with a display of bravery.

"I'll ride for help," he said.

River told him, "Chances are that anyone riding out of here won't make it but a few feet before Shiloh puts a bullet in them."

"If I ride, I have a chance of living. If I stay here without you, I'm dead for sure," Benz responded.

River could only shake his head and sigh upon hearing Benz's motivation stemmed around him saving his own ass. "So, you ride out, and if you make it, the soonest you could be back with help, if you ever find your way to help, would be nine or ten tomorrow morning. In that case, Shiloh will do just what he said he'd do. He'll wait until night, climb up and hide over our heads in those rocks and at first light shoot us like fish in a barrel."

Benz quickly came up with yet another idea, "Let me take your coat and hat. He'll think it's you trying to get out of here."

River mulled the option out loud, "If you make it out of here and into the thick woods just west," River replied, "then it might work. Shiloh will come on in here thinking I'm gone, and he'll run head on into a shit storm."

River didn't like any of their options, but this one seemed the most favorable. Benz probably had little to no chance of making it out of the rock formation. River could ride out with slightly better chances, but that would leave Benz to protect Carrie. That cinched it.

River handed his hat and coat to Benz and watched the movie hero crawl up on his horse. He turned his horse toward the opening just as River thought of something else that might give Benz a slight edge.

Carrie adamantly disagreed with River's last-minute suggestion, but River felt it best for all concerned.

* * * *

All initially went as planned. Benz went barreling out, and Shiloh reacted as they thought he might. Moments later Shiloh raced into the canyon and into River's sights. River raised the shotgun he now had loaded with double-ought buck shells, and got off a well-aimed shot. The clothing beneath Shiloh's left arm exploded into cloth confetti, and the man nearly fell from the saddle. River's first shot missed by less than an inch.

Shiloh pulled the two old-time revolvers from their holsters and shot each so quickly it stunned River, and damned near hit him. As a result, River's second shot didn't even come close to hitting the mounted man. Shiloh's third round hit and splintered the shotgun's wooden stock. His fourth shot hit the sandstone just inches from River's face, showering his eyes with rock particles and dust. Shiloh fired two more times just to pin him down and fuck with him.

River could not get the debris cleared from his eyes. He couldn't see a damned thing so dropped to his knees behind the cover of a rock outcropping. Moments later, Carrie made it to his side. Already terribly frightened, Carrie thought River was hit and grew nearly hysterical. River tried explaining his predicament when Shiloh first laughed long and hard before calling his name.

"River Yates! I'll be damned if I didn't think that was you on that horse. Please don't tell me I've already killed you!"

"I'm far from being dead, you bastard!" River shouted while clawing to clear his eyes.

"Carrie Deshazo! I'm guessing you're up there with Yates?" Shiloh giggled.

"Don't say a word," River groaned to Carrie.

"Hey, Doll!" Shiloh shouted, "At the least I've winged your man up there. You've seen how he can't stand against me. You've seen I'm the better man. You best get holt of him and bring him on down here. If I have to come up there after you two, I'll cut him up like fish bait and shoot off both your fine tits. Believe me, I'll do it!"

"I believe him, River," Carrie sobbed. "What are we going to do?"

River could just now barely make out the features of her tormented face. In his current state, Shiloh could be upon them in a matter of minutes and River would be helpless in protecting his woman.

* * * *

At River's insistence, Carrie took him by the arm and started him down from their perch to where Shiloh awaited them. River told her they had no other choice than to try and gain time for his eye sight to clear. Shiloh continued to make the most horrible threats if they didn't hurry the process. River expected to put up a better fight, but Shiloh put him out of commission so quickly and effortlessly that it left River acting both embarrassed and ashamed.

To sooth these wounds, she told him how much she loved him, and he shared the same with her. They spoke no other words on the way down to the floor of the "corral."

Billy Shiloh remained mounted. Carrie led River to within yards of the sleek gelding. Shiloh threw back his head and laughed heartily before pointing a wicked finger at River.

"Guess you're pretty disappointed with this ol' fucker, ain't you?" he asked Carrie.

"Actually, I'm very proud of him," Carrie replied, not bothering to check her defiance.

Shiloh just grinned and shook his head. "Well, then, you're a stupid bitch and deserve..."

"Shiloh!" River thundered, "I'm about tired of your filthy and ignorant mouth!"

Carrie braced herself. She feared Shiloh would explode. He didn't. River's admonishment seemed to confound him, and Shiloh didn't respond for several long seconds.

"Well, by God, you do have some balls after all. I'm glad to see that. That's going to make what's about to happen just little more interesting."

Shiloh turned hateful eyes back to Carrie. "Woman, take his guns off him and hand them up to me one at a time. With him starting to show some guts, he might try something before I'm ready for him to try something. From this point on, I want this to go exactly the way I want it to go."

River had a big revolver in the gun belt around his waist and the .45 in the shoulder holster. Carrie never touched a gun before. She didn't care to this time, but knew her options were very limited. Carrie took the one off River's waist first and turned to give it to Shiloh. Without thinking she started to hand it up to him barrel first with it pointed right at him. For a split second she considered pulling the trigger and she could tell by the look in Shiloh's eyes that he knew exactly what crossed her mind.

"Think you could do that?" he scoffed. "Let's say I wasn't fast enough to shoot you before you could pull that trigger, do you think you could put a bullet in me?"

Her mother died by gunfire. Carrie quite naturally always supported any and all gun control initiatives. That was before she'd met Billy Shiloh – before she knew how he'd murdered his wife and beaten his father-in-law – before he'd nearly raped Carrie and punched her repeatedly in the face.

"I'd shoot you in a New York second," she said without batting an eye.

Shiloh reached down and took the gun by the barrel. "Hand the next one up by the butt," he said with a wink.

Shiloh ejected the rounds from the revolver's cylinder and then threw the gun in some brush about thirty feet away. Upon retrieving the automatic he pulled out the magazine, threw the gun in the brushes and the magazine in the opposite direction.

Shiloh took a canteen off his saddle and tossed it down to Carrie. "Rinse his eyes out. I'll kill a blind man if I have to, but I'd rather him be able to see what I'm going to do to him...and to you."

Carrie took her strength from River. If he felt any fear, it didn't show. He seemed almost relaxed, and she knew he must be deep in thought. She had faith he'd come up with something. Believing this dulled her fear just enough to make it bearable.

He held is head back and Carrie tiptoed to pour the water in his eyes. She could see the particles caked in his lids and flushed most of it out. River soon held up a hand and told her thanks.

Carrie watched as River used the sleeves of his denim shirt to dab at his eyes. When finished, River turned his head to Shiloh, blinked four or five times and then held his gaze steady. Carrie's heart skipped a beat as River first smiled and then started to chuckle.

"What the fuck's so funny?" Shiloh questioned.

"Twister."

The single word brought back the story River told Carrie about the horse, the parking lot, and the bet River lost to the previous owner of the horse appropriately named Twister.

River didn't blink an eye before bringing two fingers to his lips and whistling. The horse beneath Shiloh came to life, and Carrie marveled at the ability of the gelding to chase his tail like a dog!

Carrie never saw anything quite like it. Twister seemed instantly to move so fast in tight circles that it looked to just spin in place, like a top. It quickly became apparent no one could stay on this horse for any length of time.

Billy Shiloh proved no exception. Twister catapulted his rider in mere seconds. The moment Shiloh went airborne, River began to move. The image of an outfielder rushing to catch a fly ball flashed across Carrie's mind, but she knew River had no intentions of catching Shiloh. He hit the ground rolling, and River stood only feet away.

* * * *

It appeared the only chance River would get, and no doubt his last one. Shiloh would have to be dizzy and, more than likely, stunned. River wanted both guns. He would settle for one. If he couldn't get a gun, he planned to punch, kick, and bite to the bitter end. Shiloh rolled three times, and River stood ready to spring on him when Shiloh came to rest in a sitting position with a gun in both hands, and both guns trained on River.

When a man could get no breaks he sometimes just had to go for broke. "Put those guns away and let's see what you're made of," River snarled.

"What?" Shiloh asked incredulously. "You want to fight me? An old fart like you wants to take me on?"

"Yeah, I think it's time you learned a little respect for your elders."

"Okay," Shiloh sneered. "Anyhow, I want to kick your ass for you making that horse do whatever in the hell it was that it did. That shit ain't right!"

Billy Shiloh twirled the guns back into his holster and River stepped up close.

"I'm going to let you take the first swing, kid," River said calmly. He heard Carrie behind him utter just the slightest gasp. She probably thought he'd lost his mind. But he hadn't. He'd lost his sense of humor.

"You think I need some kind of advantage?" Shiloh chuckled like he couldn't believe what he heard.

"Well, I don't know. You take the first swing. Show me what you got. Then I'll tell you," River said, standing with his hands down to his sides.

"Here's what I got!" Shiloh blurted as he threw the first punch.

River ducked under the right hook and brought his own right up and solidly into Shiloh's stomach. It brought the younger man up on his toes and caused him to grunt loudly. River stepped back while Shiloh folded in the middle.

"Obviously, you ain't got much!"

Shiloh lunged into a run at him. River sidestepped and stuck out his leg and tripped Shiloh. He went down hard, but bounced right back up. The side of his face now badly scraped. This time he started to move slowly toward River with his fists raised to cover his face.

River simply stood and waited. His arms relaxed at his sides. "It figures," River said softly. "I ain't never seen a woman beater that could do any good against a full-grown man."

Shiloh swung again with his right. River stepped into him and blocked it with his left forearm and synchronized it with a right jab to Shiloh's face. It sent the man's head rocking back. Blood spewed from his nose. River followed up with a left hook that exploded on the side of Shiloh's head, causing him to stagger.

"That one was for killing your wife and beating her ol' daddy, Walter Bates."

Shiloh shrieked in anger and came with both fists swinging wildly. River stood his place, blocking, bobbing and ducking, but not swinging. In seconds a winded Shiloh's arms drooped and River stepped in.

"And this is for treating my woman with disrespect."

River dropped his right hand down to his left side and brought it back up with a vengeance to backhand Shiloh with an open hand. It collided with his jaw sounding like a balloon being popped, and sent the man stumbling backwards.

"I normally hit a man like he's a man," River said in a gravelly monotone, "but I just bitch-slapped you, boy. You don't deserve any better."

Having his fun and revenge out of the way, River moved in to end the fight. He took two quick steps and wrapped his hands around Shiloh's neck. Suddenly River felt the barrels of both guns in his ribs.

"Back away from me, motherfucker!" Shiloh gasped.

With no other real alternative, River squeezed harder and did so until the gun in Shiloh's right hand went off.

River didn't feel a thing. No impact, no burning, no searing pain. It took him a second to realize it, but he wasn't hit. Shiloh didn't shoot at him. He'd turned the revolver to the side. "Oh, God, no! Please, please, no!" River screeched as he used the grip on Shiloh's throat to toss him to the side. River then spun to look at Carrie.

She remained on her feet but held her right forearm with her left hand. "He just nicked me," she said, her voice sounding hollow.

River turned back to Shiloh and found both guns pointed in his direction.

"I could have killed her," Shiloh rasped as he shook his head to clear it. "And if you don't do exactly like I say, next time I will."

"Okay, you sorry son of a bitch, it's your game," River hissed, "So what happens now?"

"Now?" Shiloh said as he holstered one of his guns so he could rub his neck. "Well, now, old man, it gets really fun. For me, anyway. Here's what's going to happen."

Billy walked up closer, but not too close. *At least*, River thought, *now he's leery. Now he has some respect.*

"First, Yates, I'm going to give you one of these guns. I'm even going to let you hold it on me. I'm going to give you the first chance to fire. But we both know what will happen. You know and I know that...with guns...you ain't got a snowball's chance in hell against me. So, I'll shoot you. But I ain't going to kill you."

Shiloh turned his eyes on Carrie, and they took on a darker kind of ugliness. "Cause after I shoot you, I'm going to fuck your woman, and I want you to see that. I want you to hear that. After I get finished with her, then I'm going to kill you. But I'm going to do it slowly."

River turned to look at Carrie and their eyes locked. The look in her eyes showed terror, but also a stubborn resolve.

"I love you, and I'm sorry," he whispered.

"It's not over, River. It's not over," she said forcibly.

Billy Shiloh laughed boastfully at the words, and River's heart sank even more. Try as he might, he couldn't agree with Carrie. Shiloh had already proven simply too quick with a gun.

Chapter Nineteen

"Now, you, bitch," Billy said out of the side of his mouth to Carrie, "you listen real close and pay good attention to what happens here. Because, if I let you live, after I'm finished with you, you'll damned sure want to tell how it happened between Billy Shiloh and River Yates.

"And, you, dumb ass old man," Shiloh said as he walked up to Yates and stuck the barrel of a Colt between his eyes, "you follow my directions. If you do anything I don't want you to do, I'm going to shoot her and then shoot you."

Billy unholstered the other gun and handed it butt first to Yates. "You take this and hold it down at your side until I tell you different."

Yates took the gun and did as told while Shiloh took ten steps backwards.

"Did you notice that, woman? Ten paces? You listen up, now."

Billy turned his complete attention to Yates, and he holstered the gun he'd kept to kill the man. "Okay, Yates, you know that's a single-action. You got to cock the hammer before you pull the trigger. So, right now, you can raise the gun and point it at me and put your thumb up on the hammer. When you think you're ready to bleed, then you can try to shoot me. But first..."

Billy couldn't help but grin because he loved this part so much, "...but first I have something to say. Bitch, pay attention, now!"

* * * *

River wanted to look at Carrie one last time, but he couldn't bring himself to do it. There were a lot of bad ways a man might die, but River couldn't think of any that could be worse than Shiloh explained. River never thought his prospects for making heaven very good, and he'd never really believed in an eternal hell. He'd kind of always thought he'd spend forever in the nothingness of a deep sleep. But now he knew there did exist a hell, for him anyway. It would be right here, and the last few minutes of his life would be an eternity. An eternity of watching her being frightened and hurt and defiled while River could do nothing but watch and listen.

River brought the old gun up and took aim at the center of Shiloh's mass. If by some miracle, he got a round off, he wanted the biggest target available. The Colt felt well balanced. River put his thumb on the hammer, and watched as Shiloh slowly raised his hands until the palms were parallel with the ground.

"You got any last words, Yates?"

"None I care to share with you, Shiloh."

"Have it your way then, but here in just a second, I'm going to start talking. When, I do, don't interrupt me."

Hank Sioux popped to River's mind. First, he wondered how his old friend was making it, and he felt bad for not thinking much of him prior to this moment, but he thought Hank would understand. More importantly what came to mind was what Hank told him as he lay bleeding on the floor of the Silver Dollar.

"The saying, River," Hank had emphasized, "he'll use it on you."

* * * *

Billy cleared his throat. He wanted his voice to be deep and confident. He wanted the woman to hear it clearly. If she did him right here in a few minutes...didn't fight too much, then he would spare her life, and if he did, she would go far in telling the world about the cool-headed outlaw Billy Shiloh. She would no doubt go on talk shows and do interviews for magazines about her experiences with Billy. She could tell how boldly he swept her away from the ranch and how he masterminded getting her back once she'd escaped. She would go into detail on how well he rode and shot and...well, there would be the thing on the fistfight. Billy would talk to her about that before he set her free. No man ever done him that way before. No man ever would again. His face still hurt badly. He knew Yates knocked at least one tooth loose. Now River Yates would pay.

"If you are going to point that gun at me, mister," Billy started with a cocky grin, "then you best be pulling the trigger. Because...

SHIT!

Billy didn't understand at first why that single word seemed to explode in his mind's eye. At this moment it didn't all piece together well in his brain. It felt like Yates hit him in the gut again, but this time even harder than the last. And, of course, there had been that ball of fire coming out of the gun he'd given Yates. Billy wasn't sure, but had that terrible noise been thunder?

Realization came slow, but when it came, it came with a vengeance. River Yates shot him even before Billy finished his saying. It didn't seem right for a man to take such an unfair advantage.

Billy felt himself stumbling backwards, like someone gave him a hearty shove. But who could be stupid enough to do that to the outlaw Billy Shiloh? His guts suddenly felt like someone ripped them apart with shards of glass and soaked them down with gasoline. Billy fought to stay on his feet, but sank to his knees. He didn't know exactly when, but he'd dropped his gun. He tried to bring his hands up to cradle his stomach, but they wouldn't move. He tried to control his bowels, but couldn't. Billy, on his knees, feeling a hurt like hell itself came to live in his stomach, tasted the blood filling his mouth and felt the acidic sting of hot shit running down the backs of his legs.

* * * *

River slowly lowered the gun to his side. Shiloh could now do nothing more than topple over. The man had concentrated too intently on his "saying" to react to River cocking and shooting the Colt. River questioned his own emotions. What did he feel at this moment? The answer came quickly – relief – simple but glorious relief. He didn't feel good about what he'd done, and he didn't feel bad, either.

"You gut shot me," Shiloh moaned. Blood trickled down the corners of his mouth and poured from the wound in his stomach.

River nodded his head solemnly. "Yup, I did, Shiloh."

"It hurts really bad."

"I bet it does," River agreed as he stuck the Colt in the waistband of his jeans.

"You got to help me."

River pursed his lips and slowly shook his head before saying, "Nothing I can do for you, Shiloh. You're dying."

River took a deep breath when he saw the tears starting to trickle down Shiloh's face. River could tell it grew increasingly difficult for the man to stay up on his knees. Shiloh started to sway, and began to sob.

"I don't want to die."

"Can't blame you, Billy," River said with a sad shake of his head, "because if there is a hell, I'm pretty sure that's where you're headed."

Billy Shiloh began to tremble as his eyes reflected what could only be terror before he teetered and fell face down. There, on the ground, he twitched and shuttered and sobbed pitifully.

River walked over, picked up the gun Shiloh dropped and tossed it aside. He thought about patting him down for other weapons, but didn't waste his time. Besides, he'd touched Billy Shiloh all he intended to.

* * * *

Carrie wasn't sure she could move. Her arms and legs felt numb. She had the sensation of awakening from a very bad nightmare. One of those in which the residual effects stay with you during the course of the following day, not letting you forget the parts that scared you the most.

Shiloh stopped crying by the time River took her in his arms.

"It's over," he whispered in her ear while gently kissing the swollen flesh on her face.

Carrie could not take her eyes from the bleeding form on the ground, the man who caused the damage to her face. He lay still now.

"Is he dead?" she asked.

"Don't know. If he's not, he soon will be."

"The sooner the better." Carrie said what she felt, and felt no remorse for saying it.

River just nodded his head and squeezed her tighter. Minutes later he broke the silence. "We better go check on Andre."

It felt good to walk away from Billy Shiloh.

* * * *

The bullet Shiloh fired as they'd fled earlier for the opening of the canyon struck Andre just below and left of the heart. The impact threw him to the ground, and he'd cut his chin on a rock. The cut wasn't serious, but bled profusely.

Earlier even still, when they had found the two rocks that gave them moments of rest from being pursued, Carrie learned why River had not wanted to take off his black duster. He'd hoped wearing it would conceal the bulk and form of the bulletproof vest he wore beneath his denim shirt. He'd known if Shiloh could tell he wore the vest, the man would aim for his head. River had given the vest to Andre while they hid between the two big rocks.

The act saved Andre's life. Still, the impact of the bullet had done damage. Carrie feared the impact of the bullet busted Andre's ribs. Once they'd gotten the weight of the vest off of him, Andre breathed easier but still labored to take in oxygen.

When Clive Benz rode into the corral, and he and River made the plans for him to ride back out again, River offered the vest to Clive. Benz jumped at the offer, even though Carrie pointed out that their plan would place River in close confrontation with Shiloh. Carrie felt peeved when River didn't keep it for himself. She'd stewed about it as River faced off with Shiloh. Carrie considered it intriguing how quickly things could change. Now the vest seemed no longer important.

They'd placed Andre down in a clump of foliage behind some good size rocks. He now slept soundly, but when Carrie touched his face, his eyes popped open.

"I thought I heard gunfire," he said nervously.

"You did," Carrie nodded. "But you won't hear any more. River shot Shiloh. He's dead by now."

"Bend down here, sweet boy," Andre smiled up at River, "and let me kiss your lovely face."

"Wouldn't a handshake do just as well?" Carrie heard River deadpan from behind her.

Andre chuckled, and then grimaced at the pain.

"We have a horse now, Andre," River said as he squatted down beside Carrie. "If you feel up to it, we'll put you in the saddle, and Carrie can sit behind you, help support your weight. I can get you to some help in about two hours."

"If you help get me up on the horse, I'll do just fine," Andre said.

"Okay," River said as he pushed to his feet. "I'll go get Twister."

Carrie watched her man walk away. He stood tall and erect and confident. He walked past Shiloh without even looking down. Carrie turned back to Andre.

"Are you going to be okay?" she asked while reaching to take his hand.

"Are you?"

Carrie didn't get to answer before the shot rang out. She sprang to her feet and saw Shiloh lying on his stomach and the gun in his outstretched arm. She watched as River clung to the saddle on Twister's back, trying to hold himself upright. There appeared a large and dark and growing wet spot in the middle of his back – a spot that a bulletproof vest would have covered.

Carrie heard a wailing, mournful scream that sounded as if it would go on forever. But it didn't. Like all things eventually do, it died away. The scream coming from her lips started from deep within her soul and evaporated into the heavens.

Chapter Twenty

"River managed to twist around to the direction the shot came from," Carrie Deshazo's voice cracked. "Drawing the Colt from the waistband of his jeans, River shot once before slumping to the ground. The shot was a lucky one, and he lived only a few painful breaths longer than Billy."

Carrie simply stared at the passage for several seconds before closing the manuscript and placing it on the coffee table beside her chair. Tears welled in her eyes.

"Well?"

Carrie cleared her throat, and dabbed at her eyes with a tissue. "I think it's good. It's, uh, very good."

It just struck too many nerves and rubbed salt in wounds that the past six months had been unable to heal. Her River did not fire his last round while still standing. He'd already fallen to the ground before he'd managed to free the gun from his jeans. While River took careful aim, Shiloh got off another shot from the pistol he'd hidden someplace on his body. The second shot missed River, but it killed the horse, Twister. When River did pull the trigger, his aim couldn't have been truer. The big bullet made an awful mess of Billy Shiloh's face and head.

Moe Trendle got out of his chair and started to pace. "It made you cry," he said softly. "Is that a bad thing?"

In the past six months Carrie left and returned to Oklahoma far more times than she cared to count. The Robbers' Roost Bed and Breakfast was more than a home away from home for her. Her heart lived here.

Every visit included time spent with Hank Sioux, Jim Duck, and Moe Trendle. Carrie quickly grew to adore Hank, who now walked with a terrible limp because of Billy Shiloh. It took her longer to get to know the sweet and shy-natured Jim Duck, and twice as much time to even like Moe Trendle. Now they were all dear to her. Moe could be obnoxious and stubborn, but he truly possessed a talent for writing.

"No, not at all. I'm sure it won't evoke the same reaction from other readers. They didn't live it," Carrie said with a forced smile.

"It's a novel," Moe reminded her as he often did, "just based loosely on the truth."

Moe constantly worried about lawsuits, and had reasons to. Clive Benz made it clear that he would take great exception to his role in the tragic ordeal being put in print. Clive seemed especially embarrassed by the fact he'd not found help upon leaving the canyon, but help found him. A troop of Girl Scouts on a fauna and foliage hike rescued a lost and hysterical Clive Benz. His publicist worked overtime to keep this scandalous tidbit from the media. Clive, proving to be a generous philanthropist, contributed the largest ever one-time donation to the Girl Scouts of America. So, Moe didn't have a cowardly action hero in his novel. He did, however, have a cowardly country and western singing star named Tommy King. Mo named the bad guy in the novel Billy Hanes. He penned the damsel in distress as Trish Scott. The hero was River Norman. It delighted Andre that the main character bore his surname.

"In that case," Carrie responded after a few moment's thought, "since it is in fact a novel, why don't you let this River live?"

"Impact, Carrie. You know how important that is."

"Impact," she repeated softly.

"It's my style," Moe nodded. "I like to keep a reader's emotions going up and down, exhaust them if you will, with tension that ebbs and flows with excitement. Timing it so that..."

"Time," Carrie interrupted, coming to her feet. "What time is it, Moe?"

"I've got three twenty-five."

"I've got to go," she said as she started for the front door. "I'll meet you later at the Silver Dollar for a beer. Say around six. We'll discuss publishing."

"Drinks are on me!" Moe hollered as Carrie stepped onto the front porch of the Robbers' Roost Bed and Breakfast.

* * * *

The oil level and tire pressure checked okay and the tank was full of gasoline. The clothes were packed and loaded in the front seat while the really important cargo, tied down to secure it, took up nearly the entire bed of the truck.

"Let me help you with that," Carrie said as she bound down the front steps.

"Is Moe about to drive you crazy with that stupid book?"

"It's a good book," Carrie disagreed amiably. "I think it will catch some publisher's eye."

"He told me his hero dies in the end."

"I know," Carrie nodded sadly. "Just like mine almost did," she said as she reached out and stroked the rugged face.

River Yates pulled his woman into his arms. "Bullshit. It'd take more than one little bullet in the back to do this old man in."

He didn't care to think how the bullet missed his spine by half an inch and nicked his heart. He damned sure didn't care to recall nearly a month in the hospital. That was then. This was now. River let go of Carrie and grabbed the tarp at his feet. He let her help him cover the Victorian dollhouse.

"What if you don't find her in Tennessee?" Carrie asked.

The last address River had on his daughter was in Memphis.

"If Sandy ain't there, she'll more than likely be someplace else," River grinned. "I'll keep going 'til I find her."

"Then you're coming to Hollywood, right? You promised, River."

River had never been to Hollywood, and he did make the promise.

"You said you live in a mansion in a very exclusive neighborhood."

"It's a pretty nice house in a pretty nice area," Carrie teased.

"So, is it going to embarrass you if I pull up in front of your place in this thing?" River asked, patting the dear old Chevy truck that once belonged to his father.

"Honey, I don't care if you come by a bus, just as long as you get there."

"Good to know," River smiled broadly, "because if this ol' girl don't make it, then I'll either be on foot or on Greyhound."

The time came to go.

"I'm not going to cry," Carrie said with a sniffle.

He didn't say goodbye. He held her and kissed her and told her how much he loved her. Then he drove away. River found it necessary to blink his eyes rapidly and take a number of really deep breaths.

Before pulling out of the drive he caught a glimpse in his rear-view mirror of the hulking old red barn. Not a single voice had called to him in the past six months. River Yates was beginning to believe no one lived there anymore.

ACKNOWLEDGMENTS

To Henry P. (Pat) Scully of Scully Associates, thank you for producing the cover design. It's one of my favorites.

ABOUT THE AUTHOR

Keith Remer is a retired Army colonel. After thirty-two years of service in the Army, he taught various courses as an adjunct professor before buying a horse ranch. He has to date written twelve novels and is the recipient of the *International Indy Book Award for Best in Fiction* for his thriller, *The Hiding Place of Thunder*. Keith lives on his ranch in rural Oklahoma City where he writes his novels and tends his horses.

To connect with Keith, visit his Facebook page
@KeithRemerAuthor, or his webpage: keithremer.com